Adam Fitzroy

The Bridge on the River Wye

Manifold Press

Published by Manifold Press

ISBN: 978-1-908312-78-5

Proof-reading and line editing: W.S. Pugh

Editor: Fiona Pickles

For further details of Manifold Press titles both in print and forthcoming: manifoldpress.co.uk

Other titles by Adam Fitzroy:
> Between Now and Then
> Dear Mister President
> Ghost Station
> In Deep
> Make Do and Mend
> A Pride of Poppies (anthology)
> Stage Whispers

Acknowledgements

Thanks for their constant support and encouragement to my invaluable 'first reader' Louise, and to the dear people who claim to be my 'greatest' and 'second greatest' fans, and thanks also to Chris who helped to research a matter of police procedure; all your contributions are appreciated more than I can say.

1.

July 2008

It was raining when Rupert got back to England. It had been raining when he left, too, and for all he knew it had probably rained on every one of the … how ever many days it was, eleven or twelve hundred? … that he'd been away. Not that it hadn't rained in Australia too, from time to time – big, dramatic, sky-emptying storms with blasts of wind which took down trees and houses, changed the landscape irrevocably, and then moved on – but here, in the pale dawn and illuminated by yellow lights reflected on wet tarmac, there was only the disheartening awareness that he'd gone halfway around the world in pursuit of a dream, that it had failed to materialise, and that now he was back with his tail between his legs.

It didn't matter how often he rationalised it to himself; there was no way of not seeing the whole thing – the emigration experiment, the relationship with Cameron – as a disaster. It had ended, not suddenly and abruptly like an Australian storm, but with the insidious quality of London rain - slowly and inevitably and drip by drip by drip. And Rupert had done his level best to keep it alive, too, even after he'd understood that there was no hope, simply because he didn't want to have to remember himself as the one who'd called 'time' on something which had seemed so promising at the outset. He didn't want to think of himself as a quitter, he never had – but then, with their business flushed down the pan and his very assuredly now *ex*-boyfriend on his way to prison, he'd pretty much run out of options.

So, was this a withdrawal, a tactical retreat, a flight from reality - or just a wounded animal returning to what it knew and understood, to lick its wounds and pull itself together so that it could try again? It was not as if he had any family to go back to, after all; they'd chucked him out a long time ago, and he'd headed off down the garden path with his belongings in his arms and the words 'AIDS' and 'PERVERT' screeched so loudly after him nobody could have been unaware of his supposed offence. Chalk that one up to experience, and to the friend who'd persuaded him so enthusiastically that the world had changed and it would be safe to come out to his parents now; unfortunately for Rupert the friend in question had never met his parents when he made this claim – and neither, for the past fifteen years or so, had Rupert.

The baggage carousel at that hour of the morning was its usual hellish self. Rupert had either ditched or sold off all his unnecessary belongings before he left Queensland, so what remained was really only one large holdall and the backpack that doubled as his laptop bag. That was all he'd brought with him, anyway, knowing he'd be working his arse off for the first few months and wouldn't have time to care about anything else. In due course, though - when he had somewhere decent for her to live - he'd be able to send for Rusty, the fool of a Springer Spaniel he and Cameron had adopted with such high hopes and the only thing he was bringing away from that relationship besides the scars. Her board and lodging had already cost him the last of what he laughingly referred to as his savings - the little he'd managed to keep from Cameron, anyway – and he'd had to borrow plenty more besides, to make sure she was well looked-after in his absence.

That was where Ren came in, of course. There were advantages to knowing a man like Renfrew Sheppard, arrogant and tempestuous though he could often be. He played up to that in public, shouting and stamping and smashing plates, and he'd gained a reputation as the toughest of a tough generation of TV chefs. It was always said of Ren, though, that once you were his friend you were there for life, and he'd do anything for you that came within the scope of his considerable resources. He'd been known to introduce his staff to contacts who could further their careers, for example, or bought houses to rent to them when they'd had difficulty getting a foot on the property ladder. He'd even lent them money when they found themselves in tight places, as Rupert had found out for himself. No doubt about it, Ren Sheppard was a good man to have in your corner – and that, just at the moment, was precisely what Rupert needed.

He took one look at the taxi queue, changed his mind, and headed for the Heathrow Express instead; even by Tube he could be rocking up to Ren's office at Nectarine - his flagship restaurant almost in the shadow of Southwark Cathedral - within the hour, and the walk would do him good after sitting still for fifteen hours on the last leg of the flight. Besides, all that filtered air, vacuum-packed food and the constant - but indubitably necessary – hum of the engines, had made him want to clear his head and stop being 'in transit' as soon as possible. He might just stop for a coffee somewhere for the sake of making his own decision after a day and a half of being passive cargo - simply to remind himself what it felt like to be independent.

The nice thing about passing through London at this hour of the day was that everybody looked equally shell-shocked and nobody spoke. Whether it was first thing in the morning or early evening – Rupert's insides were still on Aussie time and if past form was any guide they wouldn't be making a decision about that until later in the week – travelling made him antisocial anyway, and he preferred not to deal with frivolous conversation. He did, however, manage to order a hazelnut latte and drink it before descending into the Tube at Paddington, and half an hour later he'd punched his reactivated staff code into the keypad at Nectarine, dumped his luggage in the locker room, and was being hugged enthusiastically by his former boss. Ren looked so great, and gave such fabulous hugs, that Rupert had always secretly been devastated by the knowledge that the man was so obviously and quintessentially straight.

"'Allo, stranger!" No amount of elocution lessons, no media training - not even the nagging of his Scottish mum - had quite eliminated that genuine 'Sarf London' intonation. You could take the boy out of Bermondsey, but you could never quite take Bermondsey out of the boy. Now in his late forties, he'd grown up cooking in pubs and restaurants south of the river; south of the river he'd returned when he'd made his fortune, and set up in business in the middle of all he'd known and loved as a child. Ren was about as connected to his place as anybody Rupert knew.

They exchanged the usual pleasantries; how was Rupert's flight, how was Mrs Ren and all the little Rens?

"Rupe, you silly sod," said his friend, "you should never have left England in the first place."

"I know." He slumped into the offered chair and took a good look at Ren, the first time he'd seen him in person for more than three years. Six foot tall, wirily built, his glowing auburn hair shot through with grey, the thinking woman's *petite crêpe épaisse* was wearing a tight-fitting black tee-shirt and jeans and positively glowing with health. "Looking fine, mate. Been to the gym this morning?"

"Swimming," Ren told him. "Twenty lengths before breakfast. No smart remarks from you, young Rupert."

Rupert shook his head. "All out of smart remarks," he answered, quietly.

"Don't blame you." Ren's mood changed immediately. "Cameron's been sentenced, then?"

"Fifteen months. He'll probably be out in six, but I wasn't going to wait - it was all over long before he got himself arrested. Besides, there was nothing much to hang around for; the business was gone, we'd defaulted on the lease, all I had to do was clean the place out and hand back the keys." Which didn't tell the story of precisely how miserable those last few weeks had been, but friends and ex-staff members had generously given their time and support and together they'd handed back his beloved beach-side bar and grill in a fit state for someone else to take it on. He'd had tears in his eyes as he'd driven away for the last time, and he'd made a point of never going round that way again before he'd left town for good; Rupert had closed the door on that part of his life, and he wasn't going to open it up again for anyone.

"Bloody shame," said Ren. "I liked Cameron. I never thought he'd have gone off the rails like that."

"Nobody ever does, though, do they?" sighed Rupert. "And it might not have happened if it hadn't been for the accident; he was okay before that; we were reasonably happy." And so they had been, or at least he'd thought so at the time - living in the sunshine, enjoying an Aussie lifestyle that included surfing and sailing and phenomenal sex. Rupert would never have said he was in love, exactly, but he was certainly in lust;

Cameron knew how to push all his buttons and then some. He had, now that he looked back on it, quite clearly been led along by the dick – but even so there was no reason it shouldn't have worked out in the long run. Except, of course, that it hadn't.

"I know." Ren did, too. One long, late-night (Aussie-time) Skype conversation - with Rupert not exactly sober and Ren sitting at this very desk, giving over a valuable chunk of his working day to listening to an ex-employee's troubles - had made sure of that. Rupert had bottled it and bottled it until he could bottle no more, then he'd torn through a couple of Barossa Valley Cabernets and steeled himself to make the call. He hadn't regretted that decision for a moment, either. "So - how soon do you want to start work, then?"

"I'm going to need a day or two to get over the jet-lag," answered Rupert. "Apart from that – it's up to you."

"Right. So I won't start you as my new *chef de plonge* this evening, then."

"Appreciate it." But Rupert had only just managed to suppress a yawn. "Sorry, Ren, the flight's catching up with me a bit. What've you got in mind, then?"

"Well, as I said on the phone, you can do *sous-chef* here again while Maggie's on maternity leave – and when she comes back, you can take over running the place I'm opening in Glasgow in the New Year. I'll be honest with you, Rupe, the bloke I offered it to originally turned his nose up at the salary." Ren passed over a Post-It note with a figure written on it.

"Fuck."

"I know, right? But he was moaning about getting his kids into the right school and everything, and when the penny dropped I realised 'this geezer's winding me up, he reckons I'm going to buy him a posh pad in Glasgow'. Doesn't matter how good a chef you are, mate, there's only so far I'm willing to go to mollycoddle you." He paused. "You can manage at Gary and Steve's for the time being, can't you? Oh and I'm supposed to give you their key." He reached into a desk drawer and handed over a key with a blue Dalek fob hanging from it. "They're in the Channel Islands doing another bloody triathlon this week, they'll be home some time on Sunday."

"They're not *both* doing the triathlon?" The concept was more than slightly bizarre. Gary was good bloke, none better, but his concept of exercise didn't usually extend much beyond the bedroom. Gary was more interested in looking languid and intellectual than in actually doing anything energetic.

"No fear; Steve's running, Gary's watching. It's how they spend their weekends." Ren's opinion of the activity was clearly reflected in his tone. "I sent one of my people over with milk and eggs and stuff first thing, and you're to help yourself to anything you fancy from the freezer."

Rupert nodded slowly. "I'll have to think about the Glasgow job," he said, "I've never even been there. But I'm happy to fill in here for the time being. How soon will you need me, seriously?"

"How about Monday?" suggested Ren. "Usual time. It's still ten days on and four off like when you were here before. Details of the Glasgow job are in the envelope." He handed over a presentation folder full of papers; Rupert barely glanced at it. "Read it when you've got your brain back - and come and have dinner here on Thursday, nine o'clock, and we'll catch up. No pressure, eh?"

"No pressure – and Monday would be great. Thanks for everything, Ren."

"No worries. Welcome home, mate; there's always a job for you in my organisation if you want it. Only what you deserve," continued Ren, in the face of incipient protest. "Now, I reckon you need a kip … you look a bit green round the gills."

"Yeah, you're right; all I really want to do is grab a shower and crawl into bed … and I'm not even sure about the shower."

"Well, call me if you need anything. I'm in Norwich tomorrow - book signing in the morning, personal appearance with Delia in the afternoon - but Maggie'll be here all day. Or there's my new PA, Andrew; I've told him all about you – I think you'll have a lot in common." The innuendo was almost crushing, but Rupert barely had energy to lift an eyebrow in response. He didn't mind Ren organising his work life for him, even somewhere to live if it came to that, but he drew the line at having some hapless young PA thrown at him quite so blatantly; he was capable of finding his own thoroughly unsuitable partners, thank you very much, and he'd proved it more than once.

"Appreciate it, Ren," was all he managed to say; Ren was already on his feet and ushering him towards the door with an affectionate arm around his shoulders.

"Not a bit of it. You always were an asset, Rupert - anything I do for you is enlightened self-interest, that's all; I'll be getting the benefit in the long run. Now bugger off and get some zeds, you look like a bloody panda."

It was excellent advice, and Rupert was quick to take advantage of it; he lost no more time in heading for Gary and Steve's apartment.

Slinging his bag over his shoulder, navigating carefully through streets beginning to fill with people on their way to work – all of them too absorbed in whatever they were listening to to notice a weary man with an out-sized holdall taking up more than his fair share of the pavement – Rupert fetched up eventually at Marshalsea Road and let himself into the former warehouse where Gary and Steve had set up home. That was only half the battle, though, wrestling his luggage into the lobby and closing the door behind him, shutting out the noise and fumes of the street; the developers - bless their avaricious little hearts! - who had taken over this formerly run-down and seedy Victorian building had not seen fit to install a lift. With the ceilings as high as they were it was a veritable Everest of stairs which faced him now - nearly eighty, if he remembered rightly, although he resolutely refused to count them as he went.

On the first landing half a dozen identical doors led into smartly expensive flats, and one floor above the picture was much the same. On the next a smaller staircase led to what the developers had optimistically marketed as the 'penthouse apartment'. Technically he supposed that's what it was, too, but an earlier generation would have characterised the rooms as airless garrets and refused to touch them with a bargepole. Gary and Steve, however, being both annoyingly fit (Steve) and annoyingly wealthy (Gary), had put their pink pounds on the table the moment the doors had opened for business, buying the penthouse off-plan before so much as a pipe or cable had been brought into the building; they had viewed it with no glass in the windows and dead pigeons on the floor, and had loved it at first sight. Rupert understood, but that didn't stop him being pathologically jealous of them all the same.

Inside their apartment he set his bag on the gleaming oak floor; all was silence apart from his own breathing. The bedrooms were on this level, the door to the spare standing open with the bed made up and looking inviting. It wasn't a fussy room; minimalist to a fault, in fact, it looked like something out of a smart hotel – as, indeed, did the whole apartment. It wasn't what Rupert would have chosen if he'd been setting out to make a home for himself, and even if he'd started with the blank canvas of a newly-developed apartment he'd have given it much more personality, yet it was comfortable and free and at the moment he wasn't in any position to be giving dental inspections to philanthropic equines.

"She'll be right," he told himself firmly. He'd picked up the odd Aussie-ism along the way, whenever they were useful and worked with his normal vocabulary. He liked to think he hadn't completely 'gone native', but there'd be no way of telling until he got back into the mainstream of British life. An establishment like Nectarine was perfect for that sort of thing; it brought out differences and commonalities, highlighted individualism and imposed a teamwork ethic; it would be a bloody good way of finding out precisely who he was these days.

There was a card waiting on the bed. "Welcome home, Rupert," Gary had written – his handwriting was clearer than Steve's. "Make yourself comfortable, you know where everything is. See you late Sunday."

The kitchen was upstairs. Rupert wandered up there for the sake of wandering, inspected the contents of the fridge, took from the bowl on the table an apple he didn't really want, let himself out onto the terrace and stared around him at roofs and bricks and chimneys and a grey, damp sky. London, in its workaday garb, was no different to any other big city in outline; the shapes and locations of the buildings might vary but the sounds, sights and smells were all fairly standard. Voices, traffic, odd bursts of music, the occasional high screech of birds, you got those anywhere. But London – well, there was something uniquely reassuring about it for the returning exile. There was a sameness, a familiarity, a certainty that whatever else in life might be capricious and mutable

London would always be itself – aggravating and combative at times, but when you were in trouble it would wrap its arms around you like a dotty old aunt, hug you to its bosom and comfort you, and tell you everything was going to be all right because it was here and would hold your hand for as long as you needed it. That was the main thing he knew he could depend on now, when it came down to it; that whatever might end up disappointing and abandoning him, London never would.

Rupert was tired - he'd acknowledged that to himself long ago and he hadn't started feeling better since – but he was also home; home empty, home broken-hearted, home with it all to do again and the careful pity of his friends to face it was true, but *home*. Now, perhaps, on his own with the dear old city, he might actually permit himself to to cry at last.

And if he chose to avail himself of the opportunity, there above the morning street, only the seagulls wheeling through the sky and the half-eaten apple in his hand would ever be in any position to tell tales about it.

2.

The trouble with flying such extremely long distances, of course, thought Rupert as he made a half-hearted attempt to unpack and shove his woefully inappropriate Australian clothing into Gary and Steve's guest wardrobe, was that you left your brain and stomach somewhere above the Indian Ocean. It had been early morning when he'd set off for Brisbane, lunchtime or thereabouts when his flight had taken off for Sydney, tea-time before they'd lifted from there and mid-evening before he'd been properly on his way back to the UK. He knew for certain they were out of Aussie airspace only when Anzac biscuits stopped showing up with every meal; he imagined it must be one of the lesser-known IATA regulations, requiring Australian passengers on home territory to be sustained almost exclusively on Anzac biscuits and chilli sauce.

But if it had been tea-time when he left Sydney, and he'd been travelling for twenty four hours, it stood to reason it must be round about tea-time again. That would be logical, and his body agreed, but the world outside his window had developed the disorientating notion that it was morning.

No longer quite as sleepy as he had been in Ren's office Rupert made a cup of coffee, watched some news on the television, then headed for the shower. The brutalist granite masculinity of the guest bathroom was softened by a pile of thick white towels set out for his use, and he leaned for a long time into the pounding spray letting the aches and pains of the journey wash away. He emerged to towel his hair and stare blankly at himself in the mirror for a depressingly self-analytical moment; he was nearly thirty-five years old, not bad-looking if washed-out blond guys happened to be your sort of thing, good at his job and with ambition to spare – broke and betrayed and living in somebody else's home. Not that Gary and Steve weren't among the best friends he had – in fact, since he'd introduced them to each other, they adored him – but he'd gone from having everything (as he'd believed at the time) to having nothing remarkably quickly. Finding the energy to start again wasn't going to be easy.

Pulling on fresh underwear, draping a towel around his neck, he went back upstairs to investigate his options for breakfast – or was it brunch? At any rate there were eggs, bacon, mushrooms and tomatoes, and it was barely five minutes before he'd thrown together an omelette and another five before he'd wrapped himself happily around the outside of it. Now what? Sleep? Not a good idea if he wanted to get over his jet-lag quickly; instead he went back into his room, pulled on some clean clothes, and set off to re-acquaint himself with the neighbourhood.

On the day Rupert emerged from his parents' front door with their curses ringing in his ears he'd had his best mate – Paulie – waiting with a car. In actual fact he'd been house-sharing with Paulie at the time, although not in the capacity of a lover. There'd been four of them in those days, squeezed into a terraced house close beside London City airport, and although they'd all been gay (and probably still *were*, he conceded, apart from Paulie who wasn't anything any more) they'd looked outwards rather than inwards for sexual partners. Rupert had been the baby of the house, he'd got there through a contact-of-a-contact, and as such he'd been treated like a younger brother by the guys and he'd never felt uncomfortable with any of them for a moment.

People had come and gone over the years of course, men had moved in and moved out, but Rupert had stayed because it suited him and Paulie had stayed because he owned the place. He'd lived at Paulie's all through catering college, all through his first professional job, through the heady days when he'd first found himself working in Renfrew Sheppard's kitchen - right up until early 2005, when he and Cameron had departed for a new life Down Under leaving Paulie alone in the house. Paulie had sent them a Christmas card that first year, too, and had been planning to come over and visit them eventually – but before they'd even started to discuss a date he'd died a lonely and rather miserable death amidst the trappings of a self-bondage masturbation ritual. He'd been found trussed and dead in his own bed a fortnight later, when his employers finally got around to noticing he hadn't reported for work in a while, and with him Rupert had lost a dear friend and the most stalwart of allies.

It had been through Paulie, on the whole, that he'd received his formal culinary education – he'd never have gone to college at all if Paulie hadn't pushed him - and Paulie who'd noticed the vacancy at Nectarine and nudged him into applying. Not that Ren Sheppard had been a big media name at the time, of course; his first cookery show, *Sheppard's Pie*, hadn't even started filming then. In fact, he'd been on the brink of it and had needed to increase his staff to cope with the show's demands, and thus he'd been on the look-out for a bright young chef telegenic enough to be seen in the background helping with preparation. Rupert, although he hadn't realised it at the time, had been taken on with precisely this in mind.

Thus it was Paulie who'd indirectly led him to Ren - and Ren who'd introduced him to Southwark and Bermondsey and the areas round about. Ren had started by taking him through Borough Market and introducing him to stallholders who could make his life easier in the future; there were plenty of people who sold produce straight from the farm – everything from asparagus to watercress, in season, with the soil still on it. There were eggs in every colour of the rainbow from whatever variety of hen, duck or goose he cared to name, plus handmade cheeses, cream, stone-ground flour, preserves – in short, it was a veritable foodie paradise. And what chef wouldn't be inspired by all those glowing colours, the rich, familiar scents, the occasional exotic experiments? Rupert had plunged headlong into the life of the market, made friends there, learned from them everything he could possibly learn, and in due course he'd become Ren Sheppard's indispensable go-to man for sourcing the finest ingredients. Ren knew all about delegation, and could undoubtedly spot raw talent when he saw it.

Borough Market was one of the places Rupert had missed most, when he was on the other side of the world. He'd sometimes stood on the beach, looking out at the impossibly blue sea where it merged into the impossibly blue sky, mentally walking those halls and alleyways once more. It had even entered into his dreams from time to time, in loud, bright colours, with its extraordinary ethnic mix of traders and customers. Sometimes he would close his eyes and imagine he was sitting at an oilcloth-covered table outside 'David Cuppafield', a market tea bar owned by a man whose name was Dickens – *Harvey* Dickens - watching it all go by; that experience had been at the heart of his memories of England, and his nostalgia for it, and that was what he'd promised himself he'd do as soon as possible after he got home.

It didn't disappoint. There were new staff at Cuppafields who didn't know him, but they said their boss would be back shortly and Rupert took his tea to a quiet table – if there was such a thing – and waited. Sure enough before long Harvey himself came swaggering in - something over six foot six in height and of Trinidadian origin, although his accent didn't reflect this; it was as thoroughly south-of-the-river as Ren Sheppard's own.

"Fuck me," he exclaimed. "It's bloody Rupert!"

"It bloody is, mate - how are you?" And for the second time that day Rupert was enfolded in an affectionate hug which almost crushed his ribs to powder.

"Back for good, then, are you, sunshine?"

"For good? I hope it's good this time, Harv. I really hope it is."

Harvey dropped off the industrial-sized tins of coffee he'd brought from the cash-and-carry and returned to sit at the table.

"All right," he said, expansively. "Tell me all about it, then."

But that was easier said than done, and by the time Rupert was halfway through the story he'd seen Harvey's eyes glaze over and decided to change the subject. "Oh, mate," he said, "it goes on and on for bloody ever and it's way too depressing. What's been happening here while I've been away – any changes?"

Harvey shrugged. "Anna retired," he said. "She's living with her daughter in Lowestoft. And Brian sold up, didn't say why; one day he was here, next he wasn't, and there's a couple got his stall now. Yeah, lot of places under new management, now I think about it ... Polesworth Dairy, Something Fishy, Bun and Bagel, Garden of Eatin', Shoots and Leaves ... "

Harvey would have gone on longer if Rupert hadn't lifted a hand to stop him.

"Wait a minute. The Garden of Eatin'? What happened to that?"

"Not sure I can really tell you," was the downbeat response. "That lad that was running it, what was his name ... Jason?"

"Jake?"

"Jake, right. Something happened in his family – brother died, or something – and he had to go and take over the farm. He started doing it part time from up here – got someone in to look after the stall, and he was always up and down on the train - but in the end he decided he'd better move down there permanent."

"Down where?" It was easy to sound casual, but the mention of Jake had provoked a frisson of reaction. He'd enjoyed a harmless flirtation with Jake in the past, both knowing that it wasn't going anywhere because Rupert had Cameron and no intention of ever being unfaithful. Nevertheless it had made the days pass, the occasional smile and wink and exchange of innuendo; only a fool would have taken it seriously, though, and neither was a fool.

Harvey shook his head. "Wales somewhere," he said. "Ask on the stall, he still sends them stuff from the country; they should be able to tell you, if you're interested."

"I might," conceded Rupert, feeling an obscure impulse to play down the curiosity he was experiencing; there was no way he was capable of making good decisions at the moment, and he felt he should play his cards close to his chest. Nevertheless there was no denying that he'd be glad to see Jake again if it turned out to be possible. "I could see what they've got to say; I wouldn't mind catching up with him some time."

Harvey's face betrayed no reaction one way or the other. "Yeah, I'd like to know how he's getting on, too. And what about you; are you going back to Nectarine?"

At which point Rupert was obliged to spend a few minutes filling Harvey in on plans which were as yet barely formed, and then he excused himself.

"Time I got some sleep," he said. "I'll see what I can find out on Jake's old stall, then I'm heading for bed." He looked at his watch. "Nearly midnight my time, I'm dead on my feet; buy you a drink in the Market Tavern some time?"

"You're on," returned Harvey. "I'm there most nights 'til seven, same as usual."

"Good." Getting to his feet, Rupert clapped him on the shoulder. "Great to see you again, mate; I really missed this place, you know." And he was tired enough not to be surprised when he heard a slight crack in his voice distorting the words as he uttered them, and had to manufacture a cough to cover it up.

Wandering down the aisles, as always it was the variety of foodstuffs which impressed Rupert most. Even the humble potato, displayed in profusion in wicker baskets, produced in him an almost Pavlovian reaction; it was simply not possible to pass such beautiful stalls without buying something, and on impulse he picked up a jar of clear honey with a piece of the comb inside. Having paid for it he had nowhere to put it but kept it in his hand, establishing himself as a buyer of *something* rather than a compulsive idler, allowing him in turn to slow down and examine everything else in much more minute detail.

There were two women running the Garden of Eatin' now, wearing green and white tabards and the awkward combination of white mesh trilby and snood; they would have sold Rupert anything he wanted but were far less keen to provide information. A quick glance showed him that the stall had diversified a bit since the last time he was here; it was no longer exclusively selling home-grown produce, unless the lemons and bananas came from some British hothouse, but there were new peas, broad beans and rich red strawberries by the punnet which he could not possibly resist.

"Local?" he asked. "The strawberries, I mean?"

"Ah, no, I fink they're Scottish or somefing." The dismissive tone suggested Scotland was off the beaten track as far as the woman was concerned; if it wasn't on a direct line between the market and the Tube, she didn't really want to know.

Rupert picked out a punnet and paid for it. If he couldn't think of something to do with strawberries and honey he wasn't fit to be called a chef, but perhaps the most appropriate thing would be to eat them as they were.

"So you don't know where Jake is now?" he repeated. Again the women stonewalled, and he couldn't honestly blame them; they didn't know him from a hole in the ground, and if they had any information they were unwilling to pass it on. However, he suspected they didn't. "You're not in touch at all?"

"We deal with a bloke called Martin. We tell him what we want and he sends it." That was all he could get out of them, because they were anxious to move him on – and in his heart of hearts he was aware that there was something creepy about him asking questions like this; he wasn't surprised they were defensive. Well, it wasn't exactly urgent; he decided to let the matter drop.

"Thank you," he said, taking the bag, and he could almost feel the sighs of relief the two women exchanged as he walked away.

Back in Gary and Steve's apartment Rupert put the honey on the worktop and found a bowl to decant the strawberries into. He was washing and hulling them under the tap, mechanically, one-by-one, the way his grandmother had taught him, when his eye was taken by the unusual name of the grower printed on the punnet – SHIP MEADOW FARM. The words 'organic', 'natural' and 'sustainable' surrounded it like a halo - and under that, in smaller letters, LOWER HEMBURY, MONMOUTHSHIRE. So much for being Scottish! But then again the women on the stall hadn't looked as if they knew or cared much about what they were doing, and he had a sneaking suspicion the people at Ship Meadow Farm would be disappointed in their sales team if they knew. After all their hard work nurturing the plants, picking and packing the fruit and putting it on the train to London, it ended up under the jaded eyes and in the lacklustre hands of individuals clearly only interested in how much they were being paid.

He'd met so many people in his life who were passionate about good food – to the point of fanaticism, in some cases – that such indifference was beyond his understanding. But then there were those who ate supermarket burgers simply because they were cheap, and had no idea and even less curiosity about what chemicals they might be putting into their systems and the long-term damage they might do. At least the guys at Ship Meadow were trying in their own way - with their large, sweet strawberries - to change that. He could picture them in his mind – young, idealistic, chronically short of money, working every hour of daylight and then some, making a massive daily effort only for the harpies on the stall to metaphorically throw it back in their faces. In fact, he'd half a mind to contact them and tell them how woefully they were being served by their front-of-house team, but the chances were they already knew and couldn't do a thing about it.

He was breaking up the punnet to recycle when it occurred to his exhausted brain that Monmouthshire was in Wales, and he went below and dragged his laptop and accoutrements up to the dining table. Putting the farm's address into Google produced a website showing an idyllic swathe of British countryside under an immaculate blue sky. It explained the odd name – it was a corruption of 'Sheep Meadow', which made perfect sense to him in a Welsh rural context – and gave a small amount of information about the village, too. It looked as if Lower Hembury - which sounded like a tiny spit and a fart of a village scarcely worthy of a dot on the map – was in a fertile growing area. Well, wherever he ended up working, he'd need good suppliers – and, since his UK database was three years out of date, these people would be a good starting-point. It was never too soon to get networking again.

He clicked on the 'Contact Us' tab. The usual address, postcode, telephone number: SPEAK TO MARTIN FISHER ON 01600 …

"We deal with a bloke called Martin," the woman on the stall had said. "We tell him what we want and he sends it." And this, presumably, was the same Martin. But Martin was not the proprietor of the operation; the owners were named as H. Colley and J. Colley, which was odd in itself - a married couple would usually be listed as 'Howard and Julia Colley', or whatever their first names might be. Brothers, perhaps? Father and son, or even mother and son? Uncle, nephew; aunt, niece; grandparent, grandchild? His tired mind wouldn't let it go, and he flicked away to another tab to look at pictures of the growing operation; of a little neat wooden house with an immaculate kitchen garden; of a poly-tunnel sloping towards the river; of chickens, ducks, children, dogs, all horrendously photogenic and all apparently having the time of their lives making sure that Ship Meadow's fruit and vegetables were packed with all the fun and sunshine the place so obviously enjoyed in abundance.

And there in the midst of it all, in jeans and a checked shirt, one foot resting casually on the shoulder of his spade, stood an attractive young man in his mid to late twenties with dark curly hair and blue eyes and a cheeky grin that could light up the entire county. He was devastatingly handsome in a rooted-in-the-earth Seth Starkadder sort of way, and looked like nearly every woman's – and most gay men's – ideal of a robust but ultimately non-threatening bit of rough trade.

To Rupert the attraction was immediate, but it brought with it the shocked delight of recognition.

There was absolutely no question about it. He was looking at a picture of Jake.

3.

There was a temptation to dig further right away, but all the nerve-endings in Rupert's brain were telling him he should have been asleep hours ago - never mind what the stupid sun was doing – so he closed the laptop and took himself off to bed. He relaxed by imagining Ship Meadow Farm folded into the curve of the river, the neat rows of crops he'd glimpsed in the background of the picture – rhubarb and raspberries in the poly-tunnel, herbs in raised beds, glowing tomatoes in heavy trusses, scarlet runner bean flowers visited by drowsy bees, and somewhere an infinity of espaliered apple-trees along an old garden wall. The modest smallholding became in his mind a gracious country estate, and he slipped seamlessly into dreams of long sunlit corridors, clipped box-hedges and an immaculate formal parterre in which every known species of plant and shrub seemed to be blossoming all at once.

He awoke with a grunt at midnight, the lights of the city spangling the uncurtained sky, his insides demanding breakfast. After a few moments contemplating the injustice of Fate he got up to make tea and toast, after which he pulled his laptop towards him, booted it, and went back to the Ship Meadow Farm site.

So was Jake 'J. Colley', he wondered? He'd never actually known the man's surname, it had never been necessary before – but, if he was, who was the 'H. Colley' mentioned? The brother, perhaps, or the brother's widow? Harvey had said there was a brother who'd died, and it stood to reason that the death of a young man – no brother of Jake's could have been much more than ten years his senior – would have been reported in a local paper, if not on the village website. A search string featuring 'Colley', 'death' and 'Monmouthshire' ought to bring something to light, he reasoned, and this logic was rewarded on his the first attempt. The *Monmouth Herald* website (incorporating the *Chepstow Courant*) had a picture of a man with features similar to Jake's – older, fleshier, with straight hair rather than curls, but clearly from the same breeding-stock. **OPEN VERDICT IN DEATH OF LOCAL FARMER** ran the headline alongside it.

There was no evidence to establish whether popular local smallholder Timothy Colley, 32 ...

"Thirty-*two*," said Rupert, aloud. "Fuck!"

... died as the result of an accident or took his own life intentionally, an inquest heard this week. His body was found in the River Wye on 27 November after he failed to return from visiting his in-laws at Lower Hembury. He was thought to have had business worries, but his family strongly refute any suggestion of suicide. Coroner Karen Sneddon, recording an open verdict, said the full circumstances of his death might never be known, but that he probably entered the water from the derelict railway bridge near his home at Ship Meadow Farm.

Mr Colley leaves a wife, Helena, and two children aged eight and four. In addition to running an organic horticultural enterprise and giving talks about it locally he was a qualified referee in the Sîr Fynwy Sunday League, officiating for the last time on the day before his death.

It was an oddly impersonal piece in view of the description of the deceased as 'popular'. Still, unexpected death at that age would have been enough to plunge any family into chaos - so it was no wonder Jake had felt obliged to abandon his business in London and return to Monmouthshire to help out. And 'H. Colley' was presumably Helena; the burden of the business had no doubt fallen on her shoulders, and Jake – being Jake – had gone out of his way to help her bear it. Rupert wouldn't have expected anything else, really, little though he truly knew the man.

Over the next day and a half his patterns of sleeping and waking became less eccentric, although he was still not quite on UK time when the evening rolled around of his dinner with Ren. He'd salvaged a silk shirt from the wreckage of his Australian life and was thus able to present himself at Nectarine looking clean and tidy; he was conducted to a table in the rear corner at which – whenever he was in town – Renfrew Sheppard was widely known to hold court.

Tonight, however, it was just themselves, although they were interrupted twice by diners asking to have photographs taken with Ren. Each time he responded civilly but got rid of them as fast as he could, and each time he returned with his celebrated ruthlessness to the story Rupert had unwittingly found himself recounting – of Jake, the death of his brother, the farm, the women on the market stall. After the second interruption, and while they waited for dessert, the thread of narrative finally blundered to a halt. Ren took the opportunity of delivering his verdict on everything he'd heard so far.

"I remember you telling me you quite fancied Jake," he reminded Rupert. "A long time ago, admittedly."

"I did," acknowledged Rupert. "But I never did anything about it. I was with Cameron, remember?"

"For all the good it did you, yes. So what's this, then, Rupe, unfinished business?"

"I suppose so, in a way. But Jake's a mate, too, Ren: if he's in trouble, and I can help him … " Rupert paused there, struggling with the words. "You did it for me, after all; what's that thing you used to say about not returning a kindness?" he finished, limply.

"'Don't return a kindness, pass it on?'"

"That's it. I had people helping me, and I'm grateful. If Jake's got loads of support that's fine, he won't need anything from me – but I want to find out what's going on. I want to see if there's anything I can do to help."

"Right you are, then," returned Ren. "Keep in touch, and let me know what I can do. A good organic supplier's worth his weight in gold, after all."

"Hang on," protested Rupert, confused, "what do you mean 'keep in touch'? What exactly are we talking about here?"

"Well, *you*, you daft sod. It's obvious you're desperate to go down there and stick your nose into things that don't concern you, and you won't settle until you've got it out of your system - so I'm saying, mate, you'd better do it, hadn't you? Or you'll never be happy about it afterwards."

And that, thought Rupert later, was actually the first time that he'd realised he was contemplating mounting an expedition into the wilds of deepest, darkest Monmouthshire.

Not that it was straightforward figuring out how to get to Lower Hembury. The map didn't show a railway any nearer than Gloucester, and in the end - after a battle with a bus company website which had him spouting profanities at the top of his voice – he zeroed in on an hourly service through the Forest of Dean which called at a pub named the Ring o' Bells. There he would just have to ask his way; Ship Meadow Farm didn't appear under that name on Google Earth, and the only address he could find was 'Lower Hembury, Monmouthshire'. Nor was there anything under the name of Colley in the online phone book; the only number anywhere was the one for Martin Fisher, whoever he might be.

Well, it was too late at night to call him now – Rupert wasn't certain he'd intended to, anyway - and he'd be on his way too early in the morning to phone before he set off. In short, he'd have to take a chance, and if all else failed he could pretend to himself that all he'd really cared about was having a few days out of town before he started work. He didn't have unlimited money, of course, but there'd enough for a hotel or a B&B, and hopefully a couple of decent meals. He could leave his laptop behind and carry the backpack which would hold washing kit, a change of clothes and something to read on the journey.

In fact, he was beginning to warm to the whole idea. He hadn't taken a step into the unknown, even on such a minor scale, since he and Cameron had boarded the jumbo at Heathrow full of plans for their new life. He'd felt at the time maybe it was probably the last throw of the dice, that he'd never get another chance to do something unconventional; maybe he'd been wrong about that, though, and definitely he'd been wrong about Cameron.

Crossing London in the rush hour was easier said than done; Rupert had lost the techniques required to negotiate some of the more treacherous passages of the voyage, together with the sense of urgency his fellow-passengers appeared to be labouring under – barging ahead at insane speeds only to end up queueing a little further on. In Rupert's case this was a ticket window at Paddington where he reminded himself sternly as he walked away that travelling by rail, however expensive, had to be better than hiring a car and trying to cope with British traffic before he'd got his eye in again; no, he'd be happy enough to let the train take the strain – this time, at any rate.

So they hurtled across England, and Rupert watched the shapes of the countryside as they passed - clustered villages, spreading farmland, grey modern towns - and at length was decanted onto a cold platform in a half-hearted drizzle and changed trains. He reached Gloucester beneath lowering skies, consulted the timetable at the bus station, headed into the nearest pub and ordered a Cornish pasty and chips; there was no point being elitist about food when what you wanted was just something to eat, after all. He could be a foodie the rest of the time, as snobbish as the rest, but when it came to lining his stomach against adversity he wasn't above shovelling down the odd handful of frozen chips – and enjoying it, too. Ren would have shouted at him for it, no doubt – Ren thought life was too short to eat bad food – but there were times when one couldn't afford to be fussy, and this was one of them.

The bus was small, apparently held together by baling wire and hope, and had seat cushions flattened by the vicissitudes of time. However, being bounced around the country lanes – and being, for much of the time, the only passenger – turned out to be more fun than Rupert might have expected. The Forest of Dean, he was surprised to learn, wasn't entirely composed of trees; for the most part it was generous farmland, with pale villages and bungalows framed by lilacs or wisteria, and here and there evidence of industry on a local scale. There were ancient manor-houses and castles, riding stables, eco-retreats and living museums. Every shop seemed to do a roaring trade – especially those selling antiques – and every pub had hanging baskets, a slide for the kiddies and a menu outside. The Ring o' Bells in Lower Hembury, where the bus pulled up an hour out of Gloucester, had two of the three - if there was anywhere for kiddies to play, it was invisible from the street. The door stood open and the interior showed sunlight reflected off old polished wood, so Rupert headed in without a thought, ordered coffee and sat at the bar which - apart from himself and the woman at the counter - was deserted.

"You couldn't help me with directions, I suppose?" he asked. "I'm looking for somewhere called Ship Meadow Farm. A guy by the name of Jake Colley."

The name clearly registered with the barmaid; he could see a flicker of reaction cross her face, but it was gone again immediately.

"I don't know," she replied vaguely. "Lots of farms around here."

No doubt that was true, but if she'd lived in the village any length of time she'd probably figured out where most of them were. Still, he couldn't blame her for being cautious.

"My name's Rupert Goodall." He still carried a card identifying him as a *sous chef* at Nectarine, with a picture of himself and Ren on the back; he handed this over. "I work with Renfrew Sheppard. I've had Ship Meadow recommended as a supplier, and I'd like to take a look at it if I can." None of that was strictly untrue, he told himself; it was simply a collection of statements which didn't necessarily belong together.

The barmaid looked from the card to him, from him to the card again. "Where are you parked?" she asked.

Rupert shook his head. "I'm not parked, I'm on foot; I came in on the bus from Gloucester."

"Oh." There seemed to be a slow calculation taking place in the woman's mind, and eventually she said, "Well, I'm afraid you're in the wrong place, love." The 'love', thought Rupert, was undoubtedly a good sign.

"The wrong place? I don't understand; Ship Meadow Farm's in Lower Hembury, isn't it?"

"Well, yes, it is - as far as the Post Office is concerned, anyway. But it's on the other side of the river, you see. This is Lower Hembury in Gloucestershire; the farm's in Lower Hembury in *Monmouthshire*."

"Fuck." The word was out of Rupert's mouth before he could stop it. "Sorry, I mean … damn. You're telling me the village is actually in two different counties?"

"*Countries.*" The barmaid had relaxed a bit now, and was clearly not as nervous of him as she had been earlier. "We're in England, you see, and the other side of the river's in Wales. The border runs down the middle of the river."

Of course it did. He'd known that, hadn't he, from looking at the map? But somehow the significance of the river as a border hadn't really sunk in.

"I should have realised." He sat back on his barstool, shaking his head in annoyance. "I was so thrilled to find a bus that came to the right place, it never occurred to me there might be a river in the way. Is there a bridge anywhere?"

"Not here, there isn't. You can get a bus to Hembury Cross – the same one you came in on – but you'd have to walk back along the opposite bank to get to the farm."

"So there's no bridge here at all, then?"

"Not any more, no. There's an old one, but it's dangerous – somebody fell in the river off it back in the winter and got drowned."

Rupert had a shrewd suspicion which 'somebody' she meant. "I'm sorry to hear that," he replied. "You're right, it doesn't sound the sort of thing I'd want to mess about with." He sighed. "So, is there an alternative? Would I be able to hire a car or anything, locally?"

The woman shrugged. "There's Tricia's Taxi," she suggested. "My cousin Tricia; she takes people to Cardiff, to the airport and such. Want me to give her a call?"

"Yes please. If you would. I'd appreciate that." Somehow he hadn't expected it to be quite so simple.

The woman behind the bar grinned at him. "All right, my love," she said, reaching for the phone. "We'll see what Tricia says, then, shall we?"

Tricia wasn't in any mood to turn down a fare. She was a blonde in a fuchsia-pink tracksuit who drove a Volvo, and seemed to consider Rupert the epitome of cuteness. She explained as she drove, repeating her cousin's words, that the closest place to cross the river safely was at

Hembury Cross.

"It's a bit of a long way round," she said, "unless you can swim."

"I can," shrugged Rupert, "but I'd rather not."

"Good decision. There's leptospirosis in the water. That's the posh name for Weil's disease."

"Rat pee," he answered her, succinctly.

"Yes. Rat pee." And that was pretty much the end of the conversation.

The village of Hembury Cross was soon reached and the bridge itself – ancient, stone, only wide enough to take traffic in one direction at a time – traversed. Soon afterwards, at the top of a rise, they turned down an even narrower country road through mixed woodland and nettles which were at places higher than the car, and eventually came to a halt at a turning-space where an uncompromising five-barred gate blocked the way.

"This is it," said Tricia. "I can't get you any closer, I'm afraid; it's private land."

"Oh." Sure enough, the name SHIP MEADOW FARM was cut boldly into the wood of the gate and a red sign with white letters said NO UNAUTHORISED ADMITTANCE. There was a padlock and a chain securing the gate. How on earth did they manage for deliveries, he wondered, and everyday things like post? Did they come up here to collect stuff? Or did they go and fetch whatever they wanted for themselves?

"I'll give you my card," said Tricia, digging one out. "If you need to go back again, just give me a call."

"I haven't got a mobile," he told her, helplessly. He hadn't got round to buying a UK one yet, although he supposed it should have been his first thought; he didn't know anyone in the country but Ren or Gary and Steve who'd ever want to phone him anyway. "Is there somewhere round here I can call you from?"

Tricia shrugged. "There's a payphone at the Youth Hostel," she said. "There's a footpath through the woods; walk back up the way we came and you'll see a signpost on the left. That'll be ten quid, love."

He handed it over without protest, pulled his backpack to him and got out of the car. He watched her turn the Volvo and drive away before he hitched the backpack onto his shoulder and climbed over the gate.

Beyond, it was like being in a secret garden - a hollow lane plunged steadily downhill, but there was no birdsong and no sign of any animals, only a few wild-flowers blowing merrily in the breeze. He knew he must have seen far too many late-night science fiction and horror movies, but it was into just this sort of bucolic tranquillity that the unimaginable horror usually intruded – a terrifying creature, an army of alien robots, or maybe a goo which dissolved human flesh in an instant. In short there was a sense of foreboding hanging in the air and he was – not for the first time – starting to question his reasons for making the trip when the stone wall he'd been following suddenly turned into a pair of gate pillars with no gate between them and he stepped through into a wide, shallowly-sloping garden full of sunlight – in one corner of which stood a saw bench over which a young man with dark curly hair was leaning, making measurements and drawing in marks with a powerful air of concentration.

"Hello, Jake," exclaimed Rupert, relieved, and the young man almost jumped out of his skin at the sound of his voice.

"Fuck!"

It was not quite the welcome he'd been hoping for, and the look of annoyance on Jake's usually-smiling features completed the impression; Rupert wasn't wanted here, and Jake's next words reinforced the validity of that conviction.

"Rupert bloody Goodall! I really, *really* could have done without you showing up here out of the blue, you monumental bloody tosser, of all the fucking people in the world!"

4.

"Great to see you again, too." Rupert plastered on his biggest, brightest, dumbest-Aussie smile and began to close the distance between them.

With a sigh of exasperation Jake put down his pencil and ruler and advanced towards him, shaking his head. "I thought you were still in Australia, you mug," he said, as they drew close, throwing his arms around Rupert in a perfunctory and half-apologetic embrace. "But I mean it - I've got enough problems already without you adding to them."

"Sorry. I thought I might be able to help." And then, belatedly, it occurred to him that Jake should have been more surprised to see someone he hadn't run into for three years and had believed to be on the other side of the world anyway. "You knew I was coming," he said. It wasn't a question.

Jake shrugged. "Debbie at the pub rang Martin after you left, and he called me. Believe me, one word from me and Tricia would have run out of petrol or got you lost in the woods or something." Jake patted a little yellow gadget attached to his belt, which at a cursory glance Rupert had taken for a mobile phone; however it looked rather more businesslike up close - more in the nature of a two-way radio, in fact. "We're in what they call a 'fringe zone' here," he explained, "which means there's hardly any mobile reception on our side of the hill, but luckily we've got line of sight to Martin and Bridget's place; they're on the opposite bank, at the end of that line of trees – you can just see their chimney if you squint. Helena and the kids are over with them at the moment."

"Oh. Then Martin Fisher ... is *Helena's father?*" This piece of the puzzle had been unaccountably slow to fall into place but, if the 'in-laws' mentioned on the *Monmouth Herald* website included the Martin Fisher who handled orders for Ship Meadow Farm, suddenly it made perfect sense.

"Yes." Jake glanced back at the job he'd been doing – constructing a five-barred gate, Rupert now saw – and apparently gave up hope of making progress for a while. "Come on in," he said. "There's a bottle of cider, if you want it, and you can tell me what the ever-living fuck you think you're doing here."

They crossed the garden on a turf path and stepped into a modern wooden bungalow – it looked very much like a lodge from a holiday park – inside which a chaos of bright plastic toys was spread across chairs, tables, an old couch and the floor. The kitchen was little more than a range of units along one wall of the living-space, and three doors opposite opened into two small bedrooms and a bathroom. In short, it was just about the bottom line as far as accommodation was concerned; small, untidy, barely adequate, it had a roof and walls and little in the way of comfort. Even the TV, which in other homes would have dominated, was a tiny portable standing on what appeared to be an old bedside cupboard; obviously nobody who lived here was a millionaire just yet.

They removed a naked doll and a fire engine from the table, pulled out chairs, and sat down with a bottle of cider each – local and organic, to judge from the label. Rupert dumped his backpack on the sofa.

"Look," he said, "I'm sorry to turn up unannounced, but I couldn't find out how to contact you directly."

"You can't," replied Jake. "You have to phone Martin. If it's important, I go to his place – or the Youth Hostel – and phone you back. It'd cost the earth to get a land-line put in here, so it's going to have to wait until we've got more money – after we've dealt with things like solar panels and another poly-tunnel, anyway. We're only just staying afloat at the moment," he admitted. "I'm not sure how much longer we'll be able to keep going as we are."

"Well, I'm not here to add to your problems," said Rupert, contritely, "but I'm working with Ren again and I wanted to reconnect with you – not least because we always have a use for a good organic supplier at Nectarine."

"That's what the stall's for." Jake seemed unimpressed. "Whatever you need, Ann and Bev'll order it for you. They phone Martin, Martin contacts me. It's our apples in here," he added, indicating his cider bottle. "A lot of our income is from cider apples."

He seemed inclined to digress, and with sudden clarity Rupert realised the man was dog-tired, keeping himself going only through a massive effort of perseverance.

"You're running this more or less on your own, aren't you?" he asked. That much was beginning to be obvious.

"Well, yes - but it isn't a lot more than a hobby farm, to be honest. No animals to speak of, except chickens and a few ducks. I mean, we don't have sheep or cows or anything, just the fruit and veg. Oh, and the bees; they're new this year. We did talk about getting a goat, but they're fussy creatures ... " Jake trailed off. "It's all long days and short nights," he said. "I don't know how Tim managed it, he was always terrible about getting up for school - or why he was so keen, really, except that he wanted to build something for his kids. He thought their descendants were going to be on this land for the next hundred years. He barely lasted five." He'd covered his eyes as he spoke, and now his shoulders began to shake. Rupert, who wasn't sure what to do with such unfiltered emotion, reached out and put a hand on Jake's shoulder, gripping tightly. He'd seen this all before; seen it from himself, in fact, and - just as he'd crumpled and let it all out in one drunken midnight Skype call to Ren - here was Jake crumpling and letting it all out to him. It was obvious he'd been strong for everyone else, carried them after the trauma of his brother's death, but that he'd had nobody he himself could turn to for support. Rupert had come wandering along just when he was at a low ebb, and was a familiar enough figure to allow Jake to relax and share the burden. This was not the sort of help he'd originally set out to offer the man, but he supposed it was more useful than anything else he could have done.

"I know about your brother," he said, awkwardly. "It came up when I was Googling. 'Tragedy' isn't a big enough word for something like that, is it?"

Jake seemed to wrestle himself part-way out of his grief and turned to face Rupert, sore-eyed but apparently glad to refocus his thoughts.

"Tim wasn't a careless man," he said. "He might have taken risks in business – chucking up accounting to do this, for a start – but he had a wife and kids to look after and he took that seriously. He'd never have been stupid enough to cross the old bridge late at night, in that sort of weather; if he couldn't get home for any reason he'd have stayed with Martin and Bridget and come home in the morning, or talked Martin into giving him a lift, or even taken a bloody taxi."

"Oh, so you don't believe … ? I'm sorry, of course you don't believe it."

"The so-called 'suicide theory'? Nobody believes that around here, Rupert, except whatever lying bastard fed it to the papers."

"So you're saying you reckon it was an accident after all?" asked Rupert. Because if it wasn't, and it wasn't suicide, what other explanation could there be?

Jake was silent a long time before replying. At length he said, as though reluctantly, "If it was, it was a bloody convenient one for some people - and that's all I'm saying." There was a general pulling-himself-together and a squaring of shoulders before he spoke again. "Now, you said you wanted to talk business?"

Rupert shrugged. "It doesn't seem important after that," he said. "I just wanted an excuse to catch up with you, to be honest. Can I buy you a drink somewhere … or something, maybe?" he finished, awkwardly.

"No thanks. Not today, anyway. But I appreciate the offer." Then, as if realising more explanation was needed, "I literally can't leave the farm," Jake told him. "Helena's out with the car, and we don't leave the place unattended if we can help it. Things vanish, you know? Stuff gets stolen when we're not around."

"Out here?" In its own way Ship Meadow seemed as remote as some back-country places Rupert knew in Queensland, but come to think of it they sometimes got broken into and vandalised as well; there were mongrels on the planet low enough to steal anything that wasn't securely nailed down, wherever you were.

"Yeah, out here - I used to have a quad bike, for example. That's why there's a gate across the lane now, and why it's always locked; stuff still goes missing, but these days it's only small – whatever one guy can pick up and carry away, basically. Tell you the truth, I'm half-expecting my chisels and tape-measure to be gone by the time I get back outside." It wasn't entirely a joke; Rupert knew that from the tone in which the words were uttered. "Are you going back tonight, or can you hang on long enough to meet H and the kids?"

Rupert's eyebrows lifted. "I wasn't planning on going back immediately," he answered. "I've got a day or two to spare. On the other hand I haven't fixed up anywhere to stay; does the pub in the village do rooms, by any chance?"

"No, it doesn't. There's a guest house at Hembury Cross, they might be able to fit you in - or the Youth Hostel, of course, but if you're not a member they'll make you join. Or you can doss down here, if you don't mind a sleeping-bag; it may not be comfortable, but at least it's cheap."

Puzzled, Rupert glanced around. "On the sofa, do you mean? Or is that where you sleep?" The thing looked as if it had been trampled almost to death already, and simply clearing it of Lego would be quite an operation. It wasn't a particularly inviting prospect, he had to admit.

"No, you idiot, there's a caravan out the back; that's where I live, and it's out of bounds to the kids without an invitation." Jake sighed theatrically. "You'd better come and have a look," he offered.

Rupert picked up his backpack and bottle of cider and followed Jake outside. Beyond the poly-tunnel there was, as in his imagination, an extension of the ancient-seeming wall - although it wasn't ornamented with burgeoning apple-trees but had been used to prop up a range of semi-derelict storage sheds and workshops. One was clearly used as a garage, since its doors stood open and there was a whiff of petrol in the air. Rupert wondered if this was where the quad bike had been taken from.

The wall took a sharp turn left, and beyond it was another productive garden where cabbages, carrots, potatoes and other domestic staples were organised in rows. Here, sheltered on one side by the wall, at each end by larch-lap fence panels, and from above by an overhanging pear tree, stood a green static caravan about ten or fifteen years old which had clearly been in this position most of its life. Two pairs of Wellingtons stood beside the step, one large and masculine in design, the other small, pink and sparkly.

"They're Tara's," said Jake. "My niece. She likes to help out; she picks peas and beans for her mum."

The caravan wasn't locked. They stepped inside and were immediately in a narrow kitchen at the end of which was an L-shaped seating area with a television, table and gas fire. The whole thing rocked perilously, like a ship at sea, whenever anybody moved.

"Here's your room," said Jake, indicating a flimsy partition with a door in it. Inside Rupert saw a narrow single bed, a table under the window, a built-in wardrobe and a selection of children's pictures on the walls. "Tara used to sleep here when Tim and I were building the house, and everybody else squeezed into the other room. Tim tried to use it as a farm office for a while after that, but he gave up in the end - it was too expensive to heat in winter. There's a sleeping-bag in the wardrobe."

"Thanks." Rupert dropped his bag on the bunk and glanced around. It was all a bit pink for his taste, but it would definitely do – especially at the price.

"Bathroom." Off-handedly Jake indicated another door.

"Okay."

And really, what more was there for either of them to say? Rupert had set off from London with all sorts of unformed quixotic ideas in his head, but now he'd arrived he was beginning to feel marginally uncomfortable about the whole scenario. After all, what was he but an uninvited guest who scarcely knew his host? He'd thought maybe there was a connection between them at one time – but that had been years ago, and they were both probably different people now, and anyway he'd never been sure.

"Something the matter?" asked Jake. He was standing in the caravan's living area, seeming to occupy most of the space. This was the sort of environment in which every move had to be thought out in advance; it would probably be necessary to go outside in order to turn round.

"Not exactly," Rupert shrugged. "Only I hope you'll find me something to do in exchange for my night's lodging. Maybe I could cook for you all this evening?"

"You can cook for me, if you like," was the cheerful response. "I'm not much use at that sort of thing – H always leaves me instructions and I always end up having soup and crisps instead. The others won't be

back until later, though; it's Bridget's birthday – that's Helena's mum -
and they've booked a meal at the Ring o' Bells."

"Oh, right. Well, is there anything else I can do?"

Jake shook his head slowly. "You can give me a hand to finish off the
gate," he offered. "It'll go faster with two of us. Plus you can tell me
about Australia and Cameron. How is he, and what the hell are you
doing back in England on your own? At least, I assume you're on your
own?"

"I am," said Rupert. "Not exactly out of choice - but yes, I'm single
again. Can of worms, mate," he added, ruefully. "Can of worms."

"Yeah, I thought it might be. Well, I've got nothing but time, so I
don't mind listening – but come on outside and talk to me while I work;
the bloody gate won't build itself."

In deference, it seemed, to Rupert's belongings, Jake locked the caravan
as they left it, shoving the key into the pocket of his jeans.

"So," he prompted, "what happened? I thought you two were set for
life."

"So did I," acknowledged Rupert, wondering where the hell to start.
"But everything changed. Cam had an accident and after that he wasn't
the same person any more; then money started disappearing from the
business." It was a long story, and he wasn't ready to go into all the
details yet. "Turned out he was spending most of his time playing pokies
– that's the Aussie name for fruit machines – and by the time I realised
what was going on he'd run through about twenty-nine thousand dollars,
thirteen thousand quid. He'd maxed out all his credit cards, taken out
loans secured on the business and fuck knows what else. Then he did
something even more stupid; he broke into the RSL, which is like the
equivalent of the British Legion, and smashed open the poker machines
in there. I can see why he thought that'd be a good idea – he reckoned
they'd had plenty of money out of him and it was time he had something
back, and if he'd got away with it he'd have got about six thousand
dollars - but he couldn't even get that right. He was caught on the
premises, and as if that wasn't bad enough he took a swing at the lady
copper trying to arrest him, knocked her back against the pokies and

broke three of her ribs; only got as far as the car park before her mate rugby-tackled him, though. Meanwhile I was busy grilling steaks and making salads and running the business single-handed and I had no idea what was going on; it turned out Cameron's idea of shared responsibility involved me making the money and him spending it, and as time went on I realised that was all it ever had been. As far as he was concerned, I was just a meal-ticket."

They were back at the workshop now, where the frame of the gate was laid on a bench. Jake got Rupert started smoothing down the edges of a mortice, while he himself picked up chisel and mallet and finished cutting out a tenon.

"We had to sell the house to pay the bills, and after that there was almost nothing left," concluded Rupert, miserably. "I sold my car and all my furniture, and came out of it with more or less just what I needed to get me home. I'll have to start work soon if I'm going to get my head back above water; all my savings are gone, and I'm living in Gary and Steve's spare room. Do you remember them? You met them a couple of times in the pub."

Jake shook his head. "Remind me?"

"Ren's TV producer, Gary, and the gym bunny I introduced him to, Steve - only now he's calling himself a 'personal trainer'. They live round the corner from Nectarine, and I'm starting a six-month contract there next week. Ren's offered me a job at a place in Glasgow in the New Year, but I'm not sure about that. I mean, I don't know anybody in Scotland."

"You didn't know anybody in Australia, did you, when you moved there? Apart from Cameron, of course."

"True, but look how well that turned out. Anyway, maybe I'd be better off finding something in London, or doing agency work for a while – it's more stressful, but the money's good. On the other hand that wouldn't be regular income and I might have trouble getting a mortgage, so I'd have to rent for a while."

"Not the worst thing in the world," shrugged Jake.

"True, but I'm getting sick of not knowing what happens next and I'd like to put some proper roots down somewhere for a while. Besides, I've got a dog waiting for me in Australia and I'd really like to bring her over." Relentlessly he crushed the note of wistfulness in his voice. "You seem to have fallen on your feet," he added, more cheerfully. "This is a beautiful part of the world."

Jake laughed. "You wouldn't say that if you lived here," he replied. "There are always serpents in paradise. We're literally surrounded on three sides – except for the river, of course - by the biggest industrial farmers in the area, Diadem; they've been putting pressure on this place ever since Tim took it over. The land used to be leased to them – they wanted it to build accommodation for their migrant workers - but their plans kept getting knocked back. Then all of a sudden the Council changed their minds, but by that time Mum'd had enough and made the land over to Tim and me; she'd inherited it from my dad - he died when I was four - but she'd never bothered doing anything with it herself. The original idea was for Tim to grow the stuff and sell it, you see; I was going to stay on in London to run the stall so that I'd maybe have a chance of meeting somebody. Anyway it all caused a lot of trouble with my stepfather's family - they're the ones who own Diadem – and they've been doing everything they can to make our lives difficult. They reckon H and I should either lease the land back to them again or just sell it to them outright. Tudor – my stepfather – told H in so many words women don't belong in farming, and neither apparently do poofs."

"Delightful."

"Oh, he's a charmer all right, I'm sure you'd love him. Mind you, his brother's worse – and he's the one who actually runs Diadem. His name's Goronwy but everybody calls him Herbert – that's his middle name."

"As in 'scruffy Herbert'?" surmised Rupert, eyebrow lifting in enquiry.

"As in 'horrible Herbert'," Jake corrected, mildly. "Nobody ever knew what Mum saw in Tudor - and now she's gone where we can never ask her - but I reckon myself he was playing a long game; I'm convinced it was the land he was after all along, and he wasn't above marrying her to get his hands on it. He did everything he could to get her to sign it over while she was still alive, but Tim got her a solicitor and they said she ought to put everything in trust for him and me. Shit hit the fan when she died, though - and ever since then we've been living under siege." He straightened his back, offering up the tenon to the mortice, and seemed satisfied with the fit. "There you go," he grinned. "Only three more of these to do and we can get the gate put together. If you're sticking around for a day or two, you might even be able to help me hang it."

"Thanks," replied Rupert, aware that there was more to be said on both sides and that one evening probably wouldn't cover it. "I will, if you don't mind - as long as you promise to let me do a few odd jobs around the place."

"Well, all right, if you insist." Sighing, Jake made a superficial pantomime of reluctance. "I reckon you've got yourself a deal, there, Rupert mate," he conceded with a smile.

5.

At Jake's invitation Rupert went fossicking in the kitchen of the lodge to find ingredients for the evening meal, discovering the essentials for a perfectly acceptable pizza. Reassured that Helena and the children would not be back until bedtime, therefore, he went to work with the equipment available, fired up the Calor Gas stove, and by the time Jake had locked the workshop and wandered back over the little house was full of the scent of cooking.

"Never had a real chef cook just for me before," Jake grinned as he washed his hands.

"Don't get too used to it," laughed Rupert. "I'm not staying forever, I'm afraid."

They sat together at the scratched old table, happily tucking into their meal.

"You had your own restaurant in Australia, then?" Jake asked after a while, looking up carefully to assess if it was a safe topic of conversation.

"I did. Well, in theory, we did – Cameron and me."

"But you ended up running it on your own, you said. What was it called?"

"Roo's Beef'n'Reef. They all called me 'Roo' over there - they thought 'Rupert' was much too queer and much too British."

"But … " Jake made a helpless gesture with his fork.

"I know, I know - obviously I'm both. Blame the Aussie sense of humour, that's all I can say. Actually it's not a bad place to be gay, especially in the cities; further out, though, you're more likely to run into people who don't get it. We were lucky, our place was on the Queensland coast; you get a lot of visitors through every year so it's pretty cosmopolitan compared with places inland. Everybody knew Cam and I were a couple, we had rainbow flags all over the place, but we hardly ever had trouble. We were on a lot of websites and in a lot of guides for gay travellers so we got customers from that, but we also had local families and people who came to us because they loved the food. We served fresh-caught fish, prawns ... papayas, mangoes, pineapples, bananas straight from the tree ... Queensland beef and lamb ... bread and cheese made just down the road ... " He ground to a halt, memories almost overwhelming him. For a while it had seemed perfect, the two of them in their bungalow by the sea with the idiot dog Cameron had insisted on adopting - but which had always preferred Rupert - working and playing hard; scuba-diving, kite-surfing, sex ... But Cam had gone kite-surfing once too often, the wind had sheared, and he'd been thrown against the trunk of a palm tree and smashed unconscious onto a nearby road. His helmet had saved his life, but afterwards ... well, he hadn't quite been Cameron any more. Yet, when it came down to it, it was Rusty whom Rupert missed most; he hoped she was being well looked-after at the boarding kennel and wasn't pining for him anything like as much as he was pining for her.

"Rupert?"

He shook himself, banishing the thought before it could do more damage. He'd been determined to let it all go, the moment that Qantas steward had closed the jumbo's door and locked out the heavy, sweet-smelling air of Australia; he'd made up his mind to appreciate the good things England had to offer instead. He was returning because it was sensible, the right thing to do, but that hadn't meant it didn't somehow feel like running away. And where had it left him, anyway? In the middle of nowhere, scraping acquaintance with someone he'd barely known before he left England, that was where. He hoped this wasn't a symptom of the way his life was going to be from now on; he didn't want to think of himself as needy or pathetic.

"You know, Jake, maybe this wasn't a good idea. What on earth will your sister-in-law think when she gets back home and finds me cluttering up the place?"

"She'll think you're a friend of mine," replied Jake, "which you are. But if you ask me she'll probably be too busy to think anything; she'll have two kids to get ready for bed and another early start to prepare for in the morning. H is a bit like me, really; she tries not to think unless she has to."

"So what happens with the gate at the top of the lane? Does she let herself in when she gets back?"

"No. She calls me when she's leaving her mum and dad's and I go and open it for her. Sometimes I ride down in the car, but usually I wait – just to keep an eye on the place, in case there's anybody mucking about in the woods – and by the time I get back she's parked and put the kettle on. We've got it all down to a fine art, believe me. You'll have to introduce yourself," Jake added, with a laugh, "but considering what you've done to her kitchen I don't suppose she'll mind too much."

"Done?"

"Well, you've cleaned stuff up and tidied it away, haven't you? She won't be able to find anything for a week."

"Oh. Was that wrong? I only thought … "

"Stop panicking, you great big wuss," Jake told him, in a roughly affectionate tone. "I'll tell her you're one of the good fairies; that'll be enough." It was enough for Rupert, too, and jolted him out of his melancholy mood.

"Well," he admitted, "you wouldn't be completely wrong at that." And he returned to finishing his meal in a rather better frame of mind.

It had started to get dark when the call came through from Helena, a high-pitched squawk Rupert couldn't quite translate, and Jake set off up the track to meet her. They'd cleared away and washed the dishes from their meal, and had been sitting outside drinking coffee and watching swallows scooping over the rows of vegetables taking insects on the wing. There was a nest under the overhang of the garage roof which Jake had pointed out delightedly, but he was convinced there must also be more of them nearby. Watching as he started up the hill, Rupert was certain there were bats in the area too; he wondered if they and the swallows competed for their food supply - but concluded that, as they were apparently co-existing peacefully, probably they were not.

He spent the next few minutes inspecting the DVD collection in the lodge; there was more *Bob the Builder* and *Scooby-Doo* than was usually considered essential, but nothing else much that took his fancy. Then he heard the crunch of tyres on gravel, squared his shoulders, and went out to introduce himself.

His first impression of Helena was that she was almost painfully thin; there wasn't an ounce of spare flesh on her, and her narrow face was framed by a fall of straight dark hair which only seemed to enhance the effect. She was undoubtedly beautiful, but it was an aloof sort of beauty. She was also, to judge from the dark rings under her eyes, exhausted.

"Hello," he said. "You must be Helena; I'm Rupert." Which was the sort of thing Cameron had always suggested should win the Captain Kirk Prize For Stating The Obvious.

"Hello." She had stepped from the car and shaken his hand briefly. Hers was cold. "I'm sorry, Jake didn't tell me you were coming."

"He didn't know; I turned up completely out of the blue. Is there anything I can carry in for you?"

Helena's eyebrows lifted. "How are you with children?"

"Average." In fact, he didn't have a clue; other than the neighbours' kids in Queensland he'd rarely had much to do with them at all.

"You could carry Finny, if you like; he's nearly asleep."

Rupert glanced into the back of the car. A small boy on a booster seat blinked back at him; he was dressed in Superman pyjamas, slippers and a bathrobe.

"All right." Whilst Helena organised her daughter — who seemed disposed to do everything noisily — Rupert opened the door and unbuckled Finn from his seat. "What do you think, mate?" he said, quietly. "Going to let me take you inside while mummy puts away the car?"

Finn swallowed nervously but nodded, and put out his small round arms to be lifted. After a moment's awkwardness Rupert succeeded in extracting him, then leaned in to retrieve a knitted dog which was apparently indispensable; then he realised that one slipper had fallen off and bent down to pick that up, too. By this time he had a better hold on the child, and Finn's arms had closed around his neck, and as he hauled them both upright he began to feel that maybe this would be doable after all.

He was aware of the little girl scurrying beside him carrying something; she had long wild hair, the thinnest legs he'd ever seen - and one of the cheekiest faces, too. She held the door of the lodge for Rupert as he carried her brother in.

"Thank you, sweetheart. What's your name?" He knew he'd been told once, but he'd forgotten it already.

"Tara Michelle Colley; I'm nine and a quarter. My brother's Finn Christopher Colley and he's nearly five. When it's his birthday we're all going to McDonald's!" She announced it with such enthusiasm that it might have been the result of the Best Picture Oscar.

Rupert suppressed a shudder. He wasn't a fan of McDonald's, personally, but for parents of small children on a limited budget it could sometimes be the easy option; he wasn't going to condemn anybody for having no money and less imagination.

"All right, little feller," he said, sitting on the couch with Finn in his lap. "Let's wait for mummy and Uncle Jake. I see you like *Bob the Builder*," he went on. "You watch him a lot?"

A silent nod of the head and a wary expression were the only responses he received.

"And he's got a cat, hasn't he?" prompted Rupert. The odd trailer he'd seen had taught him that at least.

"Pilchard," said Finn. It was the first word he'd uttered, and to judge from the expression on his face he was astonished that someone he'd never met before – a grown-up, into the bargain - could possess recondite information.

"She gets lost in the rain," enthused Tara, "and when they get home they find her asleep on the chair and she just goes 'prrrp'."

"Yeah, that sounds like typical cat behaviour to me," laughed Rupert, but he was saved from further improvisation when Helena walked into the house, set her bag and keys on the table, and glanced around.

"Thank you for tidying up," she said. "You can visit any time you like. Would you like some coffee?"

"Not long had one, thanks, just before you got home – but can I make you one instead?"

Helena was shaking her head. "Thanks, but I have enough trouble getting to sleep as it is. And so do these two, usually – far too much sugar, I expect."

"Well, perhaps I'd better let you have this one back," said Rupert, rising to put Finn into her arms. "I think he's just about ready for his bed."

"Yes," said Helena, "and so am I. Maybe we'll have time to talk in the morning, if you're not dashing off too early?"

"No, apparently I'm staying on to help Jake hang a gate or something. Not that I have the first idea how to do it, but I presume he does. Goodnight, Finn," he added, "and goodnight Doggy, too." The creature was shoved into his face, and automatically he kissed the top of its knitted head. "Goodnight, Tara - sleep tight."

"Night night, man," answered Tara, cheekily, dancing from one foot to the other.

"Rupert," said Rupert.

"Uncle Rupert," corrected Helena, with a warning look.

"Uncle Rupert," he amended, "from Australia." And he didn't know why he'd added that, except that it might give him status in the little girl's eyes – which, for almost five seconds, it did. Then, with a yelp of delight, she turned away.

"Uncle *Kanga*-Rupert from Australia!" she squealed. "Boing! Boing! Boing!" And she was still making cartoon jumping noises when her mother ushered her into the bedroom and, with an expression of amused regret, closed the door between herself and Rupert.

"Making friends, I see?" Jake stepped into the lodge from outside.

Rupert was standing in the middle of the room, still mind-boggled from his encounter with the family. "Yes," he said. "Apparently I'm a kangaroo."

"So I heard. I hope you're house-trained, at least."

"More or less. Haven't had too many complaints so far."

"Good. Well, let's make ourselves scarce, shall we? H will want to decompress, and all I care about at the moment is a shower and an early night. I have to go out first thing in the morning to start the deliveries, but I'll try not to wake you up when I leave."

"What do you call 'first thing'?" They'd left the lodge and were crossing the garden again now; it was almost completely dark, although here and there solar-powered wands had been set along the path. The occasional moth flitted in and out of the little ghostly light they shed.

"Four-thirty. You don't need to move until I've gone, though – you'd only be in the way and I'm really bad company at that time of day. I'll be back before H takes the kids to school – she'll need the car then, and like I say we try not to leave the place unattended for any length of time."

"Isn't that … ?" Just in time Rupert managed not to ask whether it wasn't perhaps a little paranoid. "Are you sure that's absolutely necessary?" he amended instead, rather more tactfully.

"Walk a mile in my shoes," answered Jake, with a sigh. "Everybody's sceptical at first - Martin was, especially - but the evidence is too strong to ignore. Maybe we do take too many precautions, but it's got to be better than not taking enough."

"I know - and you're right, I don't completely understand the situation so I shouldn't comment," Rupert acknowledged. "I'm sorry; obviously you and H know what you're doing."

They were back at the caravan by now; Jake paused before unlocking it. "Have you noticed how dark it is here?" he asked. "We're miles from any source of light pollution. Apart from a few places on the other side of the valley, we could be completely alone in the universe up here."

Rupert resisted the temptation to tell him that until he'd been to the wilds of Australia he wouldn't know what true darkness - or true isolation - really was.

"Peaceful," he said instead.

"You'd think so, wouldn't you? But we're in the way here; the Roberts family have made it very clear they want us off this land."

"Why?"

Jake sat down hard on the caravan's built-in couch. "Money," he said simply. "Herb and Tudor are obsessed with the stuff, and they'll do just about anything they can to get it. They hire migrant workers from Eastern Europe, treat them like shit, pay them as little as they can get away with, fire them when they feel like it and then sit back and watch while the poor buggers get deported."

"Like gang-masters, d'you mean?" Then, into the resulting silence, Rupert added; "What? They have them in Australia, too, you know."

"I suppose they do, I didn't think of that. Well I don't know half of what they get up to over there, but I do have my suspicions. Martin's car was rear-ended once by an uninsured driver who didn't speak English, and you sometimes see a minibus full of people who look like they've been sleeping rough and haven't had a decent meal for months."

"So you reckon what? That they're being exploited? Or that they're illegal immigrants?"

"Could be either, could be both," Jake shrugged. "In any case the Roberts boys are much too slippery to let themselves get caught. They've got legal migrants living in decent accommodation, all above board, but I don't think that's the end of the story by any means. You remember those cockle-pickers who drowned in Morecambe Bay? Was that before you left England or not?"

"About a year before." Rupert didn't know anyone who hadn't been chilled by the tragic story; a group of Chinese migrant workers had been sent out to pick cockles, the tide had turned, and twenty-three of them had drowned. They'd all been illegal immigrants with barely a word of English between them.

"Well, I definitely wouldn't put that sort of thing past Herb and Tudor; they're parasites, the pair of them, and all they care about is the bottom line. Some of the stuff they use on their land would turn your hair green just to think about it, and they used to spray from a chopper until Tim complained and got it stopped. But I think it was us taking over the farm and turning it organic that upset them most; there were always going to be problems where their land ran alongside ours. What they didn't realise was that if they'd gone about things the right way and made an honest offer we might have ended up selling it to them anyway - we never had to be on opposite sides in the first place – but they didn't want to pay the market price, and now we're all suffering the consequences."

"What does it matter to them what you do with your land?" asked Rupert. He felt he was getting in deep here, as though he'd stepped through some looking-glass into a world where things didn't quite work the way he was used to.

"They call us amateurs," yawned Jake. "Dabblers. They say we're playing at it, not real farmers at all. Herb's as good as told us we're ruining the value of the land the way we're treating it, which he reckons means he'll get it for peanuts on the day we eventually go bankrupt. He's like a bloody vulture, you know? He's just waiting for Ship Meadow to die so he can get rich pickings off the corpse."

"That's disgusting," replied Rupert, absently. He wasn't sure how much of this was the product of over-work, tiredness and suspicion and … well, it wasn't impossible Jake had lost all sense of proportion about the merits of the two rival claims. Probably wisest not to say anything of the sort just at the moment, though.

"I know, you probably think I'm nuts." The remark was more pointed than was comfortable, and Rupert looked up guiltily to find Jake staring at him. "I honestly don't expect you to take my word for it, but if you were staying around for any length of time maybe you'd see what we're up against for yourself. If you want to help us, though, a nice juicy contract with Nectarine would go a long way – and maybe a few words from Ren on TV or in print about how Ship Meadow produces great organic yadda yaddas and we wouldn't have to worry about money in future. We might even be able to get somebody decent to run the market stall for a change."

Which was, at least, an aim with which Rupert could wholeheartedly empathise.

"No problem, mate," he answered, quietly. "The minute I get back to London, I promise to tell Ren you guys have the very best yaddas in the country, and I'll make absolutely certain he never buys a single solitary organic yadda from anybody else again."

6.

After the longish day he'd had, and all the travelling, and with the after-effects of jet-lag still lingering, Rupert had no objection to retiring early. When he was back at Nectarine he'd be up at crack of dawn every day anyway, and there was no reason to stay up late here with Jake crawling off to bed in a state of exhaustion before nine-thirty. Therefore he made a cup of tea and settled down in his sleeping-bag in the child-friendly bunk room to read a chapter or two of *Faceless Killers* and listen to the rural night until eventually he fell asleep – which, when he could hear soft snoring coming through the thin partition from next door, he didn't find difficult to do.

In the morning he was sleepily aware of Jake moving about but was too comfortable to get up and complicate matters. Instead he stayed where he was, drifting off again until slanting sunlight pried his eyes open somewhere between seven-thirty and eight. Then, with an effort, he pulled himself together to visit the microscopic bathroom, make a cup of tea, and clamber back into his clothes. He opened the caravan door and sat on the top step, tea in hand, looking out across the sloping garden and over the river towards the opposite bank where he could see nothing but generous, giving green, bathed in the subtle tinctures of morning pink and gold.

With one or two exceptions, Ship Meadow was much as he'd imagined it after seeing the pictures online. There were even, he'd been glad to notice, some espaliered apple trees alongside which Jake had established his beehives. The main commercial orchard was partly hidden from the house and garden by the contours of the land, falling away towards the river on the far side of a ridge which divided the farm into two asymmetrical slopes. During most of the year it was apparently simple enough for one man – with occasional assistance from family members – to take care of the trees; only for the harvest was additional labour necessary, and Jake had assured him there were always students willing to lodge at the Youth Hostel and pick apples for a week or two in October – it made a cheap working holiday and gave them extra income ahead of Christmas.

The whole scenario was idyllic. He supposed that somewhere beyond his eye-line people were robbing and raping and murdering one another as they did every day and in every country in the world - but here, now, at peace with the landscape, it was difficult to imagine. This was a moment of absolute contentment, one he would be glad to tuck away in his memory-bank to draw on whenever he needed it - when the world as a whole didn't seem so delightful, or when he was less certain of his place in it than he was today.

He was still sitting there, drowsily content, his arms and feet bare, his hair an unkempt muddle, when Jake came bustling round the corner wearing a purposeful expression.

"Oh, good!" he exclaimed. "I was just coming to kick you out of bed. H is taking the kids to school and I'm about to have some breakfast; are you hungry?"

Rationally Rupert felt he shouldn't have been; all he'd done since he arrived was cook, eat and talk, but the clean fresh air had sharpened his appetite acutely.

"I could eat a scabby donkey," he replied with enthusiasm.

"Sorry," grinned Jake. "Bang out of luck with that. Bacon sandwich do instead?"

"Brilliant. Hang on while I grab some shoes, and I'll be with you."

As they crossed to the lodge, Jake explained that they'd be on their own until lunchtime. "H does twenty hours a week at Caraways in Cinderford, and this is her weekend on." Then, in answer to a questioning look, "The supermarket?"

"Oh. That's ironic."

"How do you mean?"

Rupert shrugged. "Just that I'd have thought you hated supermarkets and everything to do with them, that's all."

Jake blew out his cheeks. "It's not that simple, though, is it? Yes, we oppose industrial farming practices and excessive food miles – but unfortunately we need a reliable income stream that we don't yet get from the farm, and jobs H can do to fit in with the kids are few and far between. She'd be capable of more if the work was available – she used to be a dental nurse - but the way things are she's lucky to have a job at all. We'd never get by if she didn't; that's seven thousand quid a year we couldn't manage without."

They were in the kitchen; Jake was pulling out supermarket bacon and sliced bread, switching on the grill, finding the tomato sauce. "Look, I know this isn't Nectarine, I know you're used to better things."

"That's not what I was thinking," Rupert protested quietly. "Nothing like it."

"No?" Jake's tone challenged him.

"No. Come on, Jake, I've run my own business; I know the compromises you have to make, I know sometimes you have to shake hands with the Devil. Change takes time; I understand that as well as you do."

Jake was watching him acutely. "Okay, sorry. I get frustrated about it myself sometimes, but there isn't much alternative; an ethical ideology is one thing, but we have to live in the real world too."

"Where not everybody sees things your way," nodded Rupert. "I know. But you're preaching to the choir, mate, so long as you realise."

"Yes. I know. Okay," said Jake, and then fell silent.

It was an uncomfortable moment. "Look," began Rupert, "I can clear out if I'm in the way. I really don't want to add to your problems."

Jake was turning the bacon in the grill-pan.

"No," he said. "We don't get many visitors - and I'm still waiting to find out why you're here in the first place; it can't all be about organic fruit and veg, now, can it?"

"Probably not," conceded Rupert. "Actually, what I was thinking was – if you're not seeing anyone at the moment, maybe you'd like to have dinner with me some time … somewhere nice, you know? You can pick the place, if you like."

"Dinner. Right." Jake wasn't meeting his eyes. Rupert didn't know what to make of that. "Well, I'm definitely not seeing anybody," he said at last. "I'm the only gay in the village, you know." A rueful chuckle followed this remark. "Actually, probably not - but I'm the only one I know about, anyway. It depends on when you're thinking about going home, I'd say."

"Have to be tomorrow night," replied Rupert. "I've got to be at work first thing Monday morning."

Jake's face twisted. "Well, unfortunately that means we're not going to be able to manage it this trip," he said evenly. "H doesn't finish until seven, which means I'm looking after the kids, and she's at work again on Sunday so she'll have the car all day. Plus there are no buses on Sundays, so if that's when you're going back it's a taxi into Ross-on-Wye and a bus from there to Gloucester. It's not a bad service, but it's definitely the long way round. On the other hand if I take you to Hembury Cross tomorrow evening after H gets back from work, you can catch the bus to Gloucester from there; if we do it before it gets dark, they should be okay on their own – they'll have the dogs for company, at least."

"Dogs?"

"We're looking after Martin and Bridget's dogs this weekend – Irish Wolfhounds – while they go to a wedding in Chester. Easier to have them here and let them run around wherever they want than to have to keep going over the other side of the river to feed them and let them out in the garden."

"I suppose it would be," conceded Rupert. "Great, I love dogs." And he was on the point of reaching for his wallet to show Jake his picture of Rusty when he realised that the subject had changed, and that any suggestion of a date had been subsumed in the practicalities of the journey home. For a moment he considered raising the question again, but there was a voice at the back of his mind insisting that maybe that was the way Jake preferred it - that now was not the time, here was not the place, and that he himself really didn't want to come off as looking desperate. All in all, it would be wiser to wait for another - and hopefully better - opportunity.

"I was useless at woodwork at school," Rupert confided, an hour later. He'd virtually shredded his hands on 40-grit sandpaper, reminding himself that his many skills did not extend to the traditionally masculine occupations of building and mending things; show him a plate of prawns to be peeled and he'd win a prize anywhere, but give him hammer and nails and he'd make an idiot of himself.

"So was I," laughed Jake. "I picked it up because I had to – Martin's been teaching me a bit at a time. But I'm the same about cooking; I suppose, if I really needed to do it, I'd probably learn quickly enough."

"Well, I hope I haven't ruined anything important."

"Only your manicure, as far as I can see. Could you pass the glue? I think this joint's about ready to fit together now." Rupert obliged. "We can get this assembled and clamped up today, and hopefully the glue'll be set by tomorrow morning and then we can hang the thing. I'll have to leave you for a while this afternoon, by the way; I've got veg boxes to deliver, and then I'm picking the kids up from Martin and Bridget's – they go there after school – and collecting the dogs at the same time. H will be here, but I don't know how much time she'll have to talk, if any."

"Not to worry," Rupert reassured him, "I can occupy myself. If all else fails I've got a book to read - or I might go for a walk, if you don't mind me wandering about on my own."

"No problem. If you're into wildlife we've got foxes and owls, and there are swans on the river. There's a footpath this side; if you follow it upriver it takes you to Hembury Cross. Downriver … " Jake hesitated.

"Ah." He didn't need to say more. The railway bridge from which Tim had entered the water on the night he died was downriver from the farm.

"Well, if you do go that way," continued Jake cautiously, "don't say anything to Helena or the children about it, that's all. It's bad enough they've got to live so close to it, without being constantly reminded."

"All right."

"We often get people fishing along the bank," Jake went on, with scarcely a flicker of emotion to mark the change of subject. "There's a local club; they reckon they get perch, dace, barbel … I forget what else, it's not my thing. There's usually someone hanging about by the old bridge; not very friendly, on the whole."

Rupert's eyebrows lifted at this. Most of the fishermen he'd encountered in Australia were happy enough to bend his ear about bait, rods, reels, boats and catches until the cows came home; he'd often bought bream, flathead and other species from enthusiastic anglers. On the other hand, maybe that was just the difference in national character; Australians tended to be outgoing and would share – sometimes over-share – just about anything, whereas the British had more of a habit of reserve.

"Maybe they don't like being disturbed," he offered. "I imagine they get a bit fed up of being asked if they've caught anything yet."

"That's probably it," conceded Jake. "Right, can you hold this steady while I put the other side rail on? I reckon we're making progress." And they returned to their carpentry, bumbling along amateurishly until finally they could bumble no more.

One of the lean-to buildings was referred to as the 'packing shed'. It was dark and small and contained little more than a bench and a series of shelves, and here Jake had been assembling veg boxes for his domestic customers – a relatively small number, since transport costs and variable supply ensured it was effectively a niche market. There were, however, some local people prepared to pay for high-quality organic produce delivered to their door, and - since word-of-mouth was virtually the only advertising Ship Meadow Farm employed - Jake had explained that the time and effort involved were being rewarded as their reputation for excellence increased.

Rupert tagged along and talked to him while he worked, eventually being promoted to assembling boxes from the flat-packs stored on the shelves – which he suspected would have been Tara's purview had she been available. Eventually, as they finished the last-but-one veg box, Jake's radio squawked at him and once again he set off up the lane.

"I didn't realise you did this even in daylight," said Rupert, walking the first hundred yards at his side. "No wonder you don't want to leave her alone for long."

"Yes. Helena's been frightened more than once by people hanging about in the woods," responded Jake, determinedly neutral. "They might just be looking for mushrooms or observing badger setts for all we know, but we don't take the chance if we can help it. Ever since Tim died, it's been belt and braces every time."

"Right. So shall I turn back and put the kettle on, then? No doubt she'll be glad of a cup of tea when she gets in."

"Thanks, mate," replied Jake easily. "I'm sure she will, and so will I."

The three of them gathered in the kitchen only long enough to consume cups of tea and a sandwich lunch, however, and then dispersed again. After helping Jake load veg boxes into the back of a Skoda which looked as if it had recently competed in the Paris-Dakar Rupert found himself temporarily unemployed, and spent the next half-hour wandering alone around the market garden. It was all firmly established, and to the limit of his knowledge good organic practices were in use throughout; it was obvious the family were enthusiastic composters, too.

Before long he had reached the bottom of the slope, where a stile broke the line of old trees revealing a luxuriant sward beyond, and a trodden path amidst knee-high wild flowers. Public footpath it may be, but it clearly didn't see a lot of traffic. The river here was untidy, deep and fast in places between little sedgy islands which had trapped old takeaway cups, plastic bags and the usual river detritus. At certain times of the year, Jake had told him, kayakers attempted to paddle from Hay-on-Wye down to Chepstow which, given the vagaries of the British climate, Rupert felt was likely to be a risky undertaking.

The weather was fine this afternoon, however, and he simply climbed over onto the path, turned right and kept going. He passed the lower end of the commercial orchard and the track which led to the Youth Hostel and marked the furthest extent of Ship Meadow land, and continued around the curve of the river until he could see at a distance what could only be the bridge where Tim had met his death. It was not at all what he had imagined; somehow a tamer picture had been in his mind, but this bridge was not only high above the water but also on a rising gradient to meet the steeply-sloping Welsh bank. There was much to admire about the way the Victorian railway pioneers had stoutly refused to be daunted by topography, although from where Rupert stood the construction reminded him of those precarious railroad trestles seen in Wild West movies – usually with the hero dangling by his fingernails from an open carriage door.

He couldn't have said, afterwards, whether it was delight in the unfolding British countryside that drew him on, or morbid curiosity to visit the scene of the tragedy; perhaps it was as much the desire to understand what had happened without having to ask painful questions of his hosts. In any case he didn't turn back on seeing the bridge but went forward again, stepping into shadow where the trees grew close to the river, following the path with no intention other than to while away an hour or so in his own easy company.

Since leaving the lodge he hadn't seen another human being. There had been cars on the opposite bank, though, moving along the road he had travelled with Tricia when he first arrived. This brought home, as nothing else had, how close the separate halves of the village were, and what a distance had to be travelled in the absence of a proper bridge. A cricket-ball thrown from Ship Meadow would easily come to earth in the back garden of a house on the English bank; it must be frustrating for anyone who lived locally to have to deal with on a daily basis.

As predicted, an angler was hunched close to the bridge on the Welsh side. Perched on a rock above the water, he had made a shelter with a couple of old boards and a tarpaulin in the lower branches of a tree, and seemed to be set up for a long wait with a flask, a newspaper and a supply of cigarettes. He wasn't taking much notice of his fishing rod, with its line curving elegantly into the water; nor did he seem aware of the midges which danced about him in profusion. Indeed Rupert would have thought he was oblivious to everything in the world, except that his head lifted as Rupert approached and there was an expression on his face somewhere between enquiry and hostility.

"Good afternoon," said Rupert, calmly. The man muttered something in return, but he couldn't quite catch what it was. "Anything biting - except the midges?" It was stupid, but it was really the only thing he could think of to say.

"Not yet." The man shook his newspaper and returned to perusing the football section in a universal gesture of dismissal.

"Well, I won't keep you talking, then," returned Rupert pleasantly, and moved away.

There were two ways he could take now; staying close to the river would mean trying to pass around the angler's line somehow, but if he went upwards and behind the man's back he could reach the deck of the bridge and get a closer look at it before he turned for home, and this was what he decided to do. It was a steep pull up a rocky path, but eventually he put his hand onto a rotten old wooden rail and set foot on slimy green timber and there he was, looking across the skeletal remains of what had once been a triumph of railway engineering. There were boards missing everywhere, the whole bridge like a gap-toothed mouth; it might have been negotiable in daylight and good weather - but after dark, in winter, only a madman would have attempted it. Or perhaps someone very, very desperate to get to the other side without going the long way round. It was all too easy to imagine Tim hurrying across here in horrendous conditions, heading for home, losing his footing and falling into the swollen river. Deceptively easy, perhaps, because having lived near the river for years he had surely known what it was capable of. What was it Jake had said? That Tim wasn't a careless man? But he'd done a careless thing, to be sure, and it had killed him. No wonder Jake was convinced the whole situation didn't quite add up.

Carefully Rupert leaned on the flimsy parapet of the bridge and looked into the water. There was plenty of depth there to drown in, even in summer; in winter, in flood conditions, it would have been deeper and moving faster, and there were rocks on which a man could be knocked unconscious. Once Tim had started across the bridge, therefore, death had been more or less inevitable – but the trouble was, Tim would certainly have been aware of that himself.

Below Rupert, on his ledge of rock, the unfriendly angler had pulled out a phone and was conversing with someone; apparently this location was one of the irregular patches on this side of the river where reception was to be obtained. The man was too far away - and the water too loud – for Rupert to have any idea what was being said, but there was something about his posture that struck him as wrong; he wasn't relaxed, as a man out for a day's fishing ought to be. So, what was going on? Had the angler been seized with an urgent desire to talk to his girlfriend or his brother-in-law only moments after Rupert had passed him on the river-bank? Or could the two things conceivably be cause and effect?

In either case the prospect of walking back past the man was one that distinctly did not appeal, and it was quite some time after that before Rupert could actually summon up the courage to make the attempt.

7.

The encounter with the angler was still on Rupert's mind when he returned to the lodge that afternoon. On re-passing the man he was ignored almost completely, although he had the distinct impression that a stony gaze followed him down the river bank and it was all he could do not to break into a run. However the scrutiny wasn't all one-sided; Rupert noticed details on the way back that he hadn't troubled himself with before. In particular, he realised that the newspaper - which he'd taken to be a classic British red-top - was nothing of the sort; it didn't even appear to be in English. Hardly surprising, since on this side of the border everything was bilingual by law, but he hadn't been aware of the existence of a mass-market Welsh-language tabloid daily – if it *was* Welsh, of course. However the world had moved on since he'd eloped with Cameron, and he wouldn't have been surprised if he was wrong. He repeated the name of the paper to himself as he walked, intending to write it down and look it up at the earliest opportunity; if nothing else, it might give a clue to the angler's national origin.

It hadn't been possible to tell much about the man's appearance without staring. He'd registered an untidy mop of hair in an intermediate colour his mind insisted on calling 'beige', a sour expression, a pair of direct dark eyes, and the fashion sense of someone who lived in a cardboard box at the bottom of a hedge. One of the migrant workers, trying to supplement his diet? That wasn't impossible, and maybe only a lack of conversational English lay behind the sullen manner. Yet the encounter sat oddly with him, and the first chance he got he was determined to discuss it with Jake.

As things turned out, this couldn't be done immediately; when Jake returned to Ship Meadow he not only had Finn and Tara with him in the car but the dogs too, shut behind a grille at the back. When released, they went gambolling about in such a frenzy that it seemed impossible anything in their path would survive the onslaught, and temporarily banished every other thought from his mind.

"That's Toffee." Jake pointed to a shaggy grey blur racing around the tidy kitchen garden in pursuit of a super-fast invisible rabbit. "And this is Fudge." Fudge was a more sedate individual with a lethally-wagging tail, currently nose-down in one of the borders like a pig hunting for truffles.

"So called because they're 'as soft as'?" grinned Rupert.

"Right. But they'll do nicely for burglar alarms until the geese arrive."

"Geese?"

"Aggressive little sods, cheaper to keep than dogs - and at the end of the day you can always eat them."

"Which you can't with dogs?" suggested Rupert.

"Which you can't with dogs. Plus the eggs are better."

"True. Not a lot of demand for dog eggs these days, is there?"

"Not much." Jake's smile was cheeky and indulgent. "They're on order from a bloke in Lydney, five geese and a gander; he'll be delivering them in the week. He reckons they go for anybody they don't like, and you don't want to be on the wrong end of them in a bad mood. But we'll have to get that gate fixed first, of course; should have it sorted by the end of tomorrow, with the two of us on it."

Rupert, who had never had any qualms about preparing *foie gras* when the occasion demanded, could only be grateful he'd be out of the way before the flock arrived. He stood for a moment watching the children – Finn stumping about on short, thick legs yelling something about tea, Tara absent-mindedly pulling Fudge's ears – then cornered Jake and spoke in a rather more purposeful tone.

"Listen, you know you told me about that guy fishing under the bridge?"

Jake's expression clouded with caution. Tara was still within earshot, so he took a couple of steps away and drew Rupert after him.

"What about him?" His voice, too, was low.

"Well, I ran into someone when I was out walking this afternoon," Rupert told him. "Creeped me out a bit, to be honest."

Jake was watching his face, his own expression shuttered. "Was it a foreign guy in a dark blue hoodie?"

"Yes, it was."

"Not exactly a wild guess. There are two or three different ones, I think, and they're something to do with Diadem, but you can never get more than a word or two out of them."

Rupert bit his lip. "Look," he said, "you probably think I'm out of my mind – I know I read far too much Scandi-crime for my own good - but do you reckon there's any possibility at all that the guy by the bridge might have been connected with … with what happened to your brother?" He hadn't known he was going to say that, exactly – his suspicions were still at the unformed stage and probably best left unexpressed - and the moment the words were out he wished he could take them back; Jake's expression had begun to change, and was no longer as sympathetic as it had been. "What I mean is," Rupert blundered on, "if I'd run into that bloke on a dark night, in rotten weather, I'd've been scared shitless; I'm not a wimp, Jake, and I'm bloody sure Tim wasn't, but there's something about him … Maybe I should shut up and forget about it altogether, though, eh? What d'you think?"

There had been a further alteration in Jake's manner, however, as if he was steeling himself not to over-react.

"Yeah, well, they do go night-fishing there sometimes - but if there was anybody around on the night Tim died they're keeping bloody quiet; nobody's ever come forward to say they saw what happened. Which they wouldn't if they'd been involved, of course. Jury's still out on that one, I suppose – there's no evidence either way."

Rupert had opened his mouth to comment again when Jake's lifted hand prevented him from speaking further.

"You'll have to watch what you're saying in front of H, mate; we don't talk about what happened to Tim unless she mentions it first – it's painful, obviously, and I don't want her upset without a bloody good reason."

"Of course," said Rupert. "You're right. Sorry I said anything."

"I'm not saying *I* won't discuss it," continued Jake, emolliently, "but not right now. I'm trying not to get in H's face if I can help it, and conspiracy theories are no bloody good to any of us unless there's some actual proof."

"I understand. Let's change the subject, shall we?"

And by the time they arrived at the lodge they were discussing the practical aspects of goose-keeping and the brainlessness of Irish Wolfhounds, and the minor miscommunication between them had already been forgotten.

The following day they made an early start on hanging the gate. Jake had rebated one post to accept the heavy iron hinges; now it was a question of digging either side of the gateway to sink the posts, positioning them carefully, and cementing them into place. There was no formal surface to the track at this point; it had been impacted into solidity by generations of pedestrians and vehicles, and occasionally had barrow-loads of hard-core, gravel or ash tipped onto it, but there was no tarmac or concrete to be broken through. Jake simply marked where the post-holes were to go, and he and Rupert took up spades and started digging. After an initial struggle they began to get somewhere with it, swinging into a steady rhythm of delving, excavating and redepositing soil as though accustomed to it all their lives. The morning was warm, with the sun unfurling above the roof of the lodge finding them already sweating from their exertions. Rupert's shirt was sticking to his back; it was a while since he'd been involved in heavy manual labour, but he had to admit that in a bizarre sort of way he was quite enjoying himself.

Jake had paused to wipe his brow, his head tilted upwards, his chest heaving. There was a hearty and abundant physicality about him – an impression only enhanced when he gripped the hem of his tee-shirt and wrestled his way out of it, revealing skin with the sheen and pink glow of a ripely blushing apple, and leaving Rupert unsure whether his own quickened heartbeat and accelerated breathing had more to do with unaccustomed exercise or the stirrings of desire. Not that he hadn't felt the same around Jake a time or two before, but he'd always controlled it carefully; there were occasions when it simply had to be ignored, for everybody's peace of mind and comfort including his own. Now, however, he felt free to look his fill - and to enjoy what he was seeing.

"What's this, then, a Diet Coke break?"

Jake's eyebrows waggled provocatively. "Liking the view?" he asked.

"Of course I am, you shameless tart; in fact, if that little exhibition's for my benefit, I've got to tell you I'm appreciating the hell out of it."

"Not entirely," Jake acknowledged. "Getting a bit warm over here, you know."

"Here, too;" although Rupert's side of the gateway had a fraction more shade than Jake's, and he'd been careful to make good use of it.

"You could always take yours off as well," was the arch suggestion, but Rupert had an answer ready for it.

"Not yet, thanks; I'm saving myself for a more suitable occasion. Rather keep you guessing a little while."

"Bollocks! You're just not doing enough to be sweating yet, you idle bugger!"

"Hey," replied Rupert, "I can assure you if there's one thing I'm definitely *not* idle about, it's buggery! As a matter of fact, you'll find I'm *extremely* energetic."

"Always good to know," laughed Jake. "Maybe you can prove it to me some time." Which was as close to an expression of interest as he'd got in the few hours of their re-acquaintance, and almost enough to convince Rupert he hadn't been wasting his time. But the children were out and about now, following Helena along the rows of beans and filling baskets whilst the dogs capered ecstatically around them, and an exchange of cautious glances brought the flirtation to a halt before it could go too far. "I reckon this hole's deep enough to take the gatepost now," said Jake, changing the subject determinedly. "Can you hold it steady while I measure up?"

"Ignoring any hint of Freudian symbolism as I wrap both hands tightly around your enormous piece of wood?" asked Rupert, unable to resist the *double entendre*.

"Of course. Grab hold and do exactly what I tell you," was the mischievous response, and for a while after that they were unable to look at one another without smirking idiotically. This did not prevent them working, however, and the post was manoeuvred into position and checked against a mark on the stone pillar, after which Jake tested the alignment one last time with a spirit level and then poured water into the hole – following it with a bag of dry Postcrete which he shook out evenly into the water. "All you need do now is stand absolutely still until it sets," he added, his lips twisting. "Don't move so much as a muscle, okay?"

Rupert's eyebrows lifted wickedly. "Any particular muscle you had in mind?"

Jake cast an eye in the direction of his family - all for the moment hidden from view behind the scarlet and green of the runner-bean canes - and then without preamble stepped over, taking advantage of Rupert's immobility to thrust a kiss, deep and dirty, into his readily accepting mouth. Considering that it was their first, and amounted to the opening bid in what would no doubt be a protracted and complicated negotiation, it established Jake's position on a number of very important questions at – as it were – a single stroke.

"The tongue," he said, pulling away after nothing like a long enough moment. "The tongue's a muscle. You cheated, Rupert; you definitely moved your tongue."

"I've got other muscles I'm having trouble keeping still, too," Rupert assured him, breathless. It was no exaggeration; apart from anything else, his arm was shaking from having been held static a fraction too long. "And anyway, you moved yours first."

"I did a bit, didn't I?" Jake was entirely unrepentant. "I enjoyed that."

"Well I hope you've got another bucket of water handy; you might have to chuck it all over me in a minute, if you're going to carry on like that."

"Yep," said Jake. "Plenty more where that came from, and I'll be happy to do the chucking. Oh, and you can move now, by the way," he added. "I think it's set." And he dodged aside rapidly, before Rupert could take the opportunity of unleashing swift and terrible retribution upon him.

Progress was slower after that. Following the opening of the gate at the top of the lane to allow Helena to set off for work at Caraways, the two men's time and attention had to be divided between working on their project and dancing attendance on two boisterous children and two even livelier dogs. The dogs did at least, from time to time, settle in strategically-placed patches of sunshine and fall asleep, but Finn and Tara had to be placated at regular intervals with drinks, sausage rolls, entertainment and first-aid, and it was only with the exercise of superhuman persistence that Jake and Rupert managed to move any further forward with the task at all. Nevertheless by the time late afternoon rolled around both posts were solidly in place, the gate was on its hinges, the two halves of the catch lined up, and the whole assemblage was working perfectly.

"I've got a feeling if we'd known what we were doing it wouldn't have taken more than half an hour," Jake said, shoving his hair back with a compulsive hand. "On the other hand, if I was on my own, I'd still have been struggling on Monday. I told Martin I could manage, but I don't think he believed me. When he sees how bloody great this thing's looking, he'll know for sure that I've cheated."

"It's not cheating to ask for help," Rupert told him, quietly. "It only means you recognise your limitations. There's nothing butch and manly about over-reaching yourself and getting in a mess." And hadn't he found *that* one out the hard way?

"True," acknowledged Jake, "but the problem is, I can't afford limitations - literally. Around here, if you don't sort something out yourself, you have to manage without it." He paused. "Tim was better than me at this kind of thing; he'd been to agricultural college and everything, he'd had proper training. I've picked up whatever I know in bits and pieces – from him, from his old textbooks, and some from asking people like Martin to show me how to do things."

This quiet admission of self-doubt was quite untypical of Jake, but the fact that he felt comfortable enough to express it to Rupert was reassuring in itself.

"Looks as if you're doing all right," he replied, calmly. "Everything's growing steadily, you've had no massive disasters … not of your own making, anyway."

"Minor bumps and bruises," conceded Jake. "But we're on a knife-edge; if I go down with flu, or break my ankle or something, there's no backup. We'd never afford to get anyone in to cover, and even if we did we'd have to teach them everything from scratch. If that happened, Helena and Bridget and Martin would have to carry on without me -

which might be okay for a week, maybe, but any longer and we'd be up shit creek without a paddle."

Momentarily Rupert was confused. "So what do other people - other smallholders - do, then? Is everybody round here in the same boat?"

"Most of us. We have to rely on family members or neighbours to help in an emergency. You can sometimes get farming students who know what they're doing, but it's a lottery - and you don't want to risk bringing in some incompetent tosser who'll run your business into the ground while you're flat on your back. When you hear about farmers not trusting people, Rupe, that's the reason; our livelihoods are shaky enough as it is."

Rupert was nodding slowly. "Well, look," he said, "I'd be happy to come down and help out if ever you need me - at least I can do the boring stuff; no reason I can't pack the odd veg box or do a bit of weeding - or even just keep an eye on the place to let you have a day off, is there?"

Jake's brow furrowed. "No," he conceded, "but we couldn't pay you, of course, and I reckon you've got better things to do with your time in London."

Rupert shrugged. "A free country weekend in return for a bit of gentle gardening or DIY seems reasonable to me," he said, wondering if he was pushing too hard. "I wouldn't mind doing something worthwhile with my time off, actually; Steve and Gary are great blokes and wonderful mates, but they're world-class party animals – loads of pretentious media types and twinks on the make, not my idea of fun at all." It had been, at one time, he wouldn't deny – but life had caught up with him in a way that made it all look rather superficial by comparison.

"Okay." Jake still seemed uncomfortable, and his next words were not exactly a surprise. "Look, if you're thinking ... " He waved a hand in the direction of the caravan. "That thing rocks like a ship on the high seas; it'd be like standing up in a hammock, and I wouldn't want the kids asking what we'd been up to in the morning. Plus ... " He trailed off awkwardly.

"Plus what?"

Jake shrugged. "I don't know about you, but if we're going to do this I reckon it's worth making a bit more of an effort and doing it properly.

Somewhere a bloody sight more comfortable, for a start."

"Yes." The relief was almost palpable; Rupert could feel a smile spreading across his face, which was met and returned in full measure by one from Jake. "I do. But I wasn't talking about that, believe it or not. What I meant was – it's been brilliant to do something useful with my time for a change, and I've fallen head over heels in love with this place."

"Only with the place?" Jake queried, teasingly. "I think I'm a bit hurt."

"Only with the place for now," was the judicious response. "Quite apart from anything between you and me, Jake, I'd love to come and help out here if there's anything for me to do. I'm totally serious about that."

Jake was still grinning at him. "Okay then," he said, "you're on. As for the rest of it – well, I get up to London about once a month to check how things are going on the stall. Usually I go up and back the same day, but if I can get Martin to keep an eye on H and the kids overnight maybe I can book into a hotel for a change. It won't be anything palatial," he warned. "Clean and comfortable is as much as we can hope for on my budget."

"All right, fair enough. If you can time it for one of my weekends off, I wouldn't have to dash away in the morning, either. I'm off the weekend after next," Rupert added, "and alternate weekends after that, Thursday to Sunday."

"Okay, then, I'll see what Martin has to say when they get back from the wedding. Give me a number where I can reach you and I'll have a go at putting something together."

"Well, whatever it is, it's got to be a damn' sight better than standing up in a hammock."

"True," returned Jake, and for a while they just smiled at one another and didn't speak. "Now, mate, much as I hate to break the mood, I reckon we ought to give these kids and dogs their tea before they decide they're hungry enough to eat the pair of *us*."

"Oh well - if you absolutely insist," sighed Rupert, and they went into the lodge together to get started on the meal.

8.

Detaching himself from the family at Ship Meadow – people he'd known, with the exception of Jake, scarcely forty-eight hours – proved surprisingly difficult for Rupert. However there was little time for prolonged and sentimental farewells; Helena arrived home looking worn out and went straight into the bedtime routine with the children, whilst Jake loaded Rupert and his possessions into the Skoda and had whisked him away up the lane almost before he'd had a chance to say goodbye.

"I'll miss the kids," he said, re-settling himself in the passenger seat after dealing with the gate. "I thought H looked completely knackered."

"She often does," replied Jake. "She tries not to complain, but I wouldn't imagine this is anything like she wanted her life to be. Martin and Bridget aren't wealthy but they're moderately well-off – they had a couple of small businesses, he was plumber and she was a hairdresser – so I don't think H knew what it was like to do without stuff when she was a kid. Tim used to worry about that; he was afraid they'd think he couldn't support her properly."

They were gliding slowly through the woods, early evening sunshine dappling between vibrant green leaves painting the scene with flecks of gold; it was almost impossible to imagine anything inimical might lurk nearby, and yet Rupert was aware that the mood could change as swiftly as the weather – and there were places out here where things, and people, could remain undetected for a very long time indeed. Months. Years. Centuries. Such suspicions, once entertained, could never be banished entirely; that was probably how people felt when they'd been burgled, he thought – or betrayed by somebody they loved. Trust was like virginity in that respect – it was far too easy to lose, and completely impossible to regain.

"I don't suppose that mattered to her, though, did it?" he asked. "She doesn't strike me as the type to care about material things."

Jake laughed quietly. "She grew up wanting to be Felicity Kendall in

The Good Life," he replied. "Explains a lot, doesn't it? By the time she met Tim we were already thinking about taking over the land and running it ourselves, and she was dead keen on the idea, so when they got married they lived off her earnings while he went to agricultural college; she was behind him every step of the way. Of course, nobody had any idea what was going to happen," he added, glumly

"Well, no. But ninety-nine percent of the time you probably wouldn't start something if you knew for certain how it ended, anyway. It's the journey that's important as much as the destination."

"True," conceded Jake. "You'd have got on well with Tim, I reckon."

"Thank you. I appreciate that."

There was pause after this, and then Jake said, "Look, about Tim's death … "

"No, honestly, we don't need to talk about that. I'm sorry I ever raised the subject."

But Jake was shaking his head. "It's not as simple as it looks, everyone knows that. Only there's a big gap between that and actually being able to charge anybody. The car ran out of petrol when it shouldn't have – so maybe the tank was drained - but then there's the question of why he didn't go back to Martin and Bridget's, or ask someone else for help, and nobody can answer that. If you want my opinion, maybe there was some reason why he felt it wouldn't be safe to turn back - somebody coming up behind him maybe - and he had to keep going forward. You've seen how far it is by road; would you have walked that, or – if you had a young family at home and you were afraid they might be vulnerable - would you have risked the bridge?"

"I don't know. I think I'd've phoned the police."

"And said what? That your car had broken down and you couldn't get home? They'd have told you to call the AA or get a taxi, and they'd've been right."

"But if there was somebody following him … threatening him … ?"

"If there was - we're guessing – by the time the coppers got out here they'd've made themselves scarce. And there's nowhere to call from anyway; the nearest phone box is at Hembury Cross, and if he could've got to Martin and Bridget's he wouldn't've needed the police in the first place - though there are other houses he could've knocked at, and I don't know why he didn't."

"So they're not taking any interest in what happened, then? The police?"

"Not a hope. In fact I wouldn't be surprised if the suicide story came from them originally, although I can't prove it of course. Whatever, they're not interested in digging deeper - and if they were they probably couldn't afford to do it. They're closing police stations all over the county, and if we see a copper here from one month's end to the next it's a miracle; the most they do these days is give you a crime number to go on the insurance claim – for all the bloody good it does."

"So what do you think happened?" Rupert knew he was taking a chance asking straight out like this, but there was no point pussy-footing around any more. If there was ever going to be anything worth having between himself and Jake, they had to get the elephant out of the room first – otherwise they'd expend a lot of valuable time and energy not talking about it which they could be putting to better use.

"Honestly? I don't know. But I know Tim didn't kill himself. It could have been an accident, or it could have been something else, but it wasn't a deliberate choice to die; he just had far too bloody much to live for."

"So, if … I mean, do you have any actual suspects?"

Jake's mouth twisted. "If I did, mate, I'd be talking to the coppers about it. Useless they may be, most of the bloody time, but if I had anything worth taking to them you can bet your arse I'd've done it by now. I know we don't exactly get along with Diadem, and I wouldn't put the thefts and so on past them – my quad bike's probably somewhere in that bloody workshop of theirs, for example – but actual murder sounds a little bit extreme even for them."

"Well - could they have been the ones who pinched the petrol, maybe?"

"They could have, just to cause him grief. That doesn't mean they planned what happened afterwards, though, does it?"

"Okay," acknowledged Rupert. "But couldn't they still be done for theft?"

"In a perfect world, maybe - if the coppers could prove it had been stolen in the first place, but they said there was no evidence of malicious damage to the car and it was probably just a dodgy fuel gauge or a leak somewhere. They weren't interested in investigating, is the long and short of it. A farmer drowns around here and nine times out of ten it comes down to suicide; they need a bloody good reason to look further than that, and in Tim's case they just didn't have one. I'm not expecting them to do anything about it now unless there's some new evidence - and I don't really think there will be."

"Does Helena agree? I mean, was she satisfied with the verdict at the inquest?" He hadn't meant it to come out as sharply as that, like a prosecuting counsel trying to demolish an alibi, and he wouldn't have been surprised if Jake had refused to answer, but the question didn't seem to have unsettled him at all.

"I shouldn't think anybody's ever satisfied with an open verdict, it just means they don't know what happened - but we're on the same page about it and so's her dad. It's not ideal, but it's what we've got and we just have to do the best we can with it."

"I understand." But there was still one question nagging at him, and he couldn't quite prevent himself from asking it. "What happened about the car, then? Was it ever properly examined? Have the police still got it?"

Jake was shaking his head, as though in disbelief. "You're right," he said, "you do read too many whodunnits. What do you think happened to the bloody car, you idiot?"

Ah. He hadn't even thought of that. It wasn't a crime scene, it wasn't evidence, and if Hafren Police had wanted to hold onto it they probably wouldn't have had anywhere to put it anyway. Also, judging by the fragile state of their finances, Jake and Helena would never have been able to afford to replace the thing, regardless of circumstances – so there was only one conclusion available; they were still using it, of course.

"Sorry. Stupid question."

"It's actually a bloody good car. It's never let us down, before or since."

Silence reigned for quite some time following this exchange, and when the two men at last began to speak again it was about other and less contentious matters.

Tempting as it was, Rupert and Jake managed to forego any *Brief Encounter*-type farewell at the bus stop in Hembury Cross. For one thing, parking wasn't straightforward; it was a question of Jake pulling onto the forecourt of the Village Hall and Rupert sprinting across the road with some sense of urgency because the bus was waiting with its engine running. It was just as well, he supposed; he wasn't sure they'd reached that stage yet, and he got the feeling Hembury Cross in general wouldn't have appreciated it anyway. He was vaguely aware of gabbling how much he'd enjoyed himself and how he looked forward to seeing Jake and the family again, and promising to phone Martin Fisher as soon as he'd bought a mobile so that he could pass the number on. Beyond that there wasn't much he could think of to say, and he boarded the bus with an odd feeling that maybe this was it, the end, and there would never be any more between himself and Jake.

He hated departures anyway; he'd always seen them as the end of something, rather than the start of something else. Life had, he supposed, turned him into one of the sort of glass-half-empty people Ren was so scathing about. Still, he managed a smile and a wave for Jake, who returned them with interest. Then, in a cloud of diesel fumes, the bus pulled away from the stop, crossed the river, and turned northward – away from Lower Hembury, from Ship Meadow, the children, the dogs, the mystery, and Jake.

Rupert wasn't given to excessive self-analysis. On the whole he took life as it came, dealing with its challenges and disasters on an individual basis, and tried not to plan too far ahead. He'd broken that rule for Cameron, though; he'd been shown a vision of what life in Australia could be – Cameron had a British mum and an Aussie dad and had grown up on a banana plantation in Queensland – and he'd been seduced by it. He'd rolled the dice and decided to take a risk, and for a while it had seemed to be working out spectacularly. Not that there hadn't been the occasional flaw, but Rupert's easy-going nature had made light of them all. Even when his relationship with Cameron had begun to disintegrate under the strain of long working hours and meagre profits he'd put a brave face on it and hoped – and worked – for better. All relationships had their ups and downs, he hadn't been stupid enough to expect anything else - and while he and Cam were having sex on a regular basis at least they were communicating; but then one of them had lost interest - or it might have been both - and it had become apparent that there was very little holding them together. Still they'd kept going, though, until Cameron's accident had changed the landscape irrevocably and Rupert had realised there could be no future for them as a couple. It was all over bar the shouting, and he was just going to have to be brave enough to acknowledge it.

Sitting on the bus, staring out at the bland, smiling British countryside – so like but so completely unlike that of his briefly-adopted southern homeland – he couldn't help remembering the way that optimism had turned to futility. Not that there was a comparison to be made between Cameron and Jake, however; Cameron was worldly-wise, even cynical, whereas with Jake there was – despite the tragedy of his brother's death – an almost Micawberish certainty that something would turn up. Jake was clearly one of the glass-half-full people, which was great – except that he and Rupert saw things in such different ways that the chance of finding themselves on the same page seemed, at the moment, quite remote. With that in mind he should probably ask himself whether he'd be doing the right thing getting involved with the man at all.

Or maybe he was just tired and cynical and too frazzled mentally to make a rational decision at the moment. At any rate, a couple of days and nights at Ship Meadow had given him new things to think about, new people to care for, new memories to treasure; some of the scars left by the Cameron débâcle were beginning to heal at last, and if nothing else he now had – after what seemed an interminable lifetime – something of interest to look forward to again.

By the time he was back in London it was late, and the party crowd were out in force. There had been a time in his life – when he was a carefree young chef lodging at Paulie's – when he would have been among them, never mind how early he'd had to start work; he could party till dawn in those days, and still be on his feet and cooking brilliantly twelve hours later. It wasn't that he lacked the physical endurance to do so now, just that life had made him cynical and there were activities he valued more. If anyone had told him three years ago that he'd be trying to readjust his life around the needs of a daft Australian Springer Spaniel, for example, he'd have thought they were insane. Add in Jake, the children, the geese and the mystery, and there was a graphic illustration of the way his priorities had shifted over the years. The problem was, he was sure Gary and Steve would still be the same people they'd been when he left London – their more settled domestic life notwithstanding.

Steve, muscle-brained and shining, met him half-way up the stairs. He'd bulked out more than Rupert remembered, his upper body now almost square and his shoulders sculpted to perfection. He'd obviously conceded defeat in the battle against male pattern baldness, though; only a thin grey stubble adorned his head. Aside from the welcoming grin on his face and the friendly twinkle in his eyes he was the sort of person Rupert wouldn't have wanted to meet in a dark alley, and for a fleeting moment he imagined pitting Steve against the hoodie from the river bank; it was a satisfyingly conclusive scenario which ended up with one drenched and exceptionally dejected hoodie.

"Hello, Rupe." Quietly-spoken for such a big man, Steve pulled Rupert into a full-body hug and ruffled his hair enthusiastically.

"Steve, mate; how was the triathlon?"

Steve shrugged. "Got to get faster," he said. "Three women got back ahead of me." Self-disgust was evident in his tone; in Steve's vocabulary, losing out on anything to a female was the ultimate humiliation.

"Really? And how many men?"

"Sixteen. I was twentieth."

"Out of how many?"

"Eight hundred and forty."

"Well, that's ... "

"It's not good enough," Steve told him firmly, and the bizarre thing was that Rupert knew what he meant.

""Never mind," he told him. "You'll get the buggers next time."

"Hope so. I'm doing an Ironman in Dorset in September, that ought to sort the sheep out from the goats."

They had climbed back up to the flat where Gary was waiting for them, still looking impossibly young. By contrast with Steve he seemed to have acquired even more hair since Rupert had seen him, and was now sporting a collar-length dark mop in artistic disarray and a crop of face-fungus which couldn't decide whether it was designer stubble or a full beard. He, too, was effusive in his greeting.

"Silly arse, you should never have gone away," he said, twining his arms around Rupert's neck.

"Well, yes, I know that now," replied Rupert, returning the hug. "Not much point in being wise after the event, though, is there?"

"We all liked Cameron," Gary went on, as though by way of apology. "He seemed fine to us when he was here."

"I think he was," replied Rupert. "And maybe if we'd stayed in the UK it would have worked out. It was when he got back to Australia that he changed; his mum said he'd reverted. But we can't turn the clocks back, can we, Gaz? We have to keep on going forward."

"Of course. Speaking of which, is there any news of Rusty?"

Rupert shook his head. "Nothing recent," he said. "I've been off the grid in Monmouthshire for a couple of days." Then, by way of explanation, "You remember Jake, from the Market Tavern?" It took a while to explain who Jake was, and to remind Gary and Steve that they'd actually met him a few times.

"Oh, yes," said Gary at length. "He was quite cute. Is he the great new love interest, then?"

"Too early to say." Rupert was on the sofa now, a cup of coffee in his hand that he didn't really want. "Could be." He'd made his mind up on the train not to say anything about Tim's death or the goings-on at Ship Meadow, but he gave them a lightning sketch of Jake as a man with responsibilities beyond his years, trying to hold together a farm he hadn't expected to inherit and a family that wasn't his. "Anything I can do to get them some publicity or push business their way would really help," he concluded. "D'you reckon you can squeeze anything into Ren's new series? Maybe something about good cooking starting with the best ingredients?"

"Possibly," conceded Gary. "I'll put it up at the next production meeting. But you do know we're not doing *Sheppard's Pie* again this time, don't you? Did Ren tell you about that?"

"No, he never said a word." They'd discussed Rupert's problems almost exclusively, which only went to show what a good mate Ren was.

"Well, we're getting more adventurous; he's going to create pop-up restaurants in a new location every week, and cook everything using local produce. We've got all our venues booked for this year - but if there's a suitable location somewhere near your farm, maybe we can do a show from there in season two."

"If they're still in business by then," replied Rupert, "it's worth considering, but they're pretty much down to the wire already; I don't know how they're holding on, to be honest. Well, yes, I do." And he told them about Helena supplementing their income with her work at Caraways.

"Ugh." Gary, who would never set foot in anywhere down-market of Marks and Spencer's, could only shudder. "What does she do there?" he asked.

"Bit of everything, I think. Shelf-filling and working the checkouts. They need every penny they can earn."

"Of course. Well, we'll get to work on Ren and see if we can come up with anything to help them out. Meanwhile, are we going to see this marvellous boy of yours any time soon? We can always give a party for him, if you like?"

"I think he'd really hate that, to be honest," said Rupert - and was then obliged to spend the next ten minutes explaining to them precisely why.

9.

Walking back into Nectarine on Monday morning was like returning to school after an extended summer holiday. There were new people to meet – all of whom fortunately had their names stitched into their uniform jackets – and renovations and innovations in the kitchen Rupert hadn't really been expecting. He walked around it all with Maggie, the terrifyingly efficient chef who had previously been his deputy, and was delighted to find everything as ship-shape and efficient as a demanding employer like Ren would naturally expect.

"Not that we haven't had our epics," Maggie said, as they got to grips with paperwork in the over-stuffed office where the real work was done. "Burst pipes, suppliers going out of business, staff meltdowns, and all the bad publicity we got when we introduced the *sous-vide* station."

"Fraud, lazy, boil-in-a-bag?" Rupert speculated. He'd heard it all before.

"That sort of thing - cheap headlines. Doesn't matter how many times you explain it to people; if they don't want to understand, they just won't."

"More interested in believing the lie?"

"Yes. Well - it's easier, isn't it? Truth is usually something you have to think about; that's too much like hard work for some people."

"Didn't hurt the business, though, did it?" The bottom line on the spreadsheet Maggie had called up was looking very healthy, even though it had to service some fairly substantial outgoings. It was as far from the hand-to-mouth existence of Ship Meadow Farm as could be imagined, and it was difficult not to experience a pang at such an embarrassment of riches.

"Nothing ever really does. Ren'd have to walk naked through the restaurant to put most people off, and even then he'd win himself a whole new following."

"Yeah, I always reckoned Jamie Oliver missed a trick with that *Naked*

Chef business; if he'd actually taken his clothes off he'd've had ten times the audience."

"Whereas if Ren did it … ?"

"You're kidding; the ratings would go off the scale!"

"Yeah, he is a bit of a hunk, isn't he?" Maggie was a product of London's racial melting-pot and claimed to be half-Jamaican and half-something else - she was never specific about what. She'd changed her hair and her man in the three years since Rupert had seen her last, and both seemed to really suit her. She was more relaxed than he remembered, and the responsibility of running a complex operation like Nectarine in the absence of its owner – which she'd found daunting at first - had been good for her. They'd exchanged e-mails on a regular basis until she'd got into her stride, but those had tailed off as she'd begun to impress her own personality on the role. Now it was clear from a glance around the office that she'd made good use of her opportunities; a new award for customer service was prominent on the wall behind the desk.

"You're going to be a tough act to follow," Rupert told her, with a shrug. "I'm hopelessly out of touch."

"Nothing you can't pick up," Maggie assured him. "Everything's documented – staff training, hygiene inspections, annual leave." She indicated a rank of lever arch files. "It's all on the computer, anyway, and of course there's Andrew. Have you met him yet?"

"The new PA? No. but Ren thinks I should. I take it Andrew's gay?"

"Just a bit, and on the lookout for someone new. Ren's been telling me for the last couple of weeks you'd be ideal for him, and I'm sure he's been telling Andrew that, too; I'm surprised he hasn't beaten a path to your door already."

"Nice of him." Rupert gave a theatrical shudder. "But Ren has no idea what I look for in a partner and I hate the idea of being 'fixed up' in the first place. I'd rather manage by myself."

"Hmmm, don't blame you – Ren wouldn't be my idea of Cupid either! So, anybody new on the horizon?" Apparently the 'business' part of their meeting was, if not over, at least in suspension; Maggie had relaxed in her chair and was clearly in the mood to be gossiped with.

"Maybe, maybe not. I'm not looking for some sort of rebound fling, you know; in fact, there's a possibility I might actually have grown up at last."

"Not you! Never gonna happen!" Maggie was shaking her head. "You're just a bit pissed off with life at the moment, that's all; you take my word for it, Rupe, you'll get through this and come out the other side eventually. You'll be fine, mate, honestly; I promise you will."

"Thanks, Mags, I'm sure I will, sooner or later. But I was actually hoping for something better than 'fine', you know? More like 'marvellous' - or 'ecstatic' or even 'blissful', maybe."

"Dream on," Maggie told him, kindly. "Sounds ambitious to me; maybe that's the problem? Maybe you've been setting your sights too high?"

It wasn't an unfamiliar notion. With Cameron he'd thought he had everything a man could want – a congenial partner and a lifestyle most people would have envied – but maybe he'd had his priorities wrong; if the man was the right one, surely the lifestyle shouldn't matter? The romantic ideal held that he should be willing to sacrifice everything for someone he loved, to go through hell and high water to be at his side; certainly the best kind of relationship ought to be worth a little personal inconvenience, which was why he'd stuck with Cameron when the going got tough – because he thought he could see the potential for something better in the future.

So maybe that was why he was here, surrounded by the best of everything, thinking back to a wobbly caravan stuck against a wall on a Monmouthshire farm and the hard-working man who lived in it. Jake would only have to snap his fingers for Rupert to drop everything and run, throwing himself into his efforts to save Ship Meadow and turn it into a going concern despite the many adversaries ranged against it - but perhaps that was only the same compassionate instinct which made him want to rebuild every tumbledown house he saw, and adopt every sad-eyed mistreated animal in the world. He was a soft touch, he always had been, but surely that was better than being so cynical that nothing would ever matter to him again.

In the present case, it would be escaping from the frying-pan only to take refuge in the fire – an appropriate culinary metaphor, now that he thought about it.

"You think I ought to settle for second-best then, do you?" he asked.

"I didn't say that. Only that maybe you want things to be perfect, and maybe they can't be. Sometimes you have to know when to stop looking, Rupe; I did, when I met Carlo."

"Well, whatever," he shrugged, "I won't be rushing into any new commitments for a while; I've had my fingers well and truly burnt, haven't I?"

"Oh, right; you'll be playing the field from now on, then? Putting it about a bit, as they say?"

He glanced at her in astonishment, meeting her gaze of dark-eyed amusement levelly. "Not really. More like trying to catch up on my sleep, if you must know; the truth is, I'm completely bloody knackered."

"Ha!" exclaimed Maggie, "and it's only your first day back, too! Wait till you get into your stride again, sunshine, and then you'll know what 'knackered' is. And if you're still in any doubt after that," she added slyly, "try doing it seven months pregnant into the bargain!"

"Chance'd be a fine thing," said Rupert, eyebrows quirking mischievously, and after that they had some difficulty concentrating on anything for a while.

The first few days were full-on, getting up to speed in the kitchen again. Ren came and went at random intervals, accompanied – like a shark with a pilot fish – by Andrew, who superficially appeared small, fluttery and nervous but clearly had a core of steel. In fact there was general amusement at - and admiration of - the way he ordered Ren around, escorting him from appointment to appointment, shoving him into taxis with scripts, travel documents, overnight bags and whatever else he needed, fielding distressed or irate phone calls at all hours and generally facilitating his existence. Before Rupert's first week was out, however, it became clear that Ren's determination to find a partner for Andrew had little to do with altruism and was motivated more by a self-protective instinct; Andrew was obviously smitten with Ren himself, and despite his nationally-acknowledged status as a gay icon this had made Ren uncomfortable enough to want to deflect his attentions. Andrew, if he knew about this manoeuvring, took little notice; he arrived early, left late, processed a phenomenal amount of information and seemed to hold the threads of the business securely in his delicate hands. He was someone Rupert could work with, and considering that they were often thrown into one another's company this was more of a relief than he'd expected.

Service at the end of the first week was hellish; Nectarine was booked up months in advance, with nights when Ren himself was cooking heavily over-subscribed, and expectations were always high. However, with the help of a well-drilled *brigade de cuisine* and an equally-polished front-of-house staff, Rupert and Maggie – now taking a back seat and spending her time in the office – accomplished the miracle. Yet it was all-consuming, and by the time it was over Rupert was aware that he'd thought of nothing – and nobody – else for almost a week. He'd focussed exclusively on the restaurant from the moment he awoke in the morning to the moment he fell into bed, exhausted, at the end of the day, and such conversations as he'd had with Gary and Steve had primarily been about work. Whilst acknowledging that there were times when this was unavoidable, however, he didn't want it to be the whole of his existence – which was why, as soon as he could summon the energy, he went round to the gym of which Steve was the manager and signed himself up for membership.

"Too much sitting around on my arse," he explained, in the face of Steve's incredulity. "I couldn't run for a bus without embarrassing myself."

"Not a lot wrong with your arse from where I'm standing," Steve said, then held up his hands by way of apology. "Just appreciating it," he explained, grinning. "I take it you want to start out with some kind of low-impact exercise routine and build up your general strength from there?"

Rupert nodded. "Anything to burn off a few calories and sweat away a bit of stress," he replied. "Rowing-machine, weights, cardio, whatever you've got. Oh, and I wouldn't mind learning some basic self-defence as well."

Steve was watching him in bewilderment. "Somebody bothering you, is there, Rupe?" he asked, suspiciously.

"Not exactly." But an explanation seemed necessary, so after a moment Rupert went on. "Jake's run into a bit of difficulty," he said. "Might be something, might be nothing, but it could be useful to have a few moves – just in case."

"It's always useful," Steve told him. "Except when it's not. It's like learning how to swim, you know? If you don't have a clue, you're more likely to avoid situations that could be dangerous."

"Good point," replied Rupert. "Only sometimes you can't avoid them; sometimes they come looking for you."

"You in trouble, mate?" Steve was suddenly serious. "Because I know a few people ... It's not Cameron and his buddies, is it?"

"No, god, no! None of that lot would have the brains or the balls to follow me half-way round the planet, they're all as bloody gormless as he is." Which pretty much set the seal on any feelings he might have had for the man, now that he thought about it; it wouldn't have required an off-the-scale genius IQ to stay out of the trouble Cameron had got himself into, just the self-discipline he'd so evidently lacked. In short, he'd been a self-centred little shit who thought the world revolved around him, and Rupert had put up with it all for far too long. "Besides, when you get down to it, I think he was expecting me to shop him; I'm half-convinced that's what he was hoping for. He knew he needed help, but he was too fucked-up to get it for himself."

"You turned him in, then, did you? What do they call that, tough love?"

"More or less, I suppose, yes, it was. I knew he was planning something but I didn't know what – although where we lived there weren't many options. I'd reported him a couple of days earlier for dipping into the till at the restaurant; the evening the coppers came looking he'd buggered off and 'borrowed' my car – without asking, of course. I was working so I didn't know he wasn't at home until they told me - although I could have put money on it. He was supposed to be looking after Rusty; she was ill." Rupert took a breath and pulled himself together. "All in the past now, anyway. Whatever's going on, it's nothing to do with Cam or his friends; there isn't one of that lot that could carry a grudge in a bucket. No – it's just that I'd like to be prepared for the unexpected, that's all."

Steve was watching him with sympathy, his mouth twisting into an indulgent smile.

"Well," he pointed out, "if you're prepared for it, technically it isn't unexpected – is it?" Then, quelling the incipient protest, "No, all right, mate, point taken, we'll think of something. Come on, let's have a walk round and see if we can work out a programme for you, shall we?"

In the same spirit of assiduity Rupert made a point of buying himself a new phone and e-mailing the number to Martin Fisher; he received a courteous acknowledgement and a promise that the number would be passed to Jake, but after that there was no further communication. He supposed it had been too much to hope that Jake would be able to get to London during his first free weekend, but with Gary and Steve out of town on a pre-determined orbit that left Rupert alone in the apartment at Marshalsea Road with little idea how to pass the time. He caught up with his laundry, went for the promised drink with Harvey at the Market Tavern, watched a couple of pleasant but forgettable movies on DVD – and then, when he felt he'd procrastinated long enough, he opened up his laptop and started investigating Diadem Wholesale Provisions.

He'd expected them to have a minimal online presence, but to his astonishment the reverse was true; Diadem had a shiny professional website with pictures of happy, diverse employees canning carrots, delivering potatoes, picking apples and so forth; in every picture there was sunshine, smiling faces, indications of the bounty of the land being harvested by enthusiastic workers. To an extent it was only the way any company would choose to be portrayed and it was hardly different in tone from the Ship Meadow Farm page, although there was one feature on the Diadem website which caused him to raise an eyebrow in bemusement. Under a tab with the heading 'Employment', Diadem trumpeted a policy of providing opportunities for workers from Eastern Europe, holding out the veiled promise of British citizenship and an improved standard of living for those willing to leave their homes to travel abroad.

Diadem, it seemed, had thought of everything; there was even a photo of their staff accommodation – Spartan, perhaps, but pleasant enough over a short period, certainly no worse than a Youth Hostel – and beside it another of their two in-house translators who were always happy to sort out any linguistic confusion. They were young men named Mirek Tesar and Vladan Resnik, smiling reassuringly out of the pixels on the screen, and the caption said they enjoyed playing football and fishing in their spare time. He wouldn't have needed that information, however, to recognise the grinning Mirek Tesar as the surly hoodie he'd run into by the bridge.

"Hired muscle," he said aloud to himself. It didn't matter how much they dressed it up, how charming and folksy they appeared, there was a coldness in their eyes which seemed to assess everything and everybody as a threat to be dealt with. He knew he'd been assessed during that encounter on the river bank and dismissed as negligible. He didn't know whether he ought to feel glad about that, or very slightly insulted.

The creeping sensation of menace which had started up his spine as he looked at the picture was allayed somewhat by the notion that this was all public information. If this much was out there on the net, there was no way Jake – or Martin Fisher – could be unaware of it. It hadn't required a tremendous amount of digging, after all – the search term 'diadem farming monmouthshire' had brought up that and Geoffrey of Monmouth and virtually nothing else. This being so, however, he was looking at a manufactured public image; nobody willing to adopt underhand business tactics to edge out a neighbouring concern would advertise it on their website; 'nothing of interest' was precisely what he should have expected to find.

So what would Kurt Wallander do in the circumstances, he wondered, or Martin Beck? The problem with the heroes of Nordic noir detective fiction was that they tended to have the resources of their local police departments behind them – and to be senior enough to send out underlings this way and that to follow clues that might be significant. Rupert wasn't anything like such an august personage; he wasn't even a police officer, just a chef with a penchant for mystery fiction and investigating what he didn't understand. He wanted to know why Mirek Tesar had been lurking by the bridge, and whether Diadem had anything to do with Tim Colley's death, almost as badly as he'd wanted to know where the money had been going from his business and exactly what Cameron was doing with it. Somehow, over only a couple of days with Jake and the family, the puzzle of Tim's death had become personal to him as well as to them; he wanted to know what had happened simply because he wanted to know, dammit! - and also because he felt somebody actually *ought* to know, and that there was no reason why it shouldn't be him.

But there was nothing more he could do tonight, anyway, and all good detectives - from Sherlock Holmes to Hercule Poirot - took time to digest their discoveries, to let information percolate slowly through their subconscious. He would do the same. He would let it run as a background operation in a mind otherwise fully occupied with Nectarine. He would let it steep, because he couldn't do anything else; because the day-to-day running of Nectarine and the trust Ren had placed in him had to be his priority - and because he wasn't sure he'd ever set eyes on Jake again anyway, since he had the distinct impression he'd irrevocably messed up his one and only chance of ever getting together with the man.

10.

By the end of Rupert's second fortnight at Nectarine life was beginning to settle down a bit. The staff had seen Maggie off, in a shower of gifts, cards and blessings, and there had been no catastrophes following her departure. Ren himself had barely seemed to register the change; he'd turned up at her leaving party and been social and said all the right things, but he'd continued working at a blistering pace afterwards and it had been left to everybody else in the establishment to keep up with him. That had been a challenge, but by the time his second long weekend rolled around Rupert had to acknowledge that he was up to speed on daily working procedures and holding everything together reasonably well. Which was only to be expected, since Ren and Maggie had assembled a successful and functional team which could have been captained by a trained monkey provided it could speak decent culinary French.

Ren's shifts at Nectarine alternated with Rupert's; when Rupert did days, Ren did evenings; when Rupert was on duty, Ren was off. They overlapped, they passed in the car park, they arranged meetings and discussed work, and from time to time one stopped by and ate the other's cooking. However for the most part each acted independently, with Andrew flying back and forth between them like a shuttle. This was how, as the second fortnight progressed, Rupert found himself warming to Andrew; there was no way he could envisage the younger man as a potential partner – there was a strong element of camp in Andrew's personality which would be attractive to some men, but which Rupert wasn't drawn to – but great professional respect had quickly developed between them. They both knew what they were doing, each learned that he could rely on the other, and they were united in their affection for Renfrew Sheppard. So, towards the end of his fourth week back, Rupert asked Andrew if he fancied a friendly drink after work – Andrew's raised eyebrow was the only indication that he understood 'friendly' to mean definitely no more than that – and ended up taking him to the Market Tavern.

"I've never been in here before," confided Andrew, as they stepped into the meticulous Victorian pub interior – imported wholesale from various reclamation yards after this part of London had been gentrified a decade or so earlier. Never mind, it looked as if had been here for generations and survived the Blitz without a glass being cracked, and that was what present-day South Londoners seemed to want from their public houses.

"It's moved up-market a bit," said Rupert, absently, then grimaced. "Sorry, you know what I mean. It used to be more of a spit-and-sawdust when I knew it before. At least you can still get a decent pint here."

"Make that a decent *half*," suggested Andrew, "and I'm your man." Rupert grinned at this, but otherwise made no comment.

It was early and the place was almost empty. A few local office-workers came in to eat before going home, and a cadre of market traders held court in the corner by the window, but the place wouldn't get busy until mid-evening. It was still possible to find a table and sit down, and to talk without having to compete with music at concert-pitch and two hundred over-excited yuppies shouting at the tops of their voices, and after a day in the Nectarine kitchen this was as close to peace and quiet as they were likely to get.

"So, you have the weekend off when Ren's cooking, do you?" asked Rupert, returning to the table.

"In theory, I do; at least I know where he is and what he's up to. Honestly, sometimes it's like keeping tabs on a randy teenager; if I turn my back on him for a minute he's off, and it takes me the rest of the day to catch up with him."

"You seem to have him pretty much under control, though," said Rupert, admiringly.

"Oh, between me and Annabel I reckon we've got him worked out," confided Andrew. "She likes me; she says he's less likely to fancy me than any of his previous secretaries."

"Oh? Has he been cheating on her, then? I've never heard anything - but I suppose I wouldn't have."

Andrew shrugged. "I honestly don't think so," he said, "but if she feels more comfortable with me around and it means I get a job out of it, who the hell cares?"

"True. Not very flattering, though, is it?"

"No, but I'm used to that. On the other hand, there are days when I definitely understand why you took off for Australia when you did; when Ren has one of his tantrums it's like dealing with a two-year-old, and some of the undercurrents in that kitchen that would make the Borgias look like the bloody Waltons. Just be glad you're only here temporarily, Rupert; you wouldn't want to get dragged back into it." Despondently, Andrew took a mouthful of beer and stared around the pub. "Not much talent in here, is there, unless you've got a thing for for chinless yuppies? Or if there is, it's all spoken for. I really wouldn't mind meeting somebody, you know – for something vigorous and uncomplicated. A one-night stand, a quick shag, no need to worry in the morning – you know?"

"I do know." But for the years and the miles, that could have been himself talking; the Rupert who'd lived with Paulie had experienced life to the full before he'd fallen in lust with Cameron and decided to try monogamy. "I haven't got any contacts any more, but my house-mates are having a party on Saturday night; if you're not doing anything, why don't you come along? You might meet some interesting people."

"Gary and Steve?" Of course, Rupert should have remembered Andrew would know them – or Gary, at least, who was Ren's producer.

"They're friendly with a lot of media types," he continued, "apparently not all over forty and perma-tanned, although I'll believe that when I see it. At least it'll get you out of the house for an hour or two!"

"You sound like my mother," grinned Andrew. "But yes - if you're sure they won't mind, I think I'd like that."

"Good. I'd appreciate having someone around I can actually talk to – someone who's on more or less the same wavelength as me."

"Oh, I'm really not sure that's true," returned Andrew, "but at least we can stand each other's company. And if we get bored you can tell me all about Australian men; all those cute lifeguards and policemen in their shorts." He sighed. "If I thought for a moment that it's anything like as wonderful as it looks on TV I'd move there in a heartbeat, if only Ren didn't need me quite so much."

"Well, maybe you could go for a holiday?" Rupert suggested. "I'm sure you'd find enough of whatever you're looking for to justify the fare."

"If only," was the wistful response. "But I'm not sure what I'm looking for exists anywhere in the world but London. That is, if it even exists at all."

Which, thought Rupert, might well be true, but he hadn't made any real inroads into cheering Andrew up – and had, in fact, only succeeded in making himself feel thoroughly despondent again, too.

"What's the occasion for the party?" asked Andrew, turning up at the front door in Marshalsea Road two days later carrying a couple of bottles of gin. "Is there anything I should congratulate anybody for?"

"Not a thing, it's just a party-party - a 'three months since the last party' party, to be accurate."

"Oh, right. Convivial types, then, are they, your house-mates?"

"They do know how to enjoy themselves, yes," agreed Rupert. "Although Steve's supposedly in training for an Ironman Triathlon. Actually I think they're doing this for my benefit, although they've been denying it like mad. It's to 'take me out of myself', they seem to think I'm getting clinically depressed."

"Really? I can't say I'd got that impression myself."

"No. Well, compared to them, I probably don't seem all that bubbly. Truth is I've done the whole life-of-the-party thing and I'm pretty much over it now; it just isn't who I want to be these days."

"I expect you're just more serious by nature," observed Andrew, airily. They were side-by-side on the polished stairs, heading for the kitchen where a jumping musical beat had drowned out any conversations not shouted at full volume. The doors to the terrace had been thrown open and tables and chairs set out there, while in the main living area the furniture had been pushed back against the wall so that those who wanted to dance could do so. Snakes of LEDs garlanded around the room gave off elaborate patterns of light that would have done justice to

Piccadilly Circus in the rush hour, bathing everything in a medley of unnatural colours from purple to green and back again. Most of the guests were male, but there were at least three expensively-dressed girls who seemed to be involved in a party all their own – one which featured drink, dancing and the minimum of intelligent conversation; not one of them looked as if she could string a sentence together without help.

"Arm candy," explained Rupert. "Some of these people supposedly aren't out yet."

"Oh, really?" Andrew was glancing around. "I don't think I actually recognise anyone," he said, after a while, "which is a relief. Oh - except Gary, of course. Good evening, Gary; thank you for inviting me."

Gary, wearing an apron with the legend 'Prick With A Fork', had a plate of canapés in one hand and a bottle of champagne in the other. "Andrew, sweetie," he said, "eat something, for fuck's sake, we've got far too much food," and had spun away – taking the plate with him – before Andrew could respond. Rupert relieved him of the gin, which he added to the collection on the kitchen worktop, and got him a glass of champagne in exchange.

"Buckle up," he said ruefully, "it's going to be a bumpy ride. Gary's in one of his queeny moods; he's been drinking since lunchtime and he's determined to catch Steve doing something he shouldn't."

"Oh, god, relationships," groaned Andrew. "They're all bloody drama and tragedy, aren't they? Much better to stay single and just have the occasional fuck when you need it."

"Be nice if it worked out like that, though." Rupert hadn't had much to drink yet, just a couple of glasses of wine to take the edge off; he'd been preparing food all afternoon and was glad of whatever put a barrier between the world and himself. "I mean, if you didn't always end up either having sex and no relationship or a relationship and no sex. 'Friends with benefits' sounds ideal, but I've never actually known it to work in the real world."

"Was that what happened to you? A relationship and no sex?" The lighting in the room had changed again; they were both purple, and so was the food. Rupert reached for a slice of purple and purple quiche and a couple of purple onion rings.

"In the end, I suppose it was. There was one time when I suggested going to bed and he said 'What for?' - and that was when I knew it was over."

"Ouch. So you're not looking for anybody at the moment?"

"Not exactly. Well, there's someone I'm sort-of interested in, but it's complicated."

"Isn't it always?" sighed Andrew. "You could tell me about it, though, if you wanted to."

It was a tempting offer, but Rupert could think of nothing that would bring a party mood crashing to the ground faster than a recitation of his own imperfectly-articulated emotions. "I know, and I appreciate the offer – but I really don't think I'm in the mood for that just now. Maybe another time."

"All right, the offer stays open. Instead, you can introduce me to somebody I've never met before who'll change my life in an instant. Who's the ripped hunk over there with the GI Joe hairstyle, for example?"

"Hmmm? Oh, that's Steve – you really need to steer clear of him, unless you've got a reason for wanting to piss Gary off."

"No, probably better not, good safety tip. But it's a shame, he is rather fine; I don't suppose he's got an identical twin brother lurking anywhere, has he?"

"Four sisters, I believe, and they're all as butch as him. But let me introduce you anyway; he knows everybody and he's bound to know if anyone's on the lookout for company." Steve was on the terrace chatting to a tall blond man with bushy eyebrows who had his arm tightly around the waist of one of the disposable girls. She was somehow accomplishing the not inconsiderable feat of clinging to him adoringly whilst at the same time looking slightly bored. "Steve," said Rupert, brightly, shepherding Andrew towards him, "there's somebody here I'd like you to meet."

"Oh, yes, of course, I've heard a lot about you," began Steve expansively, breaking away from his companions and holding out a bear-like paw. "This fucker told us flat out that you hated parties - which was why we didn't invite you in the first place - but I always thought the tart was lying through his teeth. At any rate, it's great to see the pair of you together at long last; it's really good to meet you, Jake."

It was the sort of faux-pas from which any sort of graceful recovery is quite impossible. Steve blustered and acted even stupider than usual when he was corrected, Andrew smiled and said it didn't matter a bit – and, refereeing the incident, Rupert seethed quietly and tried not to make matters any worse.

"So who's Jake, then, when he's out walking?" asked Andrew, when they'd managed to extract themselves from the awkward conversation.

"Just somebody I happen to know, that's all."

"Uh-huh. And he's the one who's complicated, is he? For fuck's sake tell me something about him, Rupert, before I go out of my mind with boredom. What does he do for a living, for a start?"

"He's a … a farmer, I suppose," said Rupert. "He used to be a market trader, but he had to take over the family business. Long story." And then, although he was scrupulous to avoid any mention of Tim's untimely demise, Rupert found he was getting into the story of the difficulties Jake and Helena had experienced as a result of being Diadem's neighbours. He ended by recounting his meeting with Mirek Tesar, complete with a graphic description of the air of menace the man projected. "I'm sure he and his mate are enforcers of some kind," he added. "They're not great big beefy bruisers, but they look as if they'd be useful in a fight. Vicious, you know. Subtle." He was beginning to wonder if he hadn't had more to drink than was good for him; the room, which was currently blue, seemed a little unsteady on its feet, and Andrew's voice was a fraction more piercing when he replied than Rupert had been expecting.

"Yes, I know. Exactly what you need if you're trying to stay below the radar."

"I'm sorry - I'm boring you, aren't I? I should really let you mingle."

"Well, yes, you should – but no, you're not boring me. Have you still got the name of that newspaper? Only I could see if I can track it down for you, if you like?" Then, in response to Rupert's look of astonishment, "What? Don't you know that if you want something done, you should always ask a busy person?"

"That's true. Well, if you're sure you've got time I'll dig it out for you; it's probably in my room somewhere."

"Yes, please. And we'd better do it now, if you don't mind, or we're likely to forget again."

"All right."

They clattered down the stairs together, studiously ignoring both Steve's gaze - which followed them – and the burst of laughter which erupted in the kitchen as they left. There were people on the stairs, too, and the always-welcome party sound-effect of someone throwing up in the main bathroom. Rupert's door, although it didn't lock, had a KEEP OUT sign on it; the room beyond was shadowed and almost quiet apart from the thudding of the bass and the sound of footsteps on the wooden floor above. Rupert was fumbling in the pocket of the coat he'd worn on the trip to Monmouthshire for the slip of paper on which he'd written the name of the newspaper when he became aware of the buzzing of his mobile phone, and quickly grabbed it from the shelf where it had been charging. There were three missed calls on it from an unknown number, timed an hour apart. There were only a few people who had this number, and most of their details were programmed in and would have shown on the display if it had been them. He'd even saved Martin Fisher's number, and that of the kennels where Rusty was lodging, so he knew for certain it was none of them. Jake, bugger it; he was almost sure he'd missed a call from Jake.

He had pressed the button to return the call before he'd even thought about it properly - before considering that Andrew was in the room. As it rang, he continued rummaging in his coat-pockets and eventually produced the relevant piece of paper.

"Hello?" said Jake faintly in his ear, sounding as if he was on Mars – or possibly somewhere even further away. "Rupert?"

"Jake, mate, where are you? What's happening?"

"Nothing's happening - not yet, anyway - and I'm in London, in a hotel room. You said I should give you a call when I got here." That wasn't the way Rupert thought they'd left it, but he wasn't going to argue the point now. "Where the fuck are you, anyway? I've been calling you for hours."

"I'm at a party," said Rupert, "and I'd rather not be." He managed to ignore Andrew's pantomime huff of disdain.

"Well then, you tosser, don't be! Be here instead! I'm at the Premium Hotel in Tower Bridge Road, in Room 418."

"I'll ... I mean, I can't just ... Oh, fuck it, hang on a minute, Jake." Rupert muted the phone and glanced over at Andrew in distress. "It's ... "

"I know - it's Mr 'It's Complicated' and you're leaving me to run away with him."

"I ... fuck, yes, I think I probably am. I'm sorry, Andrew."

"Don't you dare apologise! Off you go and have a totally fabulous time - and I hope you get a thorough seeing-to at the end of it! Don't worry about me, I'll be fine; if all else fails I'll just call a taxi and go home - but before I do I'm going back to the party to see if I can talk to that man with the wonderful eyebrows; he reminds me a bit of a U-Boat commander, and I've always had a thing about men in uniform."

"You're insane," said Rupert, making the discovery belatedly but in sheer delight. "You're absolutely bloody certifiable, aren't you?"

"Why yes," agreed Andrew blithely. "How very kind of you to notice! But give me that piece of paper before you go, and we'll meet up at work on Monday morning and tell each other all about it. Now get your act together, Cinderella - you don't want to keep the handsome prince waiting any longer than you have to, after all!"

"Thank you." Numbly Rupert handed over the paper. "Jake? Sorry," he said, resuming the call in increased agitation. "I'm on my way, I can be with you in about ten or fifteen minutes. Don't go anywhere," he added, desperately. "I'm really looking forward to seeing you again."

11.

There was a light rain beginning to fall as Rupert galloped down the stairs and out onto Marshalsea Road – not enough to make a coat or umbrella necessary, but sufficient to turn car headlights into haloed stars and the sound of their tyres to a subtle swishing music. After the warmth of the flat the evening air was a cool blessing, and despite scattered knots of people on the pavement the street seemed empty by comparison.

He made a beeline for St George's Church, bypassed it, and shortly afterwards stepped into the maze of streets where post-war housing was even now being swept aside by massive commercial redevelopment. Too long neglected, Southwark and Bermondsey were suddenly fashionable again – and much of their traditional character was vanishing under glass and steel as the money rolled in even faster than the concrete. However, as long as it was possible to scurry down alleyways between houses, across car parks and through tiny, scruffy areas of 'open space', there would always be fragments of the old London left – and Rupert knew the short-cuts like the back of his hand. He didn't have to hurry but kept up a smart pace, and was through Reception at the Premium Hotel – past two bored girls on the desk who took no notice at all – and into the lift before he'd had a chance to figure out what he was expecting from the encounter; Andrew's blunt philosophy – 'something vigorous and uncomplicated, a quick shag, nothing to have to worry about in the morning' – while it undoubtedly had its attractions, sounded facile and ultimately soul-destroying to him, but then again he'd been through the whole commitment thing once, and look how well that had turned out!

On the other hand Jake was Jake, and there was something about him that defied classification; he didn't belong in some neatly filed and docketed compartment, he was simply himself; thinking about him and the life he led, about that kiss and what it had promised, was enough to make Rupert want to run away from the sterile environs of the Nectarine kitchens forever, out into the fresh air where he could spend his days cutting herbs and taking tomatoes from the vine - an agrarian idyll he was sensible enough to realise had little to do with reality. The whole fork-to-fork scenario had always appealed to him, however - cutting down on food miles, making everything with produce as fresh and local as it could possibly be …

It was a delightful daydream, and Jake belonged in the heart of it all somewhere. For that reason it seemed wrong that he should be in London in the first place, let alone in a budget hotel in Southwark, torn from his proper context and dumped unceremoniously at the heart of the urban jungle. It was stupid and misplaced, he knew – Jake was as much a Londoner as himself - but the idea was bringing out all Rupert's most protective instincts. In fact his feelings for Jake were entirely characterised by contradictions; he wanted both to look after and to be looked after by him, to brag about him and to keep him secret, to hold back and to dash ahead with a 'damn the torpedoes' recklessness; most of all he didn't want this to be anything that played by anybody else's rules – he wanted it to be impulsive and ridiculous, to press all the buttons at once to find out what might happen. Above all, now that he was here, he didn't want to have to wait.

"There you are, then," said Jake as he opened the door onto a narrow, quiet room dominated by a massive bed with a charcoal throw and taut sheets of dazzling whiteness. "Come on in and have a drink."

But Rupert wasn't listening. He had launched himself at the man with all the finesse of a baby elephant on roller-skates, snagged him around the waist, and was pressing sloppy half-drunken kisses onto his mouth before either of them managed to establish his balance. They staggered together, Rupert's hip impacting the corner of the built-in cupboard, and he didn't care, he really didn't care, because Jake was large and warm against him and something was clearly happening that they had both done their best to postpone when the time wasn't right and they were needed elsewhere. It was impossible to go on deferring these things for ever, though; they would either happen or they wouldn't, and he was damned well going to let this happen now. The pair of them had had unfinished business for years – and this was where, for good or ill, it ended.

He was fumbling at Jake's belt, Jake was fumbling at Rupert's fly, and there was no oxygen in the room and everything had become light-headed and ridiculous but there was just no stopping it. Someone switched out the lights, someone got Rupert out of his boots and trousers and tee-shirt, someone ran a possessive hand over his chest and someone chuckled quietly against his ear.

"Steady," said Jake, "we've literally got all night, you know."

But it wasn't so much a composed and elegant progression to the bed as a scarcely-controlled collapse; they tumbled together like two dynamited buildings toppling from their foundations, functionally but without dignity, debris scattering in all directions.

"I really hope you're going to fuck me, sunshine," said Rupert, breathless, some part of his mind aware that he should make his requirements clear before it was too late. "Preferably through the bed and into the room downstairs."

"I will if you like," Jake told him, pretending not to care in the slightest whether he did or not. "Only if you absolutely insist, though, mind."

"I do," replied Rupert. "I absolutely and completely insist on it."

"Oh, all right then. If I must, I suppose I must – but I don't really think I'm going to enjoy it."

This never grew old. At least, it was always familiar and always somehow strange, this first experimental glide of skin on skin. The nondescript hotel room was comfortable enough, neither too warm nor too cold, and if the walls were made of cardboard and the cups rattled every time a heavy vehicle went past that was nothing; it was safe, it was dark, and there was newness to be explored. Jake's hands were strong, businesslike but gentle – Rupert could imagine them on a lamb or a chick as easily as on a hammer or a saw – and they read him as if he were his own instruction manual. It was a comprehensive, methodical overview, impeded only by the fact that Rupert was making explorations of his own. He had known, from seeing him without his shirt, that Jake had only the lightest scruff of chest hair high on his breastbone, although now he discovered a well-developed treasure-trail which ran across his stomach to provide an enticing framework for a straight and sturdy prick which he already knew would feel good inside him. It had been far too long a time, and he'd been striving desperately not to think about it; Rupert had been so determined not to miss Cameron, not to miss regular sex, that he'd expunged the subject from his consciousness almost completely. Monks managed, after all; they sublimated, they worked and prayed, they thought loftier thoughts; he'd tried his best to be like them, only it hadn't really worked.

"Calm down, Rupert," said Jake again. "I mean it, we don't have to do it all in the first five minutes."

"Yes, we do, of course we bloody do." He was aware of sounding petulant and demanding, but he'd completely stopped caring about that. There was going to be total honesty between himself and Jake from now on, even if that meant he showed himself in a less than flattering light.

"That fucking hot for it, are you, mate?" The words were arch but affectionate, accompanied by an indulgent chuckle. "I suppose I should be dressed for the occasion, then; do you want to do it or shall I?" In the darkness, there was the distinctive sound of him tearing open a condom packet with his teeth.

"I will," said Rupert. His hands were shaking as he took the packet from Jake, but he'd done this a couple of hundred times or more; it was all part of the ritual, like assembling the ingredients before he began to cook; preparation, careful and precise, was always the main component of success.

He went slowly, drawing the membrane down over hot, over-excited flesh, anchoring it in the bed of curls at the base and then stroking back up again, drawing an anxious hiss from his partner.

"Careful," said Jake. "Don't want to waste the good stuff, do we?"

"I know. Is there anything to use on me?"

"Under the pillow."

It was a tube of something, viscous and unscented, cool and frictionless; it could have been anything from cooking oil to liquid soap to tractor grease. Rupert sniffed it, touched it with his tongue – slightly distasteful – and then applied it to himself. It was soothing, emollient, gentle, and with it his last measure of reserve evaporated completely; it wasn't possible to be any readier for this than he was, and without thinking what he was doing he rolled onto his belly and wiped his greasy hand briskly on the fresh white sheet.

"Do it," he instructed boldly. "Now."

"Oh well, if you're quite sure that's what you want…"

There was the usual undignified scrabble for position when there seemed to be too many legs and arms to be accommodated in comfort and it ran through Rupert's mind that four pillows on a double bed was really three too many, and then like a swimmer he turned his head to one side and breathed and was glad he had when the fullness reached up inside him in one slow, strong, deep stroke and he lifted back to greet it.

Yes, this was pretty close to perfect, whatever it was; it was sweeter than no-frills sex with a stranger, and would almost have been an out-of-body experience except that his body was so thrillingly involved. Rupert had achieved some kind of separation, however, his mind clearly detached and floating elsewhere while his physical self jarred and juddered its responses. There was something gloriously crude about the way the bed shook under them, and if the headboard didn't quite slam backwards and forwards in time with their rhythm it was only because the management had had the forethought to screw it to the wall; nevertheless their neighbours could be in no doubt what was going on in room 418, and that was as good a reason as any not to hold back on the sounds of appreciation, the whimpers and guttural expletives as Jake went into him repeatedly, each time deeper, each time different, each time just that little bit more wonderful as gradually they escalated together towards -

A sound shrilled into the room, tearing the warm air into a billion jagged fragments, shattering the mood like an unexpected ice-bath. The fire alarm? Rupert's heart, already racing, lurched terrifyingly and his mind gave way to an immediate sensation of panic; he hadn't even bothered looking for the exits, how could they possibly hope to get out? And then he was naked, and -

It rang again, and in another split-second the banality of the interruption became obvious. It wasn't the fire alarm at all. It was the phone.

"Oh, fuck!" Jake had already managed to extract himself somehow and reached for his trousers, which he was clutching in front of him like a fig-leaf. His flailing left hand almost sent the phone flying, but he grabbed the receiver and said "What?" - rather brusquely and half an octave too high. Then, after a troubled pause, "No, no, wait ... slow down, slow down! Say that again, I didn't get it all. Who was mucking about? What happened to Martin?"

Rupert peeled away, sat up, snagged the bed-cover around himself and switched on the bedside light. Jake's expression was a frozen mask of horror and concern.

"The bloody idiot - he didn't, did he? But I specifically told him ... Yes, of course - it's my fault, I should have known that all along. And where is he now? And you're there with him? Got it." There was a long pause, while Jake's eyes revolved in their sockets and he was struggling visibly to pull himself together. "What about the farm? Oh, are they? That's good of them. No, I have no idea at the moment, I was in the middle of ... Well, it doesn't matter. Of course you can't, H, I know that - don't even think about it, okay? I'll be there as soon as I can. Yes, I'm leaving this very minute, I promise. No, no, you did absolutely the right thing. I'll call you on your mum's mobile the moment I've got something fixed up, okay? But I can't see me getting back there until about six o'clock at the earliest... Now go on - get some sleep if you can and don't worry about me, I'll be there before you know it. Fuck!" This last expletive, roared to the world in general, burst from him the moment the phone was back on its rest. Jake stood up, his body flushed pink, and stripped the unused condom from an erection which had lost interest in the proceedings and was no longer worthy of the name. "I've got to go," he said, beginning to reassemble his clothing. "It's an emergency."

Rupert was out of bed in a moment, helping to get him organised. After a few seconds of concentrated mayhem they were both decently dressed again, the condom and its packet flushed down the toilet, and Jake had pulled his overnight bag out of the wardrobe.

"Martin's in hospital," he said, the effort to remain calm evident in his tone. "Somebody was mucking about on the farm and he went to investigate – the silly bastard, I told him if anything happened he was to take care of H and the kids and leave the rest to the coppers. Anyway, I don't know if he saw anything or not, but it looks like he's had a heart attack and he's been taken to hospital in Abergavenny. I've got to get back right away. Got any bright ideas about how?"

"Uhhh … " The cog-wheels in Rupert's brain meshed only with maddening slowness. "Train?" he suggested, foolishly.

"Not on the ticket I've got, no chance, it's one of those cheap timed things – I wasn't planning to leave until about lunchtime - and anyway there's no service until half-five in the morning and I couldn't get to the hospital before nine at the earliest. That's eight hours away or something, and from the way H was talking that might be too late. There's got to be something that doesn't take eight hours to do a hundred and sixty bloody miles, for fuck's sake! The coaches are hopeless," he added. "I've checked them out before; the only way to get to Abergavenny by coach is not to want to go there in the first place."

"Okay, well, maybe you could maybe hire a car or something." It was a total stab in the dark. "I mean, have you got your licence with you? How long would it take you to drive it?"

"Three or four hours, I suppose. But where do you hire a car from in London at this bloody time of night? And what the fuck is it going to cost me, anyway?"

Rupert looked blankly at him. "I wouldn't know offhand," he said, "but I don't suppose it'll be cheap. Reception might know; that's what they're there for, after all - people must need to come and go at all sorts of strange hours, surely? They'll have flights to get and so on … "

"Yes, you're right, I'd better go down and ask."

"No," said Rupert. "Let me; you pack your stuff, I'll find out what's available. And don't worry about the money, you can owe it to me; just make sure you don't leave anything important behind."

"But you can't … "

"I can get the ball rolling at least," said Rupert. "I promise not to make any final decisions before you get there; just come on down as soon as you're ready, okay?"

"Okay. It won't take me long to get everything sorted out."

"I know." Rupert had stuffed his shoes back on and dashed his fingers through his hair. The mirror in the room showed him a sight that mercifully wasn't too horrifying; he was bedraggled and tired-looking, but that would have to do.

"Look ... " Jake's gesture towards the ruined bed encompassed their entire interrupted evening. "Fucking awful timing," he said, wryly apologetic. "Just when it was all starting to get interesting as well."

"Fucking terrible," concurred Rupert, "but we'll survive it, and it doesn't matter anyway. Right now this thing with Martin is far more important - isn't it?"

"Yes," said Jake. "I'm afraid it is. I'm really sorry, Rupert."

"No need to be, mate. No need at all, honestly." And Rupert was out of the door and hot-footing it back along the corridor to the lift before so much as another syllable could be exchanged.

The two girls on Reception, who at first sight – Rupert was embarrassed to admit – he wouldn't have credited with having a functioning brain cell between them, jumped on his enquiry with the enthusiasm of people desperate for something to break the monotony of a night shift. There was a car hire place at Victoria, they remembered, which was open around the clock; within seconds they'd found the website and were quoting prices at him.

"That's for twenty-four hours," said the smaller, chirpier one, peering around her colleague at the screen. "But you get Sunday free, so if you took it out now it'd be the same price for forty-eight. That's not a bad deal, really, is it?"

"No, not at all, though he wouldn't actually need it that long. Do they do a one-way hire or anything?"

"Hang on a minute ... " A couple of mouse-clicks followed. "Yes, but it's more. A lot more." So much more, in fact, that the price she quoted Rupert almost made him stagger sideways.

"Ouch. That's bloody ridiculous," he said. "Okay, well at least that makes it nice and simple; I'll go with him, and then I'll drive the car back to London. What's the easiest way to get to Victoria at this time of night, a black cab?"

"Definitely. You can do it by bus if you know what you're doing -

they run all night - but it's complicated. Would you like us to call a cab for you?"

Rupert hesitated. "Wait till my mate gets down from the room, it's got to be his decision." But even now Jake was falling out of the lift with his jacket over his arm and a look of quiet horror in his eyes; Rupert went to meet him. "Calm down, it's more straightforward than I was expecting; we can hire a car at Victoria, and it won't be ridiculously expensive if I come along with you and drive the thing home afterwards." In the face of Jake's appalled expression he continued relentlessly. "Look, I'll be honest, I've had a couple of glasses of champagne, I'm not fit to drive now – but I should be fine to return the car if I can grab a few hours' sleep at your place first. A one-way hire would be nearly three times as much and you'd have to drop it off at their place in Cardiff anyway," he added in conclusion. "It's just too much bloody hassle doing it that way."

"All right. I mean, thanks. If you're really sure you want to go to that much trouble I'm definitely not going to turn you down." Jake sounded dubious about the whole business, but willing to be guided – in this instance anyway - by Rupert.

"Don't be a prick, mate, honestly; that's what friends are for - I've said I'll do it and I'll bloody do it. Only we'll have to go round and pick up my licence first. And maybe a jacket or something as well," he added, somewhat pathetically. "Black cab, please, ladies," he continued, recrossing the floor towards them. "For Victoria via Marshalsea Road and stopping at the nearest cash-point on the way. And after that the M4, I suppose - and the road to Abergavenny, whatever that is. Sounds like it should be the title of a Bob Hope movie, doesn't it?"

But the girls on Reception were too young to know the answer to this question, and Jake was too preoccupied, and the line fell as flat as a pancake and was thankfully ignored in the ensuing general confusion.

12.

There were still people up and about at Marshalsea Road. In fact, although the party had begun to wind down, there was a die-hard bunch of revellers who clearly had no intention of going home before dawn – although by now the revelling was of the muted variety which featured a dozen or more people slumped amidst the remnants of the party food indulging in long, rambling and pointless conversations which they would have forgotten by the following day. Neither Andrew nor the man he had referred to as the U-boat commander was present, however; Rupert wondered whether or not that was a good thing.

There was no sign of Steve either, but Gary was holding court with all the elegant presence of a Noel Coward, languishing on his white couch with his feet up and a glass of red in his hand. Rupert's arrival in their midst caused a sudden hiatus in the conversation and all eyes inevitably turned towards him.

"Sorry to be a pain," he said, shrugging. "Gaz, I've got to rush off – Jake's got a family emergency and he needs my help; it's a long story," he continued, quelling any attempt at sarcasm with an upraised hand and a look of perturbation. He didn't begrudge this crowd of lotus-eaters their fun, by any means, but he wanted them to realise he was serious; what usually passed for witty banter at this hour would be wasted on him, and he'd rather they saved their breath.

"Oh." Gary performed a miracle of agility, rising in a smooth unbroken movement without disturbing the surface of his wine. "What can I do?"

"Nothing, thanks. Just came back to get my driving licence. Mind if I take some of the food as well, since there's so much left? I don't know if we'll be stopping anywhere, and I'm going to need something to eat before too long."

"Mmmm, help yourself; there's nearly a whole courgette quiche and plenty of those miniature pork pies." Gary had drifted over, set down his drink, and was pulling plastic boxes from a cupboard. "So," he continued, leaning closer, "did you get any? Andrew told us your new man called and you rushed off to see him. He's with Jørgen, by the way; I think they've gone to a hotel."

"No." Rupert went on packing for a moment, cutting slices of quiche to fit the box. "It nearly happened - but then the bloody phone rang and interrupted us."

"And you actually answered?" Gary sounded appalled. "I'm not sure a herd of rampaging elephants would have stopped me at that point, but each to his own!"

"It was an emergency," enunciated Rupert with pointed clarity. "The life or death kind; his ... a relative has been taken to hospital, and it sounds like there's trouble at the farm as well." He had no intention of trying to work out what relation Martin was to Jake, if any, and a catastrophe involving 'his late brother's father-in-law' wouldn't have sounded reason for panic in any event.

Gary's mouth twisted into a waspish pout, Dame Edna by way of Dr Evadne Hinge, but whatever remark he'd been about to make he clearly thought better of.

"Oh well - better luck next time, then. Holy Interruptus, Batman!"

Rupert was too preoccupied to take notice of what Gary was saying, or to respond beyond thanking him for the food. He had packed it – plus a change of underwear and socks – into his backpack, and was downstairs and opening the rear door of the taxi to climb in beside Jake before he suddenly became aware of what might possibly have been singing emanating from somewhere high above him and looked up to see half-a-dozen people leaning out of the windows of Steve and Gary's flat all impersonating – with greater or lesser degrees of drunken accuracy – Tammy Wynette belting out the chorus of *Stand By Your Man*.

"It's probably about time we got out of here," he said resolutely to Jake. "Come on, mate - for fuck's sake, let's go!"

By the time they'd arrived at Victoria, explained their requirements to a man in a shiny suit who had obviously been exiled from the day shift for being too cheerful, and been processed through the system, two o'clock had come and gone. It was closer to half-past by the time they found themselves side-by-side in an electric blue Corsa, following a National Express coach along Grosvenor Place to Hyde Park Corner. On the pavements around them people emerging from clubs and restaurants jostled with those making overnight deliveries, and here and there small bands of tourists dragging bulging trolley-cases were clearly either arriving or departing. There was an air of futility hanging over the entire proceedings like a pall, which the gleaming window-displays of Knightsbridge did nothing to dispel.

"I'm sure he'll be okay," said Rupert, as they stopped at one particular pelican crossing where they and a Japanese couple stared at one another in a kind of mutual empathy. "Martin, I mean. What did Helena say?"

"She said the same, but I can tell it's really shocked her. He and Toffee were at the farm with her and the children and Bridget was at home with Fudge. H said they'd heard somebody mucking about in one of the sheds about midnight; she didn't want her dad to go out and investigate but he insisted – he said he was sure he'd be okay. Then she heard a crash." There was a pause as they drew away from the lights, navigated around a double-decker bus full of blank-faced people, turned onto the Cromwell Road. "H called Bridget on the radio, Bridget called the police. H put the kids in their bedroom with the dog, switched the light off and told them to snuggle under the covers while she went out to see what had happened. She found Martin flat on his back in the garage with petrol all over the place." Jake's jaw was working overtime, as though he was chewing on a particularly indigestible fact. "She'd've had to go up the lane on her own to let the police car in through the gate," he said, "leaving her children alone in the middle of the night, knowing there were people about who were probably planning to torch the garage. Now you know, and I know - and she knows, too – that people like that are never going to stop at beating up a woman. Or worse," he added, bluntly. "That girl's got bigger balls than you and me and Martin put together."

Careful not to distract Jake while he was driving, Rupert reached out a hand and gave his knee a consoling squeeze.

"The worst of it is," continued Jake, "it was my fault. I wanted to get together with you, and I badgered Martin into staying so that I could come here."

"But you said you'd stayed away overnight a couple of times before," countered Rupert. "I didn't realise you were worried about it."

"I wasn't at the time, but I think I should have been. The last time I stayed away they got my bloody quad bike, after all; I'm still arguing with the insurance company about that."

"Bastards."

"Absolutely. But the point is I shouldn't have done it, should I?"

"Is that what you reckon Martin would tell you? Only he could have refused to stand in for you, couldn't he, if he didn't think it was right?"

"He could." They had reached the Hammersmith Flyover, a sure sign that they were getting somewhere at last, and had swooped easily around the curve of the river before Jake spoke again. "The fact remains; I was away enjoying myself and everything went to shit. I don't know how I'm ever going to explain it to Helena if Martin dies."

"It's not all you, though, is it?" challenged Rupert. "I must be at least partly to blame, if that's the case."

"No you're not," Jake told him, clearly. "Not at all. I was the one who made the wrong decision, not you. But you do have to ask yourself, don't you - with everything against us like it is - whether or not any of it's really worth doing? Or, at least, I have to. I'm going to have to think very seriously about that, Rupert."

Which was unanswerable, really, and for some time after that a depressive silence prevailed between them as they headed out of London.

"I'm sorry," said Jake, after a long interval. The road was dark, and so was the sky; sunrise was still at least an hour away, and it had been like driving through a black tunnel ever since they'd left the urban streets behind and the A4 had almost imperceptibly become the M4. The car had begun to show its paces then, gaining speed under Jake's confident direction until the miles – and the counties - were sliding away behind them with regular monotony. Which was, it seemed, precisely the trouble. "I'm getting sleepy. Maybe you could talk to me for a while, to help me stay awake?"

"Of course." Truth to tell Rupert had been drowsing a bit himself; it had been warm in the car before Jake opened the window, and there was little to take his interest outside. "What would you like to talk about?"

"Oh, anything," said Jake, "that isn't Martin and the farm and whatever's waiting for us when we get back. Tell me about your dog - what's her name again?"

"Rusty. She's a Springer, it seemed appropriate. 'Rusty spring', you know?" But it had never really been funny, and seemed even less so now.

"Oh, okay. So what made you get a dog? Was it your idea or Cameron's?"

"Not really." Afterwards, neither of them had ever fully owned the decision; it had just happened, almost by accident. "He used to say he got lonely when I was out working and he was at home. The original idea was that I'd cook and he'd do front-of-house, but there wasn't enough business to support him if he wasn't going to wait tables as well – which he refused to do – so he ended up being more a sort of event co-ordinator and party planner, which mostly meant working from home. Anyway, he'd been talking about getting a cat to keep him company – and then Ruth, one of our regulars, asked if we knew anybody who wanted a puppy. Rusty's mum had just had a litter of five - and of course she had the photos with her, didn't she? Scheming cow knew exactly what she was doing all along." It was said completely without malice, however.

"But aren't they pedigree animals, Springers? Don't people usually sell them for a lot of money? I know Martin and Bridget shelled out a fortune for those two daft lumps of theirs - they were something like a thousand quid each."

"Rusty was the last puppy," said Rupert. "All the others had been sold. Ruth offered us a discount." He paused. "Maybe it was a scam, I don't really know, but one look at that cute little face and we were suckered. Cameron fell in love on the spot, so I said I'd buy Rusty for him. I genuinely thought it would make him happy, more fool me."

"But it didn't," concluded Jake. "Is that what you're saying?"

"No, it didn't. Oh, it was fine at first - but then he began to get bored; I was the one who used to take her for walks and clean up after her whenever she'd been sick – and she was sick a lot before we found out she was allergic to beef and a few other things and got her diet sorted out. The more I think about it now, the more I realise Cameron had no more attention span than a spider monkey; it was all raging enthusiasms with him, and whenever anything got too difficult he lost interest in it quickly. The last straw was when Rusty chewed up a pair of boots he'd just bought; I think that was when he finally stopped caring about her. If she'd had any proper training she'd never have done it in the first place – but Cameron wasn't big on discipline, for himself or anybody else. At first I used to think he was spontaneous and fun, but as time went on I realised he was really unreliable; what I originally thought was a quirky personality ended up being bloody irritating. The short answer is, Jake - if Cameron could let anybody down, he would. He let me down and he let Rusty down, and I'm not in a place where I can forgive him for either of those things just yet."

"So where is she now? Why did you decide to bring her back to England? She's an Australian dog, isn't she? She won't speak the language or anything."

"Back with her breeder for the time being, but I'm having to pay rent while she's there. Cameron wanted her to live with his mother while he was in prison, but his mum wasn't having it. She told me she was sick of clearing up after his mistakes, and I can't say I blame her. She wanted him to sell Rusty, but since I'd paid for her in the first place it was my name on the paperwork and he couldn't legally do it – and that's when I put my foot down. Even if it cost me a bomb, I decided she'd be better off with me than stuck in Australia with people who didn't appreciate her. That might have been a mistake," he concluded, "but at least it was something I could do. Everything else had gone wrong, but I didn't see why Rusty should suffer. I'll need somewhere permanent to live before I fly her over, though; she's used to bounding along the beach at top speed, and a room in somebody else's flat isn't going to be enough for her for long."

"Well - we could have her at the farm, if you like," said Jake. "She could come and live with us for a while; the kids would fall in love with her, and you could see her whenever you wanted."

"I'm sure they would," replied Rupert. "And don't think I don't appreciate the offer, but I reckon you've got enough problems as it is. Besides, doesn't what's happened with Martin make things more complicated for you? I mean, if you don't know whether or not he'll be able to carry on helping with the business."

"Yes, you're right." A large green road-sign had loomed up out of the darkness. "Services, ten miles. Good opportunity to stop for a pee and a cup of coffee and I can give H a call and let her know when to expect us – what do you think?"

"Perfect," said Rupert. "And we can grab a bite to eat while we're at it; should make the rest of the journey go a bit faster, with luck."

They crossed the Severn in a pearly dawn with the mist rising off the water almost reaching deck-height on the bridge, paid the toll, and were in the car park of the hospital shortly after six. It had clearly rained here, too, overnight, to judge from the oiled rainbows on the tarmac and the dew-starred spider-webs on the vegetation in the borders. Alerted by a call from Jake's mobile to her mother's Helena was waiting for them as they drew in, wearing a cardigan that looked too thin to be of any use against the morning chill.

"How is he?" asked Jake, briskly, although he'd already been told that there was no real change.

"He's in CCU," was the reply. "He's had what they call an 'uncomplicated' heart attack; he's got a bit of a fever but they reckon he could be out of bed as early as tomorrow. It's nothing like as serious as it could have been," concluded Helena, wrapping her arms around herself against the cold. "Actually I think they want us out of here now, they've been dropping some not-very-subtle hints already, and I must say I'd be glad to get home; there's nothing we can do at the moment, anyway. Besides, the dogs will need to go out; Mum left Fudge shut in the kitchen, and as far as I know Toffee's still in the kids' bedroom – unless the police have let him out by now, of course. They said they'd leave a man at the house overnight, in case anybody came back, but he was supposed to go off duty at six. We'd probably have left here by now if we hadn't been waiting for you," she added, without a trace of reproach. "Mum's had enough, the kids look like zombies, and we're all hungry; all you can get here are chocolate and crisps out of a machine - and if you run out of cash for that, basically you're stuffed."

"There's food in the car," volunteered Rupert. "Pork pies, courgette quiche, sandwiches." They'd eaten some at the motorway services, washed down with coffee so strong it could have etched metal, but there was plenty left.

"Oh, god," said Helena fervently, "I think I'd kill for a pork pie. You haven't got any chips to go with it, I suppose?"

"Sorry, no. But I can always cook you some when we get back, if you like?"

"You've talked me into it, you silver-tongued seducer."

They were walking as they spoke, through a grim shiny corridor towards a squared-off seating area where Bridget – a little woman with short grey hair – was sitting with the children. Tara was leaning against her grandmother attempting to read a book; Finn was stretched out asleep across several chairs with his toy dog clutched in his arms and his mother's coat over him. Jake leaned in and kissed Bridget on the cheek – her hands gripped his arms briefly, but she soon let him go. For good measure he kissed Tara, too, and formally introduced Bridget to Rupert.

"Let's see about getting you lot home then, shall we? Rupert, you go with H and the kids in her car; I'll take Bridget to the cottage and join you in a little while - I'm going to have to phone and e-mail all our regular customers first, to let them know we won't be delivering today."

"I've made a list," said Helena. "I had to have something to occupy my mind while we were waiting for news of Dad. The six at the top are the most important." She handed him the paper.

"Brilliant. Now, then, ladies and germs, are we planning on staying here all day or is there anybody who'd like to go home?"

"I would," said Tara, and it was obvious she spoke for them all.

The mist was still rising from the fields as Helena drove the Skoda back through the lanes - Rupert beside her and the children in the back, happily munching pork pies for breakfast as though they were on a picnic. He didn't blame them; on a glorious morning like this death and disaster must feel very far away, and Finn at least had little or no conception of hospital as a place where anything unpleasant might happen to anyone.

The gate at the top of the lane was open, but there was a police car parked at the bottom and a constable came out to greet them as they drew up. He and Helena had obviously met before, because all she said by way of introduction was that Rupert was a friend of the family.

Rupert left them talking and wandered into the yard, his eyes drawn to the arresting sight of a couple of fat geese wandering about nibbling at anything green and growing within easy reach of their beaks. They were doing quite a bit of damage, and as far as Rupert knew the geese should probably not be out at this time of day; he'd understood that the routine involved shutting them up for the night and letting them out again first thing in the morning. He'd got as far as wondering whether they'd simply not been locked up the night before or had managed their own escape when he saw Tara opening up the door to the lodge and a grey blur shooting past her as though propelled from the muzzle of a gun. Toffee, all flailing limbs and pent-up energy after a long night indoors with people he didn't know, launched himself into the midst of the knot of geese and scattered them, chasing first one and then another with galloping enthusiasm. Some seemed inclined to stand their ground and fight, but a couple of them took flight – to such extent as they could with their wings clipped, anyway. They flapped, they hopped, they scuttled, and somehow succeeded in getting up quite an impressive head of steam, careering dizzily across the market garden at low-level with the idiotic dog in hot pursuit. Before Rupert could pull himself together sufficiently to respond Toffee and one of the geese had vanished from sight altogether, over the ridge which divided the land and towards the cider orchard – and Tara was left standing on the doorstep of the lodge with Toffee's lead dangling from her fingers, tears of frustration and sheer exhaustion coursing hotly down her narrow little face.

13.

There was an instant in which Rupert would have liked to be able to split himself in two; part of him wanted to race after the dog and the goose, to try to round them up quickly and make sure their encounter wouldn't end in a pile of blood and feathers; part of him was more inclined to run across and comfort Tara, who seemed to be suffering the after-effects of her grandfather's heart-attack and a night in a hospital waiting area as much as her immediate reaction to Toffee's break for freedom. Then again the voice of sanity cut in; known to the family though he was, an adult man hugging a child of Tara's age was likely to be viewed with circumspection in these unenlightened times; it was an instinct which would have to be suppressed until he was sure there could be no objection.

One split-second of indecision was enough, however. In the time it had taken him to make up his mind Tara, too, had raced off over the ridge.

"Fuck." Well, at least that reduced his alternatives; he wasn't prepared to allow her to vanish from adult supervision altogether, and he would have to go after her. "Helena?" He raised his voice just enough for it to reach her where she was in conversation with the policeman. "I'm going with Tara, to catch the dog!" He indicated the direction they'd taken. "That way."

"Oh, all right." The distance between them wasn't massive, but he could hardly hear her; then he realised he'd been moving all the time, and was now at the crest of the rise. Below him were the trees in their neat rows, in full and healthy green leaf, with the land sloping away towards the river and the path that led to the Youth Hostel; here the mist still roiled, water vapour hanging in the air as delicate as spun sugar, and here he slowed his pace to a walk. Over his own accelerated breathing he could hear Toffee barking, and an unearthly hissing sound which must be from the goose, and Tara's high voice calling "Toffee! Toffee!

Come back, silly fool!" He could see none of them, however, and was on uncertain ground himself, stepping cautiously down the hill as he listened for their voices, muffled and distorted by multiple echoes from hillsides, rocks, water and the fine veil of cloud.

Lower down the visibility was further reduced, and it became important to concentrate on the sounds around him. Tara had started singing – although whether to keep her spirits up or to let Toffee know where to find her was anybody's guess; the words of the *Bob the Builder* theme song were bouncing around him incongruously, seeming to come first from one side and then another.

The surreal properties of the situation were not lost on Rupert. It was early morning, a time when he was usually at work in a kitchen somewhere setting up for the day, and here he was – after being interrupted during a sexual encounter he'd really been enjoying and travelling through the night – on someone else's farm searching for someone else's child, someone else's dog and someone else's goose, all three of which were invisible somewhere in the mist.

A nasty aggressive growl, a yelp of astonishment, then all of a sudden there was a thundering of rapid paws, an awkward slithering sound, and something that looked like a small horse in a fur coat rushed full-tilt at Rupert as if he was the best friend it had in the world and leaped at him with nearly enough force to knock him over, its tail wagging at a frantic rate and its big stupid tongue lolling out of the corner of its mouth.

"Toffee, you maniac, you're absolutely bloody filthy! What happened, mate, the nasty goose attack you?" There was certainly an air of gratitude and wounded pride about Toffee's demeanour; Rusty had behaved like that once, when an encounter with a crab on the beach hadn't turned out the way she'd been hoping. It had been comical at the time, but essentially he'd been dealing with a frightened dog then – and he was now. "All right, all right, I promise I won't let it near you ever again."

Having found and latched on to someone he trusted Toffee didn't seem inclined to stray from his side, but Rupert wasn't taking any chances. After all, Toffee only knew him as somebody who'd visited once and fed him; the recognition factor would be minimal at best, and there wasn't much hope of being obeyed unless he did something to establish control. It took only a moment to unsnag the belt from his jeans and loop it through Toffee's collar, but it was time well spent. Being on the end of a lead seemed to calm the dog immensely, and a few judicious pats and words of reassurance did the rest; a docile and chastened Toffee looked up adoringly at Rupert out of a fringe of the dirtiest, stinkingest dog hair he'd seen in a long time.

"God, Toffee, what the fuck have you been rolling in, you dork? Your ma's going to be horrified when she sees the state of you. Right, come on - let's see if we can find Tara, and I hope she's not plastered from head to foot in mud as well!" As if Helena needed that or anything else to deal with at the moment, he thought ironically. But then, the heaviest burdens seemed to fall on those best equipped to bear them. "Find Tara," he said to Toffee. "Where is she, mate? Where's Tara?"

The dog stood still for a moment, his comical ears lifting and lowering apparently at random, then gave a snuffle and began to pull downhill at an angle, leaving Rupert with little option but to follow. Although nominally in charge, he was aware that Toffee was as heavy as himself – if not heavier – and suffused with an inexhaustible wiry energy for which an over-tired Rupert would never be a match.

The singing, he noticed, had stopped. There was no sound in the orchard but their quiet footfalls and the steam-engine panting of the dog. Belatedly it occurred to Rupert that if he was a nine year old girl on her own in a mist he'd probably find that rather sinister; she might be too young to have read *The Hound of the Baskervilles*, but she had doubtless seen more than enough episodes of *Scooby-Doo* to be aware that she was in a vulnerable position. Literally anything could come looming out of the fog at her; an aggressive goose, in the circumstances, would be the least of her worries.

"Tara?" Rupert called. (It might just as well have been 'Velma', he thought.) "Tara? It's me, Kanga-Rupert. *Boing boing.* From Australia. I've found Toffee." Strictly speaking Toffee had found him, but it was all good as far as Rupert was concerned. "I think the goose may have bitten him or something." If that was what geese did; he was hazy on the technicalities. And then; "He's filthy, he's going to need a bath when we get back."

They were still heading downhill slowly, taking it easy - as if they were just out for a walk, enjoying the chill white air and the rich rolling fog for their own sake, when Tara emerged suddenly from a clump of vegetation – Rupert hadn't realised they were so close to the edge of the orchard; they must have travelled on a diagonal line from one corner to the other – and, as eagerly as the dog had, she ran to him and wrapped both arms around his waist.

"All right," he said, vaguely embarrassed, patting her head with one hand while he tried to restrain Toffee with the other. "Easy." And then, because he didn't know what else to say, "I reckon it's time you had something to eat, young lady, don't you? Then maybe you ought to go to bed for a while and catch up on the sleep you missed last night. Grandpa's going to be fine where he is, you know; you don't have to worry about him. Those people are experts, they'll make him better in no time."

But Tara had worked her way out of his half-embrace and was sniffing with unladylike vigour and wiping her nose on the back of her hand.

"I know," she said, scornfully. "It's like *Holby City*, they've got machines they put people into. My nan watches *Holby City*, she told me all about it."

Yes, he could imagine that. During those hours in the waiting area, while Finn slept and Helena made notes, it would have been Bridget who had kept up everybody else's spirits; that was the way things seemed to work, for some inscrutable reason.

"I'm not frightened about grandpa at all," continued Tara, manfully. "But I did get scared when I saw the ghosts."

"Ghosts, was that? Or did you say 'goats'?" Either was equally likely, after all. Or equally *un*likely, he thought.

"Ghosts. People who disappear. They were walking up the path, and they heard me calling Toffee, and all of a sudden they vanished – like ... whoosh!" The gesture she made mimicked a bubble bursting or a dandelion seed-head exploding; something which had seemed substantial a moment before disintegrating into thin air.

"They vanished? Honestly? Are you sure they didn't just turn a corner?"

"There aren't any corners," returned Tara. She had threaded her fingers with his and was tugging him towards the path. "Come on, come and see!"

"Come and see where they … aren't?" Rupert felt he was getting in deep here, and might not find his way out again. "What about breakfast? Toffee's hungry, even if you're not!"

"I am," she said, "but I want to show you. Here. This was where they were." She had brought him to a place where the hedge around the orchard was broken by a locked gate with a PRIVATE sign on the outside. "They went that way." She was pointing up the hill towards the Youth Hostel.

"Ghosts," he repeated, in befuddlement.

"Lots of them, walking in a line and not talking."

Well, silence was typically ghostlike - but he'd never heard of a group of ghosts walking in single file before. "Are you sure they weren't just hikers?"

"They weren't carrying anything," was the firm response. "Hikers always have loads of stuff. And they'd be going the other way, wouldn't they?"

This was irrefutable logic; at this time in the morning it was unlikely anybody would be arriving at the Youth Hostel; they'd be more likely to be leaving, so they'd be going down the path and not up it.

"Well, I don't suppose it was anything important," Rupert said, comfortably. "They weren't really ghosts, you know, Tara."

"No," she agreed, "because ghosts don't exist - but they looked like it. They were pale and shivery, and the man who was with them had a gun."

"A gun?" No, this was going too far! There were no armed cowboys roaming rural Wales, and even if there were they'd hardly be around at this ungodly hour on a Sunday morning. "Are you sure you haven't been watching too much TV?" he asked, sceptically.

"It was a shotgun," she said. "He had it over his arm." And that was the moment Rupert realised it was no use arguing with a girl brought up in the country who had been around such things all her life; she ought to recognise a shotgun when she saw one, after all. "Like people use when they're going after rabbits," she added, more convincingly still.

Rupert was leaning over the fence. He was no tracker by any stretch of the imagination, but even to him the footprints on the muddy path looked recent – and there were, as Tara had suggested, several sets of them; it certainly seemed unusual, considering that this path didn't see much traffic. Even so he was inclined to place little importance on it until he became aware of something shining at the edge of his vision and screwed up his eyes to make out what it was.

"Looks as if somebody's dropped a credit card," he said, half to himself. Then, with a sinking sense that he should probably try to get it back to its owner, he pulled himself up and over the gate and reached into a clump of weeds to retrieve the thing. It was not a credit card, however; it seemed to be an identity card for a young woman of foreign origin; the name on the card was Zdeňka Jahodová, and she was twenty-two years old. "I'll take it to the Youth Hostel later," he told Tara, tucking the card into his pocket and returning over the gate to take Toffee's makeshift lead from her. "Now – let's get you two home at least; the bloody goose will have to manage by itself for a while, if it's stupid enough to run away like that. Maybe we'll have another look for it when the mist's burned off a bit." Which, judging by the speed it was rising from the ground, wouldn't be long now.

"It wasn't a goose," said Tara firmly. "That was Gandalf, he's a gander."

"Ah. Well, whatever it is," Rupert told her, tolerantly, "it'll probably be all right on its own; we can always come and get it later on."

"Unless the ghosts have eaten him by then," said Tara, falling in beside him without demur. She didn't sound too appalled at the prospect, he had to concede; maybe she wasn't very fond of Gandalf.

"Unless they've eaten him, of course," he acknowledged, as they pulled back up the side of the hill together.

Between them he and Helena concocted breakfast for the children. It amounted to little more than bacon and fried bread, and Finn fell asleep at least twice while he was eating his, but at length the food was disposed of and the children shepherded towards their bedroom – "No, you don't need to put your pyjamas on, you can sleep in your underwear for once" – while Rupert washed the dishes and poured another coffee. Toffee, steeped in filth to his eyeballs, had temporarily been fastened outside the house; there he'd taken a pragmatic view, settled his chin on his paws, and immediately fallen asleep.

Helena reappeared after a short while, to pat Rupert on the shoulder and thank him for his help. "And how are you feeling?" she asked him kindly.

It was the first time in a while that he'd paused to take stock of himself; he was tired, obviously, but there was also a sort of low-level adrenalin buzz going on which was keeping him alert – or perhaps it was all the industrial-strength coffee he'd been drinking.

"Not bad, on the whole," he replied. "If you want to have a sleep yourself, I'll stay awake until Jake gets back. He shouldn't be much longer, should he?"

"No. He'll see mum settled and make his calls, and then he'll be right back. Half an hour or so, maybe." Helena looked at her watch.

"Then I'm fine; you have a rest - and don't worry about anything out here, okay? I've got it covered."

"Thank you." Helena was smiling tiredly at him. "I like you, Rupert; you fit in - the children trust you, and so do I. If you don't mind me asking … are you and Jake actually a couple? Or is it something else between the two of you?"

"I don't mind at all," he said, "but I can't give you a coherent answer all the same. At the moment we seem to be trapped in a permanent state of not-quite-getting-it-together." He shrugged helplessly. "I don't know if we're a couple or not, to be honest. It probably depends on how you define the word 'couple'."

"Oh," she said. "Like Schrödinger's Cat?"

"What?"

"Well, it was simultaneously alive and dead," explained Helena. "And you're together and not together, both at the same time." She stopped. "I think I probably watched too much *Star Trek* when I was younger; I had a bit of a thing for Data, if I'm honest."

"Oh," said he, "good choice; I wouldn't have kicked him out of bed on a cold night either! Except, you know, as an android … "

" … it's difficult to know what he'd have been doing in your bed in the first place," concluded Helena, grinning at him. "I had the same problem. So, when I met Tim … well, there wasn't any similarity but I knew I loved him anyway – right from the start."

"Of course. I'm sorry I never got the chance to meet him, you know; from everything Jake's told me, it sounds as if he was a really nice person."

"He was, actually. Really, *really* nice." Helen shook her head. "But maybe it was all too good to be true, you know?"

"Yes, I do. I've … well, it isn't comparable, obviously, but I do know a bit about loss. From personal experience, I mean."

"So I understand from Jake."

There was a silence that fell between them then, although it wasn't an awkward one – more a shared moment of reflection.

"For what it's worth … " began Rupert hesitantly, when his thoughts had had a chance to form, "I think Tim would be proud of the way you're carrying on without him. I mean, everybody's putting everything they've got into keeping this place going; you all believe in his dream, don't you, and you all want to make it a success – for him, as much as for yourselves?"

"Yes. Absolutely." But Helena was staring at him, wide-eyed. "You'd be astonished how many people don't get that," she said. "Even my mum asked me, once, if I wouldn't rather sell the place and settle down somewhere else – on an estate with other young families – and do without the worry of it all. I probably would've had to, too, if it hadn't been for Jake. He's the one making it possible for us to keep living here; he's the one making his brother's dream come true. It was never Jake's dream," she pointed out, although he had realised that already.

"I know. He still cares about it massively though, doesn't he?"

"He does. But it would be nice to see him having something for himself as well. The least he deserves is a partner who'll support him in whatever he does. And if that partner turned out to be you, Rupert - well, let's say that it wouldn't break my heart."

"No," said he. "It wouldn't break mine, either. I could get used to this, you know; I like the place - and you all, as a family - and I like Jake very much."

"Good. Then maybe it'll all work out for all the best, although at the moment it's difficult to see how."

Slowly, so that she'd have the chance to stop him if she chose, Rupert reached out a hand and gently squeezed her shoulder. Helena made no attempt to evade the gesture, however, simply smiling in return.

"Things worth having are never easy, are they?" he asked her, quietly. "And if they were, I suppose they wouldn't be worth having in the first place."

14.

An hour later Rupert was beginning to feel tired and irritable. There had been no sign of Jake, and not a squawk from the radio handset Helena had shown him how to operate before she went to grab some sleep, and time was passing slowly. The kitchen was immaculate, he'd drunk as much coffee as he could without his kidneys floating away, and although he'd half-formed a plan for giving Toffee a scrub-down now that it was warm enough to do it without risking hypothermia – to either of them - one look at him spark out and snoring was enough; Toffee looked so peaceful, he wouldn't have disturbed him for the world.

He stared for a while at the picture of Zdeňka Jahodová on her identity card. Apparently she was a citizen of the Slovak Republic and her place of birth was Bratislava, which he had a vague recollection was the capital city. He couldn't really imagine what it might be like, but coming to the UK had probably been something of a culture shock. He'd always pictured the former Soviet Republics, when he'd pictured them at all, as heavily industrialised and having a standard of living that didn't quite match the one he was used to, although whether that image was accurate or hopelessly out of date he had no idea. He did remember somebody telling him once that, in East Berlin before reunification, if you broke a window you just boarded it up and forgot about it – glass was almost impossible to get hold of and you might be waiting a very long time. That seemed to indicate life was a struggle generally, and in his mind the scenario in Bratislava was similar; shortages, queues, limited opportunities, labyrinthine bureaucracy …

But then, what did he know? The Slovak Republic might be a haven for musicians, artists and writers; it might be The Next Big Thing for entrepreneurs; it might be the ideal place for Ren to expand his Nectarine empire – Glasgow today, Bratislava tomorrow – and maybe Rupert should volunteer to go and open up a restaurant over there instead.

He was wondering whether Slovakian cuisine had anything to rival the legendary Glaswegian deep-fried Mars Bar when he became aware of the sound of the Corsa's engine and snatched himself from the brink of sleep to go out and greet the returning Jake.

"On your own?" asked Jake, getting out of the car. Rupert had made an impulsive move towards him and faltered, and now lingered irresolutely in the gateway.

"Everyone's asleep," he shrugged. "Even Toffee. The geese were out when we got back; Gandalf's still missing, he's probably in the orchard somewhere."

"He'll have to wait," said Jake. "I'm going to need a kip before I go rounding up bloody geese. You got the rest back all right, though, did you?"

"Yes, but not before they'd got into the salad stuff and had most of the radishes," Rupert told him, with a sigh. "Helena reckons they were locked up last night as usual but the copper who was here said they'd been wandering around the whole time and he hadn't known what to do about them. He's a townie, he wouldn't have had a clue how to deal with geese."

"Okay, well, Gandalf will have to take his chances. I'm going to get my head down for an hour, but first I want to see what sort of mess they've left us to deal with; might as well know the worst."

He led the way over to the garage, the doors of which were closed. On pulling them open, the acrid stink of petrol hit them strongly in the face.

"Oh, god. I suppose we'll have to get some kind of industrial detergent on that – but not before the guy from the insurance company's seen it. I called them from Bridget's; they're sending somebody first thing tomorrow morning."

"Is that your petrol?" asked Rupert, glancing around at the scene of devastation. "Or did they bring it with them?"

"Probably ours; we always keep a couple of cans for the car – and stuff like the mower and the chain saw use petrol too. Whoever did this must have known where to find it, but if they were the same lot who helped themselves to my quad bike they know the place inside-out anyway."

"And Martin heard them and came out to try to stop them, did he?"

"Apparently. I wish he hadn't, but then this whole thing might have been no more than a heap of ashes by now – and it could have got the house as well. Not to mention H and the kids," continued Jake, in a more subdued tone. "Martin probably saved the farm - but maybe the price was too high, you know? He could've died, after all."

"I know," said Rupert. "How's Bridget coping?"

Jake shrugged. "Surprisingly well," he said. "She's a tough old bird. She's got great neighbours who'll look after her – Tricia, who drives the taxi, lives next-door - and of course she's got Fudge for company, but I said I'd go over again this evening."

"You can't be in two places at once," Rupert reminded him. "You're going to have to spread yourself even thinner, aren't you, with Martin out of the picture?"

"Well, yes, but what's the alternative? If we took the kids to live with Bridget for a few days H and I could manage the farm between us, but there'd still be times when we'd have to leave it on its own and hope for the best. And it's not really the sort of situation you can put up with on a long-term basis; if Martin isn't going to be well enough to come back for a while – if he ever is - we're really going to have to think about whether we can carry on at all. There's too much working against us at the moment; we need something to change for the better or we're going to be buggered."

Rupert resisted the temptation of making a knowing quip in response. Instead he slid his arm around Jake's waist and gave him a squeeze, and Jake in turn slung an arm around his shoulders and pressed a half-distracted kiss against his cheek.

"Look," said Rupert, "I've been thinking about that. Maybe I could ask Ren for time off, to help you out in the short term."

"Time off? You've only been there a few weeks, you can't be due for any holidays yet!"

"That's true, but ... look, Ren's a mate as well as a boss. We watch each other's backs, have done for years. He knows I wouldn't ask if it wasn't important, and ... well, I reckon he'd want to do whatever he could to help. My job only needs somebody with a certain level of skill, and there are plenty in London – all you have to do is pick up the phone. If I hadn't come back from Aussie when I did, Ren would either have got in an agency chef or promoted someone from another department. He put me in there because I needed a job - not because he needed me, specifically, though he pretended he did. He does want me to open the new place in Glasgow for him, though," he added, wryly. "I reckon he'd give me a bit of leeway now if I agreed to that. I'll ask, anyway; he can only say 'no', after all."

"Okay." Jake's tone was cautious. "So, what - we leave the kids with Bridget and you and me and Helena ... and maybe Toffee ... keep the farm going until Martin's out of hospital?"

"It's better than nothing, isn't it? I could do the deliveries and the cooking at least, to let the two of you get on with the important stuff."

"Yes, you could." Jake was thoughtful. "You really mean it, don't you?"

"Of course. I wouldn't have suggested it otherwise."

"All right, then, let's see what Ren says about it. You're going to have to go back to London anyway, to take the car back."

"Yes. I'll go to work in the morning as usual, but I'll grab the first chance I get to talk to Ren, and with a bit of luck I could be back here by the end of the week. You and H can manage that long, can't you?"

"I expect so," grinned Jake. "We'll do our best. It would be really great if you could swing that, Rupert."

"Swing what?" It was Helena's voice, subdued and sleepy, and they looked around to see her emerging from the direction of the house. Instinctively Rupert pushed the garage door shut before she could reach them, thinking the sight of the chaos might upset her, but he should have realised she was made of sterner stuff. "Don't worry, I've seen it all before," she said. "I found him, remember? What exactly is it you're hoping to swing, Rupert?"

In a few words they explained the plot to persuade Ren to release Rupert for a few days. It was possible, even as they spoke, to see some of the burden lifting from Helena's narrow shoulders; she was standing more uprightly by the end, and there was even the tentative precursor of a smile around her lips.

"That would be brilliant," she said, quietly optimistic. "And Dad might be back sooner than you think; I've just had a call from Mum on the HT – that's what woke me up, I could hear it blasting away in the living-room - and apparently he's doing really well. I knew she wouldn't be able to resist phoning the hospital every couple of hours," she added ruefully. "Tricia's going to take her to see him this afternoon; I thought I'd probably wait and go some time tomorrow."

"All right," said Jake. "Then we've potentially got a way of carrying on without him for a while. You'll be able to tell him that, when you visit him."

"I will," replied Helena. "Otherwise he's likely to feel guilty about letting us down, and that wouldn't do him any good. Oh, sorry!" She clapped a hand over her mouth, having been unable to stifle the yawn which had crept up on her surreptitiously during this speech.

"No problem. Are you going back to bed?"

"I don't think so, not now I'm up. I've got a headache and I want to work it off, so I'm going to give Toffee a bath before he sets solid, and then I'll do something about lunch. The kids will be up before long, anyway, if I know them."

"Oh god - and bounding with energy, too," groaned Jake. "I'm not sure I can cope with that."

"Well, you go and grab some shut-eye," Helena advised him calmly. "I'll call you when lunch is ready – in about two hours?"

For a moment Jake looked as if he might be inclined to turn the offer down, but any potential resistance crumbled almost immediately.

"You're right," he said. "I could definitely do with a power nap."

"So could Rupert, by the looks of him. Why don't you take him with you?"

Jake laughed, a half-embarrassed sound. "Matchmaking, H?" he asked her, his mouth twisted into an odd smile.

"Don't need to, the pair of you are a perfect match already. Seriously, Jake, this one's a keeper; you need to do everything you can to hold on to him."

"Hey," said Rupert, "I am actually *here*, you know!"

"Yes," said Helena, "you are – for which I'm profoundly grateful and so's Jake, for all that he's doing the shrinking violet thing. I don't know why men have to be quite so stupid when it comes to talking about emotions but you can take my word for it, Rupert; my brother-in-law is really glad to have you around."

"She's right, of course," Jake told him in the caravan. It smelled a bit of petrol – Rupert supposed everything on the farm would, for a time anyway – but was shady and familiar and somehow more welcoming than on his previous visit. A quick glance seemed to suggest Jake had tidied up a bit, and maybe even vacuumed; it now seemed less like some rancid student digs and more like a place where civilisation might eventually flourish. "I mean, I appreciate your help. But I'm getting a bit muddled about whether we're friends, or lovers, or both or neither. It's great having somebody you can rely on for stuff - but I wouldn't want to push it all too far, you know."

Rupert shook his head in confusion. "Do I have to remind you of what we were doing when the phone rang?" he asked. "That wasn't even twelve hours ago!"

"I know. But things can change quickly, can't they? Up in London, in a hotel, we could be … just two people who fuck, I suppose. Here, well … you're more like family, somehow. I don't want to get it wrong, that's all."

"No, neither do I. And for what it's worth I'm still not all that keen to have sex in your grotty caravan, mate."

"No, me neither. But come to bed anyway and we'll see if we can fall asleep instead, shall we?"

"Oh, I thought … " Rupert gestured towards the door of the little room he'd used before.

"Not this time, no. Come on, through here."

The so-called double bedroom of the caravan was only just larger than the bed, with two flimsy wardrobes and a pathetic attempt at a dressing-table separating them. It was difficult to imagine how Tim, Helena and Finn could possibly have managed to share this tiny space even for a short time, but Finn would have been a baby and the carry-cot should just about have fitted under the dressing-table; hardly luxurious for any of them, but at least it would have been warm and dry. At each side of the bed was a triangular shelf the right size to take a cup or an alarm clock, but probably not both. The bed, however, looked inviting – it had a decent mattress, pillows, and a duvet in a clean cover. On the other hand a pile of sacking in a shop doorway would have looked good to Rupert right now; he wasn't sure how he was managing to put one foot in front of the other without falling into a comatose heap. He sat on the bed and unfastened his trainers, toeing them off.

"Hey, listen," said Jake, closing the door and tugging the thin curtains across the window, "I know it's not romantic, and I know we're both shot to pieces, but there's no reason this has to be boring – is there? Do you realise I've never seen you properly with your shirt off?"

That was true. They'd undressed so fumblingly quickly at the hotel, and in such poor light, that it had been difficult to get more than a general impression of one another's physique. Actually, and for a good reason, Rupert had preferred it that way.

"Ah," he said. "Well, yes. I mean, fine, but … there's something I should warn you about."

"You're really a woman?" Jake took hold of him and looked warmly into his eyes.

Rupert shot him a glance of apology. "Nothing so simple. What I wanted to say was … never let your partner get you drunk and steer you into a tattoo parlour. We passed through Hong Kong on our way to Aus, and … I can only tell you that it seemed like a good idea at the time."

In one swift movement Rupert stripped off the sweatshirt he was wearing and the tee-shirt under it to reveal, tattooed on his left breast, a livid-looking heart with a long-stemmed red rose threaded through it and the name 'Cameron' in copperplate script beneath.

"Oh, right." Jake's calloused fingers touched the place softly. "That's a constant reminder, isn't it, I suppose?"

"Yes, it is - a constant reminder that things you do quickly and without thinking can't be undone anything like as fast. Like Cameron, and like a lot of other decisions I've made and afterwards thought maybe

I shouldn't have done. What I mean is, Jake, I'm worried about getting in too deep too fast - if you see what I mean."

"I do," said Jake, "and I understand it, too." He paused. "Look, I'm sorry things went wrong with Cameron but I think I'm actually impressed by this." He was still stroking the tattoo. "Impressed it meant so much that you wanted to have his name there permanently, I mean; nobody's ever had *my* name tattooed over his heart, after all. Things must have been really wonderful for the two of you at the time."

"They were, for a while," shrugged Rupert. "And then they weren't."

"Yeah, I get that. Clean break, start again. Makes sense to me." Jake leaned in and kissed him, not a prelude to anything, just by way of comfort. "We kind of started in the middle," he said, "and everything's been in the wrong order since, but all the same I'm very glad it's happening."

"Yes," replied Rupert. "Me too."

Which made it much easier, somehow, to scramble out of his jeans and crawl into half of the double bed wearing only his boxers.

"Silk," laughed Jake, matching the movement and sliding to meet him under the bed-covers. "Very nice indeed. Very sexy."

"Hmmm. 'You don't need to put your pyjamas on, you can sleep in your underwear for once' – that's what H said to the kids."

"Yes, that sounds like her. I bet they thought it was wonderful, too. They're great kids, you know, never whine or moan about anything. Their mates at school have got computer games and all sorts of expensive stuff, and they've got … " Jake yawned, snuggling closer, pulling Rupert into his arms " … geese and home-made honey. Personally I reckon their friends should be jealous of *them*."

"Maybe they are," drowsed Rupert. He'd buried his face against Jake's shoulder and was inhaling the scent of him, skin and the faint odour of sweat and something that might be a lingering trace of deodorant or shampoo. Whatever it was it was pleasant, and the rhythm of Jake's breathing was hypnotic; the slow rise and fall of his chest lulled him like the motion of the sea.

"Bugger," said Jake. "Looks like your credit card's fallen out of your pocket. Don't forget to grab that when we get up; you'll be stuck without it."

"It's not mine and it's not a credit card," murmured Rupert softly. "Apart from that, your logic's flawless. It's an identity card for somebody called Zebinka Jonka or something; I found it on the footpath. I'll hand it in at the Youth Hostel before I leave."

"All right. That sounds like a plan."

And shortly after this, with Jake's arm around his shoulders, Jake's legs tangled with his own, and Jake's scent warm in his nostrils, Rupert's brain finally parted company with his body and allowed him access to the grateful oblivion that is sleep. For both himself and Jake, it was a desperately long time overdue.

15.

One of the happier accidents of Rupert's life – and there had been enough of the other kind, heaven knew – was the ability to sleep more or less anywhere under more or less any circumstances, as long as he was tired enough. It had come in useful working unsocial shifts at Nectarine and in other commercial kitchens over the years, and on flights from one side of the world to the other, and it did not fail him now. In fact, when he awoke, he was scarcely aware of having been to sleep at all; there was no blissful drift towards the consciousness of a comfortable bed and a comfortable partner, no luxuriating into a soft pillow reassured that duty was hours away and he could stay there as long as he wanted. No, this time – worn out and distracted though he had been – Rupert awoke to the uncomfortable knowledge that his body had started to think about sex before his brain had been copied in on the memo, and his instinctive reaction was that it was inconvenient and just plain wrong in the circumstances. What was worse, they were pressed so closely together in the snuffling, half-awake space that Jake - if he was anything like conscious - must be aware of it already.

Rupert tried a subtle movement, imperfectly disguised as a sleepy wriggle, putting space between them. The shape of the mattress wasn't exactly co-operating, but he'd succeeded in peeling himself from Jake's thigh when there was a quiet grunt close to his ear and Jake murmured, "You too, huh?"

"Me too," he acknowledged, embarrassed. "Couldn't have chosen a worse time or place, really, could it?"

"Probably not." But a hand was already stealing slowly down Rupert's side, and a finger under the waistband of his boxers. "On the other hand, maybe our bodies are a lot smarter than we are; if you're always waiting for the perfect time and place, you're probably never going to do anything at all."

"True." Rupert gave this a moment's thought. "You're sure the kids can't walk in on us?"

"Quite. The door's locked."

"All right, then."

And there followed the undignified business of squirming out of two pairs of underwear and losing them in the bed, Rupert surging into Jake's arms, and Jake's hand wrapping itself around his balls and tugging gently to produce a gasp of delight.

"Nice bum," said Rupert, only half-coherently, stroking the smooth contour as he spoke. "Strong."

"Thank you," answered Jake softly. "Very proud of it myself. And you know what they say, it takes a big hammer to drive a big nail." He paused. "Want it, then, do you? My bum?"

"God, man, don't tempt me, I'd love to — but maybe another time, all right? You're good either way, then, are you? I'm not sure I'd ever've guessed that to look at you."

"Can't judge a book by its cover, Rupert. Yeah, I'm fine either way, honestly. Any way, in fact. I hope that's okay with you?"

"Yes, it is. It's very okay, actually. Only this time … " Rupert's hand returned to grip Jake's manhood fully, squeezing perhaps a little too tight. "Ages since I've done this," he volunteered. "Nice to take it easy for a change. No performance anxiety or anything."

"You don't want me to suck you, then?" Almost as an afterthought.

"Not really, thanks, but I appreciate the offer. Just hands would be good this time. Your lovely big hands and nice long fingers. But as for that mouth… "

Rupert edged closer, and Jake's lips parted to receive him, and somehow a simple kiss turned dirty all at once with their tongues entwining wetly and urgent sounds escaping as their grappling hands sought for and found a rhythm which was never, ever going to be enough. It was too difficult to co-ordinate anything, whatever the romantic novelists — or the authors of internet pornography - might imagine; one of them was bound to reach a climax before the other, and Rupert was desperately hoping it wouldn't be him. After all the build-up, all the missed opportunities, he didn't want to disappoint Jake by going off like a rocket within a few moments of being touched; it should all be more dignified, he thought, more considered somehow - but there was nothing that resembled dignity in their urgent groping, in the hands that tugged and squeezed, in the incoherent grunts punctuating their wet, lascivious kisses and the deep, deep thrusting of their tongues.

"Oh, fuck," gasped Jake, clapping his large hand over Rupert's where it was working on his prick and rutting awkwardly into them both. There was barely time to notice how impressively focussed he was, how he put all his energies into that swelling, rocking motion, his eyes closed, his mouth open, his shoulders heaving – and then with a muttered obscenity he lost control and his body flexed and bowed as he spurted into and over Rupert's hands, warm and wet and abundant. "You stupid son of a bitch, too soon. Not you," he added, half-apologetically. "It."

"I know," said Rupert, but he wasn't really concentrating. The place between them was slippery and primal and inside himself he was seething with unspent energy, the urge to rub and grind and lose himself in the mystery completely overpowering. He groaned in his throat, shoving irrationally at Jake's wet hand, feeling powerful fingers closing round him, and abandoned himself to sensation. A moment later he could hear his own harsh breathing, louder even than Jake's, and the tension within him had broken apart completely.

"Yes," whispered Jake, stroking him gently as he came. "That's it, that's right, that's absolutely fucking fantastic." And Rupert kept thrusting and coming until he thought he would never be able to do so again, until he was dry inside, until he had nothing left to lose.

"My god," he said at last, aware that his teeth had cut a red mark into Jake's strong shoulder, "you're fucking good at that, you know?"

"Fucking good at fucking?" Jake laughed. "I fucking hope I am." There was a pause, during which he appeared to be trying to regain his breath and also to consider his answer further. "Actually, I reckon we're both better than average – and I really want to go further with you. A hell of a lot further. This was just – what do you call it, the appetiser?"

"Oh, my fucking god. If that was the appetiser, I can't wait to try the main course."

"No, me neither," replied Jake. "And after that there's the dessert - and then the coffee and the After Eight mints."

"The works," approved Rupert. "You can serve a banquet for me any time. But what happens after we've worked our way through the menu?"

"I don't rightly know," was the response, accompanied by an affectionate kiss which landed just below Rupert's ear. "We'll probably go back to the beginning and start again. We'll have had time to work up a whole new appetite by then, won't we?"

Rupert considered this for a while, then delivered his verdict as concisely as he could.

"All right, I think I could get used to that idea," he said. "As long as you make sure there's always an interesting variety of dishes available."

By the time either of them thought of looking at his watch, the two hours Helena had suggested for their rest had somehow morphed into more — almost three and a half, in fact.

"Oh, god," groaned Rupert. "I thought she was going to call us. I've still got that bloody car to drive back."

Jake was out of bed and wriggling into his underwear and jeans. "Want me to come with you and share the driving?" he suggested, unexpectedly.

"No, don't be daft, that would defeat the object. Anyway you're needed here, the place would fall apart without you; you've got to help H through this thing with her dad."

"I know," sighed Jake. "But I don't like the thought of sending you off on your own like that. At any rate, you'll have to have something to eat before you go."

"Probably, but … "

"It wasn't a question." Jake's eyebrows lifted and his mouth took on a wicked twist. "You're not leaving until you've had something filling inside you," he said. "Unfortunately this time it's only going to be food, but you can come back another time and have the rest."

"All right," said Rupert, "if you absolutely insist." They'd finished dressing and were about to leave the bedroom, but he'd suddenly noticed the identity card sitting where Jake had left it on the triangular shelf. "I'm not going to have time to deal with that before I go, am I?"

"No, but you can leave it with me - I'll sort it out. I'll go up to the hostel tomorrow, after I've done the deliveries. Don't worry, I won't forget about it."

"All right, then." And a moment later they were out of the caravan and on the way back to the lodge, and the identity card and the woman pictured on it had fallen out of Rupert's mind with the closing of the door.

Getting away from the farm took longer than Rupert could ever have imagined. Helena, it appeared, had unilaterally decided to let him and Jake sleep - 'or whatever', as she said without a blush - longer than intended, but had been distracted by the return of Gandalf who had wandered up to the lodge bloodied and minus several important feathers and honking as if it was somehow Helena's fault. She'd taken the time to clean him up and examine his wounds – deciding that they were superficial and he'd probably acquired them in a battle with a bramble bush – before coming to her senses and realising she should have woken Jake and Rupert at least an hour earlier. Now she was all apology and embarrassment, but since she'd also had the foresight to put a casserole and jacket potatoes into the oven – and since neither of these had suffered from an extra hour's cooking – there was little reason for reproach.

And, despite the circumstances, it was a relaxed and comfortable meal. Helena had lost her hollow-eyed look now that her father was in capable hands, and was taking the view that no news was good news. Finn and Tara, recovered from their disrupted night, were only marginally inclined to be niggly, and even Toffee seemed to have regained his usual *joie de vivre.* He stood and watched beef and gravy being spooned onto plates with the wistful expression of one who had never been fed in his life and was expecting to expire of malnutrition within the hour – a perception undermined by the continual and enthusiastic wagging of his tail.

By the time they'd finished eating the afternoon was well advanced and the drive to London was weighing on Rupert's mind. He'd decided to take it easy, perhaps with a break for coffee to make sure he stayed awake for the rest of it; even so it would mean arriving in the city centre in mid-evening when it would still be busy, and he was not certain his brain - more used these days to Australian driving conditions – would be up to the challenge. However, the only way to find out for sure was to go ahead and do it; what was the worst that could happen, after all?

The children, told that Uncle Rupert would have to set off soon, expressed their disappointment loudly.

"No," said Tara. "Stay and have tea instead! We can watch DVDs!"

"I wish I could," he told her, "but I've got to be at work in the morning and it's a long way. Like you, you have to go to school every day – don't you?"

"It's the holidays," returned Tara briskly. "You could have a holiday too."

"I could, but I'd have to ask my boss first. Anyway, the car's got to go back to the people we borrowed it from."

Pouting, Tara seemed to accept this only with reluctance.

"But Uncle Rupert's going to be back to see us as soon as he can," put in Jake. "He likes it here - don't you, Uncle Rupert?"

"I do indeed. I like all of you very, very much – as well as your house and your dogs and even your silly geese. I'd love to come and see you again, if it's all right with your mummy and Uncle Jake."

"It's fine with Uncle Jake," said Jake, although the matter had never been in doubt. "How about you, Mummy?"

"No problem," grinned Helena. "You're welcome any time, Rupert."

"Thank you." He returned her smile. "I might take you up on that. In fact, you could have trouble getting rid of me in future."

When the time came to leave, both children insisted on accompanying Rupert to the gate; it was only with difficulty that they were persuaded to leave Toffee with Helena. Since Jake was also in the car, brandishing the key to the padlock, it was a full cargo which jounced up the lane and drew to a halt to allow Jake to open the gate. Here they all got out, and here the children demanded hugs.

"Bye-bye, soldier," said Rupert to Finn. "Look after your mummy and I'll see you again soon." To Tara he said, "Keep an eye on Gandalf; I might not be around to go after him next time."

"It wasn't his fault in the first place, it was Toffee's," she explained, kissing his cheek. "He's the one to blame, not Gandalf!"

"Well, keep an eye on them both; I reckon they're as bad as each other."

Turning to Jake, he had half-expected either a brotherly handshake or the sort of perfunctory hug he'd exchanged with the children - but was alerted at the last moment by a glint in his eye that something else was in prospect; Jake grabbed him, pulled him close, and kissed him there and then without a shred of reserve. Rupert was powerless to do anything but respond in similar kind, and it seemed to go on for a very long time indeed – like an epic movie kiss, the sort that leaves its protagonists stunned and exhausted and usually happens at an important turning-point in the narrative.

"And you take care of yourself, too," said Jake, releasing him. "I don't want to hear you've wrapped that bloody thing round a lamp-post somewhere, okay?"

"All right, but … " The more urgent question seemed to be what on earth Jake imagined he was doing, being so demonstrative in front of a juvenile audience. " … are you sure … ?" A helpless gesture indicated his confusion.

"You seriously think I'm not out to my entire family?" asked Jake, shaking his head in pretended exasperation. "The kids know; of course they know. Wouldn't want them thinking it was the sort of thing you had to keep hidden, after all; they're growing up in a more tolerant world than you and I did, remember?"

"Of course. Just took me by surprise, that's all – but it wasn't the first time for that, and I don't suppose it'll be the last."

"Hope not," grinned Jake. "Have to think of something even sneakier for your next visit, though."

"That's fine with me," replied Rupert, "as long as I know there's going to be a 'next visit'." Which seemed as good an exit line as any - and therefore he got back into the car and, with Jake and the children grinning as he passed, turned out onto the road and waved from the open window. He was almost sure he could hear Tara yelling at the top of her voice as he pulled away - "Uncle Rupert kisses *boys*!" - and shortly afterwards they'd disappeared from view and he turned his face and his thoughts resolutely towards London.

As he'd expected, it took all Rupert's concentration to get the car – and himself – back safely. Once he got properly into the rhythm of driving he began to gain in confidence, though, and by the time he reached the Severn Bridge and the M4 it was almost as if he'd never been away; however the entry to London and the approach to Victoria was tricky even with the benefit of GPS. Long before he'd found his way to the car hire office, returned the vehicle and signed off on the paperwork he had a pounding headache and the desire only to stand for a long time under a lukewarm shower and then tumble into unconsciousness for a few hours.

Gary and Steve, predictably, had other plans. As he stepped into their kitchen a short while later they rounded on him demanding to be told Absolutely All in minute detail, and preferably Right This Very Minute.

"And how was t'trooble at t'farm?" asked Steve, in a Pythonesque Yorkshire accent. "All sorted out now, is it?"

"Not exactly. A man's in hospital." Briefly Rupert sketched the saga of Martin and the heart-attack, together with the improved prognosis. He left out all reference to the sequel featuring Toffee and Gandalf, but concluded by informing them he'd be going back to Wales as soon as he could persuade Ren to allow him time off. "There's nobody else," he added, quietly. "At the very least I'm hoping Ren'll be willing to support an independent organic producer having a hard time, who could go out of business any minute. We need more people like that around, not less."

Gary's dark eyebrows had lifted quizzically throughout this peroration. "And what about you?" he said. "Have you had a hard time, too?"

"Yes, I did, actually," replied Rupert – and, after a pause, "although that's not what I went for, and not what I was expecting. It wasn't just a booty call, you know?"

"Of course not," acknowledged Gary, his tone so burdened with irony it was clear he didn't believe a word.

"I thought," said Steve, laughing as if he expected Rupert to find him charmingly clueless, "that the little shrimpy one was Jake, the one you brought to the party."

"I know you did," said Rupert, "but that was Andrew. He's a friend from work, that's all."

"Oh yes? And how would you describe the wondrous Jake, exactly? More than a friend? A friend with benefits? Your bestest friend for ever and ever and ever, cross your heart and hope to die? Or maybe the great new love of your life?"

"I don't know," conceded Rupert, wearily. "Could be some of those things, I suppose; could even be all of them. Just at the moment Steve, mate, I haven't got the least fucking clue."

16.

The first person Rupert saw in the locker-room at Nectarine the following morning was Andrew, chirpy and in command of the situation as always.

"Someone's in a good mood," grinned Rupert. "I take it your weekend went according to plan?"

"Just what the doctor ordered, thank you. It turned out he wasn't a U-boat commander after all – he's Danish, not German - but he said he wouldn't mind wearing the uniform for me some time. How about you, plenty of no-strings sex with Mr 'It's Complicated'? Or maybe you like the strings, I don't know."

"I wish," Rupert sighed, before recounting the saga of Martin's heart-attack and the late-night dash to Wales.

Andrew's eyes grew huge and round. "Well, you were right about it being complicated," he said. "Is the poor man recovering, at least?"

"Yes, the last thing I heard. Only there's more." They were in the office now, glancing through the diary, checking the machine for messages; fortunately there were none, because by the time Rupert had finished his description of chasing Gandalf, Toffee and Tara through the orchard Andrew would have been quite incapable of dealing with them. "None of it went the way I thought it was going to go," he concluded, "but I did have quite an interesting time."

"In the Chinese sense of the word, by the sound of it," Andrew chuckled. "'May you live in interesting times'."

"Possibly," Rupert conceded.

"And what about sex? For fuck's sake, man, tell me you did it at least three times in between wild goose chases?"

"Once. We were both too knackered for anything else."

"Which is a sad indictment on your age and general state of decrepitude, although just this once I'm prepared to make allowances."

"You're only showing off because you spent the weekend biting lumps out of some Danish bloke's pillow. Not that I'm jealous, you understand."

"Oh no, no, no, of course you're not! Besides, it wasn't all pillow-biting - the hotel had a swimming pool as well."

Rupert was torn between envy and hoping that the pool had a bloody good filter. However there was no opportunity to make any response; Andrew was still speaking.

"Oh, and I found out where that newspaper came from," he said, "the one your fishing-gnome was reading. *Nový čas* is a Slovakian rag published in Bratislava. I don't know how you get it over here, maybe they send it, but it hasn't got much to do with news so presumably it wouldn't matter if it was late. It's like the *Sun*," he added. "All naked tits, celebrity gossip and football."

"Slovakian? That's odd. I found a Slovakian identity card when I was looking for the goose."

"Well, maybe it belonged to the gnome, then?"

"No, it was a woman's - but all of a sudden there are a lot of Slovakian people in one very small corner of Wales, which is unusual to say the least."

"*Doodoo-doodoo doodoo-doodoo*." It was a reasonable approximation of the old *Twilight Zone* theme. "It couldn't just be that you're paranoid and see conspiracies everywhere?"

"No - I think it's more than that, or the police wouldn't have bothered leaving somebody at the farm overnight. They decided Martin'd interrupted somebody trying to steal the car, but they're going to find out if he remembers anything else. So it's not 'nothing', but it still might not be much. On the other hand," Rupert added, "being without Martin is going to bugger things up at the farm; how do you think Ren'd react if I asked for a couple of weeks off to help them out?"

Andrew considered a moment before replying. "He wouldn't," he said. "He pays me to react to things for him; he's too busy negotiating book deals and trying to nick Michel Roux's recipe for *Coquilles Saint Jacques à la Parisienne*." Andrew flipped open the diary in which, in defiance of electronic equivalents, Ren's busy schedule was maintained. "It's my job to solve problems before he knows they exist," he said.

"I present him with the solution, and then I tell him what it's the solution *to*. It'd be easier if I could tell him you're definitely taking the Glasgow job."

"I know, I've already thought of that – so make it a twelve month contract and I'll sign it on the spot."

"Eighteen," countered Andrew, "and we'll find you a nice one-bedroom flat to live in as well."

"Ground floor. With a garden."

"What for? Oh, the dog! Yes, of course, I'm sure we can manage that. So, do we have a deal?"

"We do," said Rupert, "as long as I get time off to help out at Ship Meadow."

"Fine. How does four weeks sound?"

Rupert released the breath he'd been holding, feeling his chest relax as he did so. "Generous," he acknowledged. "You're quite sure you can get that past Ren?"

"I expect so. We were going to have to bring in cover before long anyway; Ren's decided to take Annabel and the kids to Florida for a week before they go back to school, I had an e-mail from him over the weekend. We can usually borrow Graham from the Trocette, he never minds a few weeks in the real world, and I'll get on to the agency and see if any of our regulars are available. You can stay till the end of Friday, can you, at least?"

"I can," replied Rupert, his head spinning.

"Good, then I'll get the Glasgow contract prepared and you can sign it tomorrow - assuming you haven't changed your mind by then. Honestly, Rupert? I think he'll be so grateful to have that sorted out he'll be happy to give you time off for good behaviour. He can get chefs whenever he needs them, and they'll do a decent job, but he really, seriously rates you. After he gave up on Malcolm Seward for the Glasgow thing your name was the one he kept coming back to; I genuinely think he'd move heaven and earth to get you running that kitchen, if only for the first year. Or, more likely, he'd get me to move them for him," finished Andrew wryly.

"I didn't realise he felt that way about it. He was actually quite casual when we talked."

"Of course he was. You were coming out of a bad relationship and your life was in the crapper. Friends don't put pressure on friends at a time like that."

"No, you're right; I should have thought of that. I owe him a big one this time, don't I, Andrew?"

"In my opinion," said Andrew, "you owe him more than one, but this'd be enough to wipe the slate clean. Do what he needs you to do in Glasgow and I'll make sure of it myself."

Rupert leaned back in his chair and regarded Andrew across the desk with more than a hint of amusement running through his mind. The 'little shrimpy guy', as Steve – who tended to respect brawn rather than brains – had called him, was clearly a force to be reckoned with; you underestimated Andrew at your peril.

"Tell me," he said, mildly, "have you ever considered a career in the Mafia? Only I think you've just made me the proverbial offer I can't refuse."

True to his word, Andrew not only had the paperwork for the Glasgow job lined up by the time Rupert arrived for work the following day, he'd also downloaded and printed off details of half a dozen flats which he thrust into Rupert's unprotesting hands.

"Do you want me to start making arrangements for Rusty to come over?" he asked, without preamble.

"Not yet. She's fine where she is until I know for sure what's happening. The company only need ten days' notice – her rabies vaccinations are up to date and they're keeping her in quarantine conditions at the kennel, so it won't take long to arrange when the time comes - but I don't feel settled enough to send for her yet."

"All right. Tell me when you're ready and I'll get the ball rolling immediately."

Rupert thanked him and they left it there, although in truth he was becoming concerned about maintaining a connection with Jake now that he'd committed himself to working in Glasgow for eighteen months. If they'd found it difficult getting together with one in Wales and the other in London, how much more awkward would it be when they were at least twice the distance apart? But then, as he reminded himself, he'd been the one to insist that they didn't turn over two pages at once and start assuming there was more between them than there was; he'd had enough life-changing decisions for one year already, and from now on he was determined to do things on his own terms or not at all.

Which, with the way his luck usually ran, would probably end up being 'not at all'.

So matters stood until Thursday, when Andrew was able to confirm that both Graham and a girl named Sabrina – who was, apparently, fabulous – would step in to fill the impending vacuum at Nectarine; come Saturday Rupert would be free to return to the Wye Valley to lend what support and assistance he could. He'd just pulled the computer keyboard towards him to send an e-mail to that effect – presumably to Bridget, although under Martin's username – when the phone on the desk rang and all of a sudden he found himself speaking to Jake.

"You're not going to believe this," he said. "I was in the middle of e-mailing you. I'm coming down again on Saturday - and this time I can stay for four weeks."

"Fuckin' brilliant," Jake replied. He sounded as if he'd been inhaling helium. "But you'll never guess what's been going on here!"

The tone of his voice, while odd, was at least encouraging. "Not bad news about Martin, I hope?" asked Rupert cautiously.

"No, thank fuck. He's looking great, I went to see him yesterday - you wouldn't know there was anything wrong with the guy, they reckon he's going to bounce right back."

"Oh, good. But he won't be able to work for a while, though, will he?"

"Not a hope, unfortunately, so I'm glad we've got you. That wasn't what I was calling about, though, funnily enough."

"It wasn't?"

"No. Listen, you remember that card you picked up and I said I'd turn it in at the Youth Hostel?"

"Yeeees?" Uncertain, because it sounded from Jake's tone as if there was another shoe about to drop.

"Well, I forgot all about it," said Jake. "I was going to do it Monday, but I was so knackered most of the day I could hardly remember my own name. I forgot about it Tuesday as well, but I came up here Tuesday afternoon to see the kids and I ran into a mate I haven't seen for a while – Idwal, Tricia's son, who lives next door. Well, he doesn't live next door - his mum does, and he was visiting her. He lives in Cwmbran, because it's handy for his work."

This all came out at such a frantic pace that Rupert had trouble following it. "Wait a minute. Tricia, who drives the taxi and lives next door to Bridget, has a son called Idwal who lives in Cwmbran – is that right?"

"Right. Only you know what's in Cwmbran, Rupert, don't you?"

It could have been anything, thought Rupert, from a pin to an elephant. "I really don't," he admitted, laughing at Jake's enthusiasm. "The Holy Grail?"

"Nearly, mate - nearly the Holy bloody Grail, I kid you not! What's in Cwmbran is the Hafren Police Force Headquarters; Tricia's son is only Detective Sergeant Idwal bloody Morris of Hafren CID, isn't he? Anyway, when I saw him, I realised I'd still got the card in my pocket and I reckoned I could hand it over to him and he'd make sure it got back to the owner, right?"

"Right, good idea." But that could hardly be all of it, or it wouldn't have merited such an urgent-seeming phone call in the middle of a working day.

"Bloody great idea, as it turned out. He took one look at it and went a funny colour. 'Where did you get this?' he says, so I tell him about you and Toffee and Tara looking for the goose, and how Tara says she saw ghosts walking up the footpath – and he thinks it over and says, 'Only, you see, we've had a briefing about these - there's been a lot of them turn up just lately and we'd like to know where they're coming from.'"

"Oh, fuck," said Rupert, in astonishment.

"Oh, yes, very fuck indeed," replied Jake. "And there's more. He got a bit serious then and started asking about the old railway tunnel and who owned it, and I told him Diadem were using it for workshops. Then he said did they have electricity and water and I said probably but I'd never been inside and I wouldn't mind having a look round some time to see if they've got my quad bike … and that led on to me telling him about all the shit that's been happening on the farm. You'd think, with his mum next door to Bridget all this time, he'd've heard about some of it at least, but he says not - well, only bits and pieces anyway - and by the time I got to the end he said he was going to talk to somebody about it at work and see if there was any action they could take."

"What - they think somebody's making fake ID cards in the old railway tunnel, is that what you're telling me?"

"Well, maybe; I didn't follow everything he was on about, to be honest, but he said it might be worth setting up a camera to monitor the footpath and get some idea of who's been coming and going that way, and would I give them permission to do it from our land, and of course I said yes. So that was that and he took the card off with him, and he must have spoken to somebody first thing yesterday because when I got here to Bridget's in the afternoon there was a message for me to ring him and it turned out he wanted me to come in and meet his boss. Top and bottom of it is, mate, I've been over to their place this morning looking at pictures and picking out those blokes in the hoodies. Idwal reckons that card was probably dropped deliberately, and when you think about it that makes total sense."

In his cluttered office at Nectarine, with London traffic outside his window and pale London sky showing above the rooftops opposite, Rupert heard the barely-contained excitement in Jake's voice with a rush of longing that was physically painful. He almost couldn't process how much he wanted to be there with him, to be part of whatever was happening, to have a share in all his joys and sorrows. Then his rational brain cut in, and he did his best to respond coherently.

"Deliberately?" he repeated, giving Jake time to organise his thoughts.

"Well, what he said was, if it'd been lost or dropped by accident somebody would either have been back to look for it – or, if they thought it was a real one, they'd have reported it missing and applied for a replacement - but they didn't do any of that. And it's an EU identity card, so it's not something you lose and just forget about – not unless

144

you've got a box full of them somewhere; you need to have it with you all the time."

"Right, so ... "

"So maybe it could've been dropped deliberately. Maybe the girl, Zebinka whatever-her-name-is, heard you and Tara in the orchard and dropped it hoping you'd find it – and maybe the bloke with the gun was in a hurry to get her and the others out of there and didn't notice what'd happened."

"Hang on." Rupert's head was spinning. "They're taking that gun business seriously, then? No, scratch that - it's Tara, of course; Tara doesn't make stuff up."

"No, she doesn't - not important stuff, anyway. They're going to get her to look at the pictures, too, but they'll do that later on today at Bridget's, when her mum can be there with her – they won't bring her to the station if they don't have to."

"Fuck, so ... they think it's illegal immigrants or something, do they?" It was almost too much to take in. "Over-stayers, maybe?"

Jake's uncertain pause was eloquent in itself. "I don't think they know," he said. "Sharon – Idwal's boss - reckons there's something going on but they won't know what it is till they can get in and have a look, and that's what they're planning to do some time next week. She had me go over the map and show her where the tunnel entrance is, and the air shafts and everything, and tell her what's there as far as I know. See, it's all on Diadem land, there could be all kinds of stuff happening and we'd never know a thing. She said it'd be a brilliant hiding-place and if you could get a train in there you could get other things in as well, which made a lot of sense to me."

"Right. Except ... "

" ... except there's that one end near the bridge, and if you got a stray punter wandering off into the bushes for a pee or something they could get a bit too close ... "

" ... so they'd want somebody on watch there all the time, and it might look better if they pretended they were fishing," concluded Rupert. "Of course."

"Yes, that's what she said. All the time, Rupert, all the time –

morning, noon and night, rain or shine, hailstorm or heatwave, they'd have to be there. All. The. Bloody. Time."

"Oh." The implications were suddenly more massive than Rupert could cope with. "So have they said anything at all about what they think happened to Tim?"

"Nothing - and I reckon they're hoping I won't ask - but it can't not be connected somehow, can it? Seriously, Rupert," Jake went on, his tone changing from high to low, from what had almost been delight to verging on despair, "I think we might actually get a bloody answer out of this at last, and I was ringing to find out if you could get down here at the weekend because I reckon it's all going to kick off soon. I could do with having you around, mate," he finished, earnestly, "I really could."

Which was, thought Rupert, all he had ever really needed to hear from Jake.

"Well, look," he said, "I'll be there on Saturday. Don't worry about meeting me, I'll make my own way – I'm not sure what time I'll be able to start in the morning anyway. But I've got Tricia's number, so I can always get a ride in with her."

"Yeah, I was going to talk to you about that," returned Jake. "H and I've come up with a bit of a plan, and we think maybe it'd be better if you walked down the river from Hembury Cross ... come in the back way so nobody knows you're there. We're thinking if her and me went out with the kids and made it look like the place was empty except for Toffee ... you never know, they might just get tempted and come snooping round again. You could stay in the house with the door locked and keep the HT with you, and maybe take pictures if anything does happen."

Rupert digested this proposal slowly. "What does your pal Idwal have to say about this?" he asked. "I presume you ran it past him before you mentioned it to me?"

"I did. He says the thefts from the farm are low priority where they're concerned, and between ourselves he doesn't really see what happened to Martin leading to a prosecution either, but if we can come up with evidence of our own that might all change. In other words they're not going to put a lot of resources our way, but if we want to do something that's up to us. On the quiet, he said that's what he'd do himself – but he couldn't advise us officially. Only he says to make sure you stay well out of the way, whatever happens."

Wistfully Rupert thought of all the self-defence training he'd been putting in with Steve, all the moves he'd learned in the hope that sooner or later he might be granted the opportunity of kicking the surly hoodie in the nuts. Now it looked as if the chance was going to pass him by after all.

"Oh well," he said, resignedly, "I was quite fancying a punch-up, but I suppose I can keep a low profile instead. Only if you absolutely insist, though, mind."

17.

On Saturday, this conversation still ringing in his ears, Rupert found himself repeating his first journey to Wales – the swooping high-speed ride through smiling countryside, the change of trains, the pub meal and transition to the local bus - although this time he stayed on after it left Lower Hembury, despite more than one lingering glance towards the Ring o' Bells. It was busier this time than he remembered, though, and he was glad not to be jostling for position at the bar. Instead he got out at Hembury Cross, walked to the river bank, and stepped onto the waterside path; now that he had an idea of the lay of the land, and was certain he could recognise both the stile into Ship Meadow and the gate between the orchard and the lane, he should have no difficulty finding his route.

The river was quite populous at Hembury Cross. There was a deep pool under the bridge where someone was hiring out rowing-boats, although Rupert couldn't for the life of him see how they made a living. There were also children paddling in the shallows – nobody had warned them about leptospirosis, clearly – a couple of kayakers who had stopped to buy coffee, and a gaggle of teenage boys with bare feet sitting on the parapet in defiance of the notice which warned that jumping from there could be fatal. Rupert turned his back on them all, shouldered his pack, and – confident he made a reasonable-looking hiker – set out to cover the last few miles in long, easy strides.

It was almost a relief. He enjoyed the work he did, but there was something about city life which felt wrong to him nowadays. Maybe the wide skies and gleaming beaches of Queensland had spoiled him, or maybe he wanted more out of life than to be packed into a city like a sardine in a can and to stumble through his days in a state of near-exhaustion. Now, with the shouting of the youths on the bridge behind him and only the plash of the water and the occasional wing-beat of a swan for company, he could feel knots melting from his spine and his heart beginning to expand. He could belong to a place like this, he decided, if only life would allow it; he could stay for the rest of his days and be content. Maybe he ought to think about putting out feelers for a job around here after he'd completed the assignment in Glasgow, even if the thing with Jake didn't work the way he was hoping it would; there were plenty of worse places in the world to end up, after all, and having lived in a few of them already he really ought to know.

But then, he acknowledged, he was getting ahead of himself. For now there was Jake - and in the fullness of time there would be Glasgow - and anything beyond that must be in the realm of speculation. He'd been caught out before, thinking things were forever when they weren't. One day at a time, that was the way he was going to live his life from now on; he would take nothing for granted ever again.

Away from Hembury Cross there was nobody on the footpath except a couple with a black Labrador who grinned at him in passing. The kayakers, too, having finished their coffee-break, came skimming past at speed and were soon out of sight around the curve of the river. Thus he was alone and unobserved an hour later as he clambered over the stile and trudged up the rising land, to knock on the door of the lodge and be greeted by Jake, Helena and the children.

"Oh, mate," said Jake, "you're a fuckin' sight for sore eyes!" taking him by the shoulders and kissing him in delight.

"We're going to pretend Uncle Jake didn't say that word," Helena told the children. "He knows he shouldn't have, in front of the pair of you."

"Ah, yes." Jake looked mildly discomposed but accepted his rebuke with good grace. "Sorry, everybody, but your mum's right – it's not a good word and I shouldn't have said it. Doesn't mean I'm not ... er, very pleased to see you, Rupert."

"I got that impression, strangely." There was novelty value to being kissed and acknowledged in front of the family. Such openness was not familiar to Rupert except among his gay friends, but he was determined not to allow himself to register the astonishment he was feeling while the children were present; the sooner they got used to the idea that love between couples of the same gender was not only possible but quite normal, the better-adjusted they would be as adults. He wouldn't have forced the matter himself, but since Jake and Helena were comfortable with public displays of affection he was happy to go along with that.

He was ushered to a chair at the table, Lego and colouring-books cleared to one side, and a cup of tea and piece of seed-cake appeared as if by magic. "Bridget made it," was the explanation. "She's on a baking kick before Martin comes out of hospital – she says she won't have the time after."

Jake and Helena joined him, the children being relegated to the couch, and for a moment all three adults stared at one another as if nobody knew who ought to speak first.

"So," said Rupert, "tell me about this plan of yours."

Not surprisingly, it was Jake who took up the invitation.

"Well, they've put a remote camera in the orchard – they came and did that yesterday, making out they were the Soil Association checking our organic credentials; they even had a van with the logo on it. I asked if they'd put one up here, too, to catch whoever's been nicking our stuff, but like I told you they said it wasn't a priority. Only they said there was nothing to stop us setting up our own camera - and that's what got me thinking, okay?"

"Okay. Go on."

"Right, so – we can't afford to install a remote camera, but maybe we've got the next best thing. We were thinking if H and I took the kids out somewhere and you stayed behind, you could get pictures of anybody who comes snooping around. We're pretty sure they're keeping an eye on the top gate so they'll see us leaving, and if they didn't see you arrive and they think the place is empty ... " He trailed off awkwardly, as if only just understanding the scale of the favour he was asking.

"Hence you asking me to sneak in by the tradesmen's entrance," laughed Rupert. "That makes sense, I don't have a problem with it at all; I meant what I said about helping you out, and if this is what you need fair enough - I'm more than up for it." The relief in the room at this was almost palpable. "So where are you thinking of taking the children?" he asked.

"We're going to pretend it's Finny's birthday – it's really three weeks away still, but they won't know that, of course. We're planning to drop the kids at Bridget's so she and Tricia can take them to McDonald's, and the two of us are meeting Idwal and Sharon to talk about next door. But you have to promise not to be a hero, okay, Rupe? I don't want you and Martin in hospital at the same time, side by side; cost me a bloody fortune in grapes, that would."

"I promise. I'll keep a very low profile, believe me."

"Great. We'll leave Toffee tied up outside so the place doesn't look too deserted, but he won't be much use in a crisis."

"Is he ever?" asked Rupert, rhetorically.

"Well, he can bark at people ... and he could probably knock them over with his tail ... but I've never known him to actually bite anybody, I admit."

"They won't know that, though, will they?" put in Helena. "He does look a bit like a guard dog. From a distance."

"Only in pitch darkness and a very thick fog," added Jake, mischievously. "Bloody dog's so stupid they could steal his dinner from under his nose and he'd probably just lick them. You definitely can't rely on Toffee for back-up, Rupert, is the short answer to that. Best not let yourself get seen at all, okay?"

"Okay. So where do you want me to be? In here?"

"The bedrooms are the best place to watch from," said H. "Mine's got a good view of the farm, the children's looks over the lane and the buildings. But you might have to wander about a bit, since we don't know which way they'll be coming in."

"If at all," completed Jake. "Only we're not going to get that many chances to do this, so I reckon we ought to make the best of this one while we can. We'll have to lock you in, and you won't be able to do anything that makes a noise like running water or flushing the loo, but we'll set you up with a flask and sandwiches and another chunk of seed-cake. If you need help get on the HT – I'll be the other end of it, over at Bridget's – and if you can't actually talk for any reason just keep pressing the button on and off and somebody'll be here before you know it. How does all that sound to you?"

"Perfectly feasible," said Rupert. "It sounds fine, Jake – just don't worry about it, okay?"

Part of him was convinced this would be a waste of time anyway - it would, he thought, be a massive coincidence if someone from Diadem chose tonight of all nights to wander over looking for something to steal - but he supposed they probably had a poor view of the inhabitants of Ship Meadow since they seemed to feel entitled to traipse all over their land and help themselves to whatever they wanted. Perhaps, once you'd decided to go against the law, you looked on all those who stayed within it with equal contempt; there must be a feeling of invulnerability, of being immune to consequences, whether the crime was large or small. In short, there was a better than even chance of somebody from Diadem taking the bait - and here was Jake assuring him he was resigned to losing more property if it resulted in better evidence against them.

"So there are absolutely no circumstances in which you'd want me to intervene?" he reiterated, for the sake of clarity. "Theft, vandalism, fire - if they go after the chickens or the geese - I'm just to let them do it, am I?"

Jake swallowed. "Yes," he said, although clearly it was costing him some grief. "Let them do it. I know it's a high-risk strategy, Rupe, but we're getting low on options here - and sometimes you just have to take a chance, okay?"

"Okay." But neither of them mentioned Toffee in this context, and for a very good reason. No doubt Jake was aware that Rupert wouldn't remain in concealment long if there was any actual danger to the dog.

"We'll be back before it gets dark, at any rate," said Jake. "Are you sure you'll be all right?"

"I'll be fine - but that doesn't mean I don't appreciate the sentiment, though, mate."

He watched them set off a few hours later, Tara in a spangly pink top with butterfly-shaped slides taming her long wild hair, Finn in a replica Cardiff City football shirt with Doggy tucked firmly under his arm. On the surface it looked exactly what it was supposed to be, a simple family outing; only the exaggerated care with which Jake locked the house and made sure Toffee was secure at the end of a long chain would have given indication of any concern about leaving the place to its own devices for a while.

Once the sound of the car had receded up the lane, Rupert wandered into Helena's bedroom and sat on the bed. There were net curtains at the window and he peered through them anxiously for a while, but the only movement anywhere on the farm was Toffee somnolently licking his private parts. It took Rupert longer than it should have done to realise that if his canine companion was relaxed enough to do that there couldn't be much for either of them to worry about. Thus he took out the Glasgow flat details, which he'd brought with him - although Andrew had been careful to point out that they were only a snapshot of what was available - and began to look through them in earnest.

He spent the next confusing half-hour trying to figure out if Muirpark Street would be better than Alfred Terrace and whether G11 or G12 would be a more appropriate postcode to live in. All the flats looked lovely, and would all have suited his requirements, but with no idea of the geography of the city and even less about transport and facilities he had no basis for making even a preliminary selection – and at this point it was nothing but a sterile and ultimately unfulfilling intellectual exercise. Never mind, though, it had passed the time – and he hadn't yet been obliged to revert to watching *Bob the Builder*.

He got up, stretched his legs and back, and glanced across to where Toffee was tethered. The silly beast was on his feet again, and seemed to have taken an interest in something happening over by the chicken run. At the moment he was not exactly on high alert but his tongue had unrolled like a pink carpet and his floppy ears had lifted as though he'd caught a sound and was endeavouring to analyse it to his satisfaction.

"Good lad, Toffee," whispered Rupert, although the dog's posture didn't necessarily indicate the presence of another human being. There were foxes in the woods, their sign and scent making its presence felt and their short barking sometimes audible at night - and Jake had mentioned that badgers, too, regularly prowled the orchard; apparently badgers had a fondness for apples, which he hadn't known before. But whether the predator was four- or two-footed – or, indeed, whether there was a predator at all – it was impossible to tell from Toffee's behaviour. "You keep an eye on it, mate, and tell your Uncle Rupert all about it." But at the same time he reached for the camera Jake had left with him – borrowed, it appeared, from the endlessly-accommodating Bridget and Martin - and made certain he was ready.

For what seemed hours – but was, in fact, only minutes – both Rupert and Toffee strained their senses towards the distant corner of the market garden where the chickens lived; as with the geese, they were close enough to be seen but far enough from the house for the smell not to be intrusive. Rupert's human eyesight was at a distinct disadvantage, and he had the added impediment of trying to observe through both window-glass and a net curtain without being seen himself; nor could he hear or sniff any interloper as easily as Toffee could. However, by lifting the hem of the curtain slightly, pressing the camera lens to the glass and selecting maximum zoom, he at least went some way towards redressing the shortcomings of his merely-human eyesight.

"Right, you bugger," he whispered. "Bring it on, I'm ready for you." And then it was simply a question of remaining as still as he could – of not breathing too deeply, even, in case the camera shook, in case it rattled against the glass and alerted the invader – and of waiting for something to happen.

Toffee was leaning forward now; not quite at the limit of his range, he was poised for action and making soft noises in his throat. At one point he turned and looked back towards the house, almost as if asking whether the human indoors could see what he was seeing - then appeared to recollect that it was an undercover operation and strained again towards the corner, huffing in frustration and disgust.

"Easy, boy," whispered Rupert. "Just watch for now. You can bark at the nasty man as much as you like later on." For there was distinctly a figure to be seen, hooded of course; a lithe young man in jeans who moved confidently and almost with arrogance but nevertheless didn't take any foolish chances. He stuck close to the cover of the trees, slipping behind the poultry shed, and a moment later a distinctive 'ping' echoed like a rifle-shot around the garden and drew a whimper of displeasure from Toffee – and it was followed by another, and another. "The bastard's cutting the wire," said Rupert to himself.

Still it was not possible to make out any detail on the man, but Rupert had succeeded in locating the camera's continuous shooting mode and was snapping away like a paparazzo pursuing a super-model. Given the number of pixels the thing was capable of capturing, and the amount of information it could store, he had high hopes of the electronic eye being able to retain and process more information than he could himself. Not that the man – the way it moved, he knew it was a man – turned to face the house at any stage, but his clothing should be identifiable, and that might be enough to secure a conviction in itself.

One outraged squawk only was heard to disturb the evening calm. Toffee crooned in sympathetic answer, and there followed the sound of a collision between something soft and something hard which no doubt indicated the demise of the unfortunate stolen chicken. Having, presumably, got what he had come for, the intruder turned away then and melted back into the shadows from which he had emerged, and at length Rupert sagged back onto his heels and managed to stop the camera. Then he flopped to the floor and untangled his legs only with difficulty, allowing the blood to return to them. He realised he was shaking, although whether from nerves or from the insult to his circulation he could not properly have said.

"Fuck, that was ... " But even if he hadn't been talking to himself he would never have been able to summon up the word. 'Intense', perhaps, was the closest he could get to it, but even that didn't seem to do it justice. He was wise enough, however, to recognise that his earlier bravado about kicking the hoodie in the nuts had been just that – bluster, designed to impress, or perhaps to cover up a want of physical courage. He wouldn't have liked to tangle with that man at close quarters, and even observing him at arms' length had been a nerve-racking experience. Not for the first time he asked himself what Tim Colley would have done if he'd encountered something similar; would he have stoically faced down the oppressor, or would have been more likely to turn and run? And could he, perhaps, in like circumstances, have found himself running towards something still worse and even more malign?

It wasn't, on the whole, a subject he expected to find himself discussing with Jake at any foreseeable point in the future.

A short while later he had sorted himself out enough to put a call through on the HT. Speaking softly, in case there was anybody still around, he recounted what had happened.

"I think you're a chicken down," he concluded, "but Toffee and I are fine." He was looking out of the window at Toffee as he spoke; the idiot actually seemed to have fallen asleep again, which Rupert was disposed to regard as a good sign.

"And you've got pictures of it all, have you?"

"Yes." He'd made sure he reviewed them before making the call; the intruder should certainly be identifiable, even though he'd kept his face hidden. "That wasn't actually about stealing a chicken, though, was it? I mean, it's not as if they're going to be cooking and eating it or anything?"

"I wouldn't put it past them, as a matter of fact – but no, it was more about being a bloody nuisance. Anything they can do to get up our noses, you can bet you bloody arse they'll do it; they're trying to wear us down to the point where we give in and give them every bloody thing they want." There was a silence at Jake's end of the conversation, and then he continued. "Look, I'm heading back now - apart from anything else I'll need to fix that chicken shed so the rest of the buggers don't get out – and I'm bringing Sharon with me; she says she wants to meet you, okay? Tricia can drop H and the kids off later later."

But Jake had actually completed the call and moved on to the next thing before Rupert had been given time to form a conclusion about whether it would be okay with him or not.

18.

Sharon turned out to be a brisk woman of indeterminate age with brown eyes, short iron-grey hair, heavy-framed spectacles and a pixie-like grin. She was casually dressed in jeans and a tee-shirt and had with her both a handbag and a bulging shopping bag – not at all, as she said when she was ushered into the lodge, what anyone watching would expect a police officer to be carrying.

"So you're Rupert Goodall," she said, looking him up and down. "You work for Renfrew Sheppard. Is he as big an arsehole in real life as he seems on TV?"

"No. not at all!" His instinctive defence of Ren was almost too vehement. "He takes no prisoners, admittedly, but he's a good bloke and I owe him a lot; there's nobody in the whole world better in a crisis than Ren."

"Good." Sharon's combative mood softened immediately. "I like a man who stands up for his friends. Jake's been very complimentary about you, for example - and if you've managed to get any decent pictures of our friend in the hoodie I think I might be, too."

Rupert held up the camera. "They're all in here," he said. "See for yourself."

Sharon took it and flicked quickly through the images. "Oh yes," she said. "Just what we were looking for. It doesn't matter that you can't see his face, I've got … wait a minute." She fumbled in her shopping-bag, and drew out a sheaf of papers which had been stuffed down beside a packet of cornflakes. "Yes," she said, thrusting them at him, "here's Vladan Resnik wearing exactly the same outfit; we downloaded that from our remote camera earlier today. You don't mind if I take the memory card, Jake? I'll give you a receipt for it."

"No, that's fine; there was nothing else on there anyway, we made sure of that before we started."

"Very efficient of you," approved Sharon. She had drawn out a small book and was writing industriously. "This is my personal official receipt - and here's my card for you, Rupert; you can reach me on that extension number, or leave a message if I'm not in."

Rupert scanned the card quickly, and discovered that he was dealing with Detective Chief Inspector Holt. For some reason he'd expected Idwal's boss to be an Inspector, but this woman was clearly a rank higher – which was formidable fire-power for what was beginning to look like a larger operation than he'd imagined.

"We'll make a copy of the memory card and return the original to you in due course," she was saying now, "but we have to be able to prove a chain of custody for the evidence whenever the matter goes to court."

"And will it?" asked Rupert, bluntly. "Is there actually anything you can charge these people with?"

Sharon smiled. "Well, yes," she said. "I don't want to say too much about it at this stage, obviously, but we've got enough evidence to obtain a warrant to search the premises; neither Mirek Tesar nor Vladan Resnik has any kind of a permit or certificate allowing them to use firearms in this country, and since we've got proof they've been doing precisely that we're entitled to seize whatever weapon or weapons they were seen with. Young Tara makes a very impressive witness considering her age, but we've also got pictures to support her story; at any rate, we'll know more in a day or two. Our intention at the moment is to go in early on Monday morning; I'm going to have to borrow a few bodies and a couple of vehicles first, and there are some more bureaucratic hoops to go through, but we should have everything squared away by then. What I'd like you to do, if you will, is keep a discreet eye on your neighbours over the weekend – and let me or someone else in my department know immediately if there are any unusual movements of vehicles or if anything out of the ordinary occurs."

"It sounds as if you're planning a big operation?" asked Rupert, cautiously.

"Yes, we are." She looked from one of them to the other, apparently weighing their reliability. "You've both been very helpful in the course of this investigation," she said. "And we couldn't have done any of it without you. In fact, without you, there wouldn't have been an investigation in the first place. I hope I can continue to rely on your discretion?"

"Yes," replied Jake for both of them. "Of course you can."

"Very well. I'd appreciate it if what I'm about to say didn't go any further – although feel free to discuss it with Helena if you think that's advisable."

The two men nodded in response.

"We'll need to bring people in from all directions on the day," said Sharon. "Along the river, through the wood, and of course through the main entrance to the Diadem site on the other side of the hill. It would help if we could use your property as a vehicle staging area; we'll have two minibuses and at least one other support vehicle, and you've got plenty of room for them here."

"No problem," Jake was quick to assure her. "Anything you need."

"It must seem on the surface to be a perfectly ordinary day, so you'll need to start by doing whatever you would normally do. When my people and I arrive on the plot, however, we'll need you to get out of the way and *stay* out until it's over. The same goes for that stupid mutt of yours - I mean it, shut him away somewhere – and it would be better if the children weren't here at all. I'll have armed officers with me in case things kick off, and I'd prefer not to have children within a hundred miles if it was up to me – but keeping them indoors should do if you can't get them off the premises altogether. Can you arrange that, do you think?"

"Absolutely. The kids can stay with Bridget - and I'll leave Toffee tied up where he is at the moment, only on a shorter chain; how's that?"

"Just the job." Sharon's manner had been businesslike but upbeat, but now it suddenly became more serious. "One other thing," she said, "and I can't stress this enough – we want absolutely no heroics from civilians; we've seen that these people are likely to be armed, and I don't want to have to deal with the paperwork if one of you gets hurt or killed. My officers are trained for this and you're not; let them get on with their jobs, and whatever happens don't get involved unless one of us specifically asks you to do something. If you get under our feet and muck things up for us I'll personally have your guts for garters – is that understood?"

"Yes." But Rupert couldn't help registering surprise. "Is that really a thing?" he asked, bewildered. "I mean, do people get in the way and bugger things up for you during an operation?"

"You'd be amazed," replied Sharon. "It happens more often than most police forces admit; everybody reads crime books and watches detective shows and they all seem to think it's easy. It isn't, of course – far from it. Just let us do the heavy lifting, all right? It's what we're paid for, after all."

"Fair enough," said Rupert. "I wouldn't ask you to my job, and I'm not going to get in the way of you doing yours."

"A wise decision," returned Sharon, laughing. "Because my cooking is absolutely awful."

Sharon's outline of the proposed operation was just that – only an outline. She was careful not to give too many specifics but asked for the gate between the orchard and the path to the Youth Hostel to be discreetly unlocked and went off at the end with the spare key to the main farm gate in her pocket, promising not to lose it. Her departure, however, coincided with the return of Helena and the children – their faces painted with extraordinary patterns and carrying an eclectic assortment of balloons, crayons and little plastic figures they had been given in the restaurant. They had also, it seemed, had blue ice cream, which Helena was convinced had been laced with something which had made them zoom about hyperactively like demented gerbils.

"Good luck calming this lot down and getting them to bed at any time this millennium," she grumbled mutinously. "Everything I've always tried to do, feeding them the best of everything – no artificial colours, no E-numbers, everything fresh - all undone in a single evening."

"It's in a good cause, though," suggested Rupert, mildly.

"I know. I keep trying to remind myself of that. And it's not that I wouldn't have taken them there myself another time – although I wouldn't have let them have that blue ice-cream. My mum's too indulgent with them sometimes," she ended, shrugging.

"Give her a break, H," suggested Jake. "She's worried about your dad, and what's going on here. She doesn't say much, but she's got a lot on her mind; maybe spoiling the kids is the way she gets it out of her system."

"I'm sure it is, and I'll grant you these are extraordinary circumstances – but, all the same, I'm the one who has to calm them down." She drew in a breath. "Maybe just this once I'll let them run it off; I suppose they can't do any real harm, although they do sound like a herd of rampaging elephants. I'm going to grab a cup of coffee and sit outside where I can watch them."

"All right." It was Jake who spoke. "We'll join you in a minute; still got a couple of things we need to discuss." But the look he shot Rupert as Helena turned to put the kettle on spoke volumes that did not require words - Helena, too, would have to be kept out of the way while the police operation on the farm was taking place. Sexist and patronising though it might appear, the instinct to protect her from any actual potential harm and from the stress and worry she would experience in the run-up to it was almost overwhelming. "We'll tell her it's going to be a week from now," decided Jake, speaking quietly so that Helena couldn't hear him. "She'll be off to Caraways first thing Monday anyway – she's got a couple of extra shifts this week - and with a bit of luck it'll all be over before she gets back. Then we'll argue about it, probably, but I'd rather do it that way round. Sometimes it's easier just to go ahead and do stuff and apologise afterwards, don't you think?"

"I do," said Rupert. "She's going to hate our breathing guts, of course, but I'd rather do that and save her the worry in advance." He made a gesture which indicated zipping his mouth shut. "She won't hear a word from me," he said, "I promise."

"Great," replied Jake. "You're a bloody brilliant mate, you know, Rupert." And he slapped him roughly on the shoulder by way of benediction, and went out to join Helena with the children.

That night there was no debate or discussion about who would sleep where; when Jake and Rupert retired to the caravan for the night they naturally turned in the same direction, and after a certain amount of matter-of-fact shucking of clothes and organising themselves for the morning they gravitated together naked in the middle of the bed and Jake's mouth was warm on Rupert's neck and shoulders.

It was so simple then just to turn to him, almost taking him for granted now, and to slide beneath him while he slid on top; there was no need to talk about what they were doing or to prepare anything, a natural rhythm building easily between them. On other nights, in other circumstances, they could be more ambitious; tonight was solely about the uncomplicated comfort of having someone to be with who didn't make demands it was impossible to supply; it was about the kind of heedless pleasure which is so rarely encountered but without which no life is ever truly complete.

Jake kissed Rupert with the dedicated concentration he gave to everything he did, as if every detail mattered and he was determined not to disregard anything important. His large hands were assured and confident but asked rather than demanded, positioning him with care rather than clutching him assertively, and the strength of his rocking body was mitigated by an exaggerated tenderness which treated Rupert as if he was made of glass. Jake, in short, was clearly conscious of his good fortune, and not inclined to risk it with an unconsidered move. That, presumably, was why he made no attempt to suggest anything that might involve the use of lube or condoms, and seemed content to settle for a primitive and earthy sort of rubbing-off, hot groin to hot groin, accompanied by all the animal sound-effects of a more ambitious endeavour.

"Next time," he said, "we're going to do this properly, and you're going to remember you've been fucked."

"Oh, really?" There wasn't much capacity for rational thought in Rupert's seething hind-brain anyway, but what there was he devoted to refuting this proposition. "And supposing I'd rather do it the other way around? Supposing I prefer to fuck you?" Upon saying which, he took advantage of their respective positions to adjust his hold on Jake's rump, to insinuate a dry fingertip into his anus, to push it up just as far as it would go. "You're not going to tell me you don't want me to fuck you sometimes, are you, Jake?"

"Of course I do, you know I bloody do."

162

"And I'll make sure that you won't forget it, either," promised Rupert, before the thread of logical thought drifted away again and he was locked into a jolting, shattering pattern of force which deconstructed him atom by atom and left him naked, helpless and incoherent beneath Jake's splendidly surging form.

It was a good thing, thought Rupert as he awoke, that Jake had taken the precaution of chocking up the four corners of the caravan with a few extra bricks; it was far less likely now to bounce about like a boat on a stormy sea, and they would be saved the necessity of coming up with some innocent way of explaining to the children what they had been doing to make it rock so much. With the return of full consciousness, however, also came a certain measure of regret. It was not for anything they had done - or would presumably continue to do - however, so much as the promptings of an unsettled conscience. If Rupert wasn't honest about the future before things went too far to mend, he would always have to live with the knowledge that he could – and should - have spoken sooner.

"There's something I need to tell you." His fingers on Jake's mouth effectively silenced any attempt at repartee. "Just so we know we're both on the same page, I've signed the contract to open up Ren's new kitchen in Glasgow; it's an eighteen month deal, starting in January."

He took his fingers away then, permitting Jake to speak, but still he made no sound.

"Ren helped me out when I needed him, and I'm doing the same in return; I suppose - until I met up with you lot, anyway - Ren and his friends were the closest I had to a family. Anyway, I owe him … Plus it'll help me get the ghost of the Beef'n'Reef off my back once and for all; that place needn't have failed if Cameron hadn't been systematically leeching money out of it, and maybe I need to prove that to myself before I can get on with my life."

Jake rolled onto his back, fingers laced across his chest. "You're not asking my opinion, are you?" he said. "You're telling me you've made the decision."

"To be honest, no, I'm not. Whatever you and I are going to be at some stage in the future, Jake, we haven't reached the point yet where I'd be involving you in my career decisions. You know I want to give this a proper go – but I've got promises to keep, to a friend who's backed me since the first time I met him, even when he thought I was out of my mind. It's about loyalty," he finished in desperation. "It's not about what I want to do, although I admit I do quite fancy this project of his; it would make a change to be able to start somewhere from scratch and have the money to do it properly. Only I thought I'd come back to live around here afterwards, if you didn't object too much."

Jake let out a sigh. "Of course I don't object," he said. "I'd like you to stay here permanently, we all would, but I don't know what there'd be to keep you. You've got a proper career, not like me – I bummed about in art school like everybody else did back then, but I never even finished the course. Then I had a couple of jobs in retail, and admittedly I did pick up a few skills that way, so when Tim asked me to run the market stall for him I was fine with dropping everything and doing that instead. I wasn't leaving anything I cared about, you see; I'd never had a job I liked until I ended up here – and even now I'd be glad not to be doing it if it meant Tim was still alive."

In the darkness Rupert reached out and quietly took his hand.

"But just because you end up somewhere accidentally," went on Jake, "it doesn't mean that's not where you're supposed to be. I never had a plan for my life at all - but maybe something else had a plan instead, you know? Maybe what I was meant to do all along was finish what my brother started."

"Possibly," replied Rupert, considering. "But there will be a time, eventually, when you realise it isn't still his project – it's yours. That might be when you've gone through a whole year and the things you're harvesting are things you planted yourself, or when you've got enough money for those solar panels and another poly-tunnel and you're not living from hand to mouth any more. One day you'll realise Tim's stopped looking over your shoulder, and Ship Meadow Farm's really yours and Helena's at last. No-one's suggesting you'll ever forget him, or stop caring about him, but you'll move on from the place you were when he died ... just like I'll move on from where I was when Cameron was arrested. We rebuild our lives slowly, Jake, but we all get there in the end."

"Yes. You're right, I know you are. And I'm with you about it taking time. I don't want to rush things any more than you do - but this could be something, Rupert, couldn't it? You and me, I mean?"

"Yes," said Rupert, "it could. I think we ought to give it a chance, anyway, to see if it'll develop into something worth keeping. But there's one thing I do know, and it might be useful to hold on to."

"Oh? And what's that, then?"

"It's not complicated," replied Rupert, gently. "It's just that ... even if we stopped being lovers one day, I don't think we'd have any difficulty staying friends - do you? And sometimes that's even more important. I'd like to be your friend, Jake, for as long as you want me to be. The rest of it, I reckon, will take care of itself."

"Yes," returned Jake, after a pause. "You're right. And I can live with that, Rupert, just so you know."

"Good," said Rupert, snuggling into his shoulder. "I can, too."

And within a very short space of time after that he was sound asleep - and so too was Jake.

19.

On later reflection, preserving an air of normality throughout the following day would turn out to have been one of the more challenging assignments Rupert had ever undertaken. It was true that in the hospitality industry it was often necessary to imitate the action of the swan – to portray serenity above whilst paddling frantically below – but the dichotomy between appearance and emotion had rarely been as marked as on this occasion. However - as a result of Martin's absence and the patched-up and hand-made nature of the growing operation without him - there was more than enough work to keep everybody busy that Sunday, with even the children being pressed into service fetching and carrying until they too were exhausted.

In the evening, after they had eaten, Jake took Finn and Tara back to Bridget's house; Helena had been in two minds about that, but her mother – pleading Martin's imminent return – had insisted. When Jake returned to the caravan later, Rupert learned the reason why.

"Sharon's been in touch," he said, as they were preparing for bed. "And Idwal had a quiet word with Bridget. It's all on for tomorrow morning; they'll wait until Helena leaves for work, and then they'll move in immediately."

"God. It doesn't seem real at all, does it?" In fact he was beginning to wonder if he had fallen into the pages of a Henning Mankell novel, which was a notion he found quite reassuring given the clear-up rate of his detectives.

"No." Jake waited until they were under the duvet and the light was off before continuing. "Did you hear a helicopter earlier?" he asked. "First thing this morning, it would be."

Rupert thought back. He'd been half-aware of a buzzing sound as he was waking up, but he hadn't really taken a lot of notice; the occasional microlight had been known to wander along the valley from a base in Coleford, and if the air was still enough their engines could be heard from a considerable distance.

"I think I did," he answered. "Why?"

"It was some of Sharon's lot," Jake told him, "using an infra-red camera to look for heat sources around the tunnel. She says they got a response from one of the air-shafts which looked as if somebody was cooking something in there. She said it was probably our chicken."

"Ugh, I hope not. Not for breakfast, anyway," groaned Rupert, his professional pride outraged.

"Who knows? Anyway, she reckons it's evidence somebody's living in there – and you wouldn't live in a railway tunnel if you had the choice, would you?"

"No." The mental image – of somewhere dark, slimy, echoing and full of bats - was hardly an appealing one. Then again people often built successful businesses in the space under railway arches, so if it was adequately prepared and ventilated … But how much effort would you put in for a bunch of migrant workers who didn't have the right to complain, and who could be shunted off to someone else if they gave you any trouble? Whatever it was like in there, it wasn't going to be the Ritz. "It's probably pretty horrible."

"Probably. But they'll be out of there tomorrow, with a bit of luck."

"Yes," said Rupert, "and then what?"

"I expect they'll send them home, eventually. It couldn't be worse than where they are now, could it?"

"I don't know," said Rupert. "Maybe it could. Are you absolutely sure we're doing the right thing, Jake?"

Beside him in the darkness, Jake seemed to shrug uneasily. "Honestly? I haven't got the faintest bloody clue - but it isn't up to me, is it? It's up to Sharon and the … whatever they are, the Borders and Immigration lot. We'll just have to trust that they know what they're doing."

The following morning, the pleasant balmy weather seemed to have deserted them again. Helena set off for work in a light drizzly rain, and surely could have missed seeing the incoming police convoy only by a whisker – if at all. There were two minibuses and a communications vehicle of some sort – it had a satellite aerial on top, at any rate – out of which stepped Idwal.

"Sharon's co-ordinating the operation from the Youth Hostel," he said. "Just the two of you here?"

"And the dog," said Rupert.

"Tied up?"

"Yes."

"Good. I suppose there's no point me telling you to stay in the house this morning, is there? No, I thought as much. Well, then, you can stick with me if you like – I'll be carrying a taser, though, so make sure you keep me between you and whatever's going on or you could be collateral damage - and whatever I tell you to do you'll do, right away, no arguments. That includes running away," he added wryly, "terribly fast."

Rupert's eyebrows lifted in surprise. The notion of a policeman in an operational situation quoting *The Hitch-hiker's Guide to the Galaxy* hadn't occurred to him before, but from the way Jake reacted it was clear the remark had a shared relevance for them.

Idwal was wrestling his way into something which was all straps and Velcro. "Is that a bullet-proof jacket?" asked Rupert, feeling at somewhat of a disadvantage.

"No fear, it's a stab vest - people often carry knives or needles hidden in their clothing; we have to be prepared for that."

"Are you expecting much resistance, then?"

"Not much, but some. Usually in a ganging situation the workers are only too glad to be taken into custody if it means they get a decent meal and somewhere warm to sleep – and the blokes who pull the strings don't tend to put up much of a fight, either, because they've all got lawyers to do that for them. What we're looking out for here is those two so-called translators, Tesar and Resnik; Tesar's got previous for affray, but for some reason the witnesses against him seem to have changed their minds and decided not to give evidence."

"Oh, really?" Jake sounded far from astonished. "I wonder why?"

"Precisely." The last buckle was done up, the last Velcro flap fastened down. "We're trialling these," said Idwal, taking the taser from its box; it looked like a ray-gun, a child's yellow and black plastic toy. "Should be enough to stop 'em, but we've got firearms on the plot as well, in case it all kicks off." He looked at his watch. "Time to get into position."

They filtered down through the orchard, slowly, in company with two other officers; a further pair remained with the communications vehicle. Toffee whimpered softly as they passed, but other than making big, reproachful eyes at the prospect of being left out of the fun he seemed to grasp the gravity of the situation and remained impassive where he was. Within sight of the footpath Idwal held up a hand and indicated that Jake and Rupert could go no further.

"Take cover here," he said, quietly. "You'll be able to see what's going on, but you won't be in the way."

Rupert shrank behind the bole of a tree, crouching - it didn't offer much protection, but was better than nothing – and in the pause that followed he glanced around in all directions; Jake was next to him, equally silent, the rain slicking his hair; there were wood-pigeons calling somewhere, but otherwise all was stillness and rest apart from the flashing red and yellow of a pair of kayaks approaching down the river.

Rupert tugged Idwal's sleeve. "Kayaks," he said urgently. Surely they'd be in danger if they got too close?

"Hush," said Idwal, "they're ours."

And that was when Rupert knew it was all right, and that Sharon really had thought of everything, and he stopped worrying and waited to see how it would all turn out.

In fact, the wait was shorter than he'd expected. Having mentally resigned himself to anything from ten minutes to half an hour, Rupert was startled when – only a few seconds later, as it seemed – a voice issuing from Idwal's personal radio gave the order to move in. Even then there was no rushing pandemonium; whatever was happening up ahead, out of sight, it seemed to be happening very quietly - and although Idwal tensed and stared ahead of him with the same sense of urgency Toffee would have adopted in the circumstances there was, to Rupert's eyes, equally little to be seen. He was desperate to ask what was going on, but not only did Idwal's expression discourage conversation but Rupert was also far too terrified of being the idiot who ruined everything with an unconsidered word to utter a sound. However he turned his eyes briefly towards Jake and found on his face the counterpart of his own pensive expression, and when Jake reached out briefly and squeezed Rupert's hand in a reassuring gesture he realised from the slight lifting of Idwal's eyebrows that he had seen it too.

"All right," said the voice. "We've got Resnik in custody and we're in at the northern end. Looks like ... half a dozen caravans in here."

"Copy," said someone else, and then the airwaves went silent except for a kind of airy static and what might have been the sound of running footsteps; someone somewhere had left a connection open; whatever was happening, it was being broadcast live to all the officers involved. There was a snatch of a language Rupert didn't recognise – it could as easily be Slovak as anything else – and somebody said, "This way, please," - and then a new voice cut sharply through the static.

"We've lost the other one, he's out somewhere on the river bank; all units in that area close in, repeat all units in that area close in."

Idwal was up from his haunches, his legs unwound, and running almost before the words had been uttered. Jake grabbed Rupert's hand and pulled him upright and a moment later they, too, were running, out through the gate and onto the footpath, aware of the converging trajectories of several police officers it was difficult – but imperative – to avoid. They almost had to throw themselves into a hedge not to trip up one particular lumbering beast who came down the footpath in uncontrolled fashion and swerved dangerously at the bottom, and when Rupert looked up after this near-collision it was to see – and to recognise with astonishment – the couple with the black Labrador approaching along the river-bank, this time wearing police uniforms.

"Oh my god," he said. "It's them!"

"What?" Jake turned so abruptly towards him that whiplash could have been a genuine possibility.

"Nothing, I'll ... later." He knew it was incoherent, but it was the best he could do.

"He's on the bridge," someone said. "He's armed!" And they all hustled round the corner together, Idwal firmly in the lead, keeping as close to cover possible.

"Armed police, Mr Tesar." It was Sharon's voice, clear as a bell and much amplified through a loud-hailer. "Put down the weapon; my officers have instructions to fire."

Mirek Tesar, the fishing-gnome from the river-bank, was picking his way carefully across the gap-toothed deck of the bridge, the shotgun in his right hand being used as much for balance as anything else – like a tightrope-walker's umbrella; it was certainly not at an angle where it could be fired except accidentally, which was no doubt why the armed officers had so far succeeded in restraining themselves. His head was down, he was clearly watching where he put his feet, and he was hobbling forward one precarious step at a time – which, presumably, was why he'd completely failed to notice that two dark blue figures in body armour had appeared at the far end of the bridge and were closing in quietly from the direction of the village. They remained there, unmoving; it was not necessary for them to approach him, and in any case it would not have been safe. Like the cat who still waits at a mouse-hole after the mouse has died of old age, they had all the time in the world – and he did not.

"I know you understand English, Mr Tesar." Sharon's tone was unfailingly polite, yet held a commanding edge only a fool would have chosen to ignore - and Rupert didn't think Mirek Tesar was a fool, whatever else he might have been. "Put down the weapon," she repeated, with the infinite patience of a mother persuading a toddler that it wouldn't be a good idea to eat a wasp. "Walk towards me with your hands in the air. Do it now, Mr Tesar, please."

Tesar was caught in the centre of the bridge. There were armed men on the village side – not moving, just waiting for him to make up his mind – and armed men on the tunnel side, and they could easily stay there all day. The next move was up to him, and the decision-making process seemed interminable. He paused, took a step first in one direction and then the other, glancing anxiously at the unstable structure of the bridge beneath him as if convinced it was liable to fall apart at any moment.

"He can't go forward," breathed Idwal, "and he can't go back."

Rupert's fingers were caught, clutched, crushed; he looked around to see Jake's attention firmly fixated on the figure on the bridge, his expression as stony and impassive as an Easter Island statue, and with dawning comprehension Rupert also turned to watch. Yes, transpose this damp daytime setting to a freezing midwinter night and reverse the allegiances of the parties – put the good guy on the bridge and the bad guys at either end – and here, surely, was the scenario which had cost Tim Colley his life.

Tesar seemed to come to a conclusion. Holding the shotgun above his head, with clear and unequivocal movements he plainly broke it open, shook the cartridges into the fast-flowing river - and then threw the gun over the parapet as well.

"Oh, fuck," said Jake, so quietly that only Rupert heard him. "*No.*"

"What?" Spinning to look at Jake in that moment, to find out what was distressing him, was the result of a mental process which had scarcely even begun to join the dots together. He knew Jake was worried, and it knew it was to do with the bridge - but in his concern for his friend Rupert had allowed his attention to wander at precisely the wrong moment, and thus he missed the most crucial and defining action of them all.

Someone shouted an incoherent warning – "Stop him!" - but short of putting a bullet in the man there was little they could do. A fraction of a second later somebody else said, "He's in!" - and when Rupert turned his head again to look back towards the bridge, the central span of it was completely empty.

"Kayak team, move in," said Sharon, calmly. "Ambulance, stand by. Tunnel team, you can start preparing to move the detainees out now."

Rupert's head was spinning. He could see the flailing figure in the water, and the bright shapes of the kayaks moving towards him, but quite how Tesar had gone from standing on the bridge waving a gun to being a sodden and struggling figure battling the currents between the pylons he hadn't the remotest shred of an idea.

"What happened?" he asked Jake, in bewilderment. "Did he fall?"

"No," came the stunned reply. "He didn't fall, he jumped - he just climbed up onto that bit at the side and threw himself into the river. He didn't even stop to think about it, just ... down he went. Which," concluded Jake, in a grief-racked and oddly sepulchral tone, "by a staggering coincidence which is nothing of the sort, is *exactly* what I reckon happened to my brother."

Idwal herded them back up through the orchard after this, sat them on the doorstep of the lodge and told them not to move. They interpreted this instruction literally and remained there – holding hands and not talking – until he returned to speak to them a few minutes later.

"Well," he said, "the kayak team got the bloke out; he's in an ambulance on his way to hospital – conscious, but he won't be talking for a while; too busy puking, apparently." His tone was redolent of satisfaction, as if the words 'serves the bastard right' were on the tip of his tongue but he was too well-trained to utter them. "We'll be bringing the detainees out this way in a minute or two, and I can confirm that your young lady – Zdeňka Jahodová – is among them. She'll be taken to the immigration detention centre at Yarl's Wood, together with the rest of the females; the men will probably be going to Haslar."

"So they'll be deported, will they, then, eventually?"

"Not necessarily. They'll be given the opportunity to return home, and some of them might well take it – sometimes they realise they were better off before they came here. The rest will probably put in asylum claims, so they'll stay in detention until those are processed. At the end of the day, though, most of them will probably be deported."

"Back to sunny Slovakia? Well, maybe it isn't quite so bad there after all."

But it was Idwal's turn to look bewildered. "They're probably not Slovaks," he said. "Slovakia's in the EU, it has been for the last four years; if they wanted to come here from Slovakia they could do it perfectly legally. This lot are far more likely to have been trafficked over the border into Slovakia from somewhere further east; they could quite possibly be Ukrainians," he added, with a shrug. "The languages are similar, it wouldn't be difficult from somebody from Ukraine to pass themselves off as Slovak."

"And Ukraine isn't in the EU?" asked Rupert. He had to admit, he hadn't been keeping track; away on the far side of the world he'd had more immediate concerns.

"Not yet, no. It's a long way to come, isn't it, to end up living in a caravan in a railway tunnel?" Idwal stopped speaking then. A line of cold, glum and dishevelled people had appeared, walking up slowly through the orchard; the police officers with them were not armed, and seemed to be going out of their way to behave sympathetically as though conscious of the detainees' distress. "They're victims," he added. "Willing victims, in a sense, but nobody signs up to be treated the way they were treated; I wouldn't be surprised if they were bloody grateful to be out of there, myself."

"And which one's ours?" asked Jake, seeming to extract himself from his reverie only with a most almighty effort.

"Near the back, in the light-coloured jacket."

"Oh, yes, I can see her."

They both could, but for a frozen moment had no idea how to react. She was prettier than the picture on her ID card, and looked younger, and there was an awful temptation to wave and smile as she passed – but of course she could have no possible idea of who they were, because she had left her card to be found by an unknown person – by someone she had probably never seen. The connection - if there was one - was all on their side, not hers. Nevertheless she seemed to become animated as she approached them, and turned to speak a few words to the officer beside her. Then, a few paces further on, she raised her voice and called out quite distinctly.

"Toffee? Toffee?"

The idiot dog huffed, rose to his feet, dashed to the end of his chain and stood there waiting, wagging his tail nineteen to the dozen, as Zdeňka Jahodová broke away from the line of detainees, crossed the grass towards him, wrapped both arms tightly around his neck, pressed her face against his hairy shoulder and burst into an overwhelming flood of grateful tears.

20.

"So Toffee saves the day again, does he?" asked Jake, when the last of the sad parade had passed and gone. Zdeňka Jahodová, having hugged the mutt for all he was worth and briefly and wordlessly shaken hands with Jake and Rupert, had been loaded into one of the minibuses with the other migrant workers and driven off, waving from the window. Rupert wondered whether they would ever see her again, or even learn how her story would turn out.

"Oh, mate, he's a marvel, that stupid bloody dog." There was emotion in Rupert's throat which he couldn't quite contain, and which he was certain set the seal forever on any chance of achieving true Aussie blokedom – as if being gay wasn't enough in itself.

"Where there's a dog there's usually a human being," explained Idwal, who'd been having a word with the escorting officer. "She gambled on Toffee's human finding the card and doing something with it. Smart move, in the circumstances."

"Do you think they'd really have shot her?" Rupert asked.

"It's not what I think that matters," shrugged Idwal. "If she and the others thought so, that would be enough; these people work on a basis of intimidation."

"I reckon they intimidated my brother," said Jake, abruptly. "I reckon that's what happened to him that night … one bloke waiting at each end of the bridge, leaving him in the middle with nowhere to go but down."

"It's possible," replied Idwal. "Believe me, Sharon will be asking them about that. Resnik's already on his way to Cwmbran for questioning; I don't suppose we'll be allowed access to Tesar before tomorrow morning, since he's suffering from concussion."

"And what about Herb and Tudor? There's no way they didn't know this was happening, is there? It's their bloody company, after all."

"True, and of course we'll be talking to them, but you can bet your arse they'll blame it all on Resnik and Tesar." Idwal squared his shoulders. "Look, I've got to start getting the crime scene processed; the satellite vehicle will stay until we've finished with that, which could be a day or two, and we're leaving officers on the main gate for the time being. Any of them will be able to get hold of me if you need me - but I'm going to have to abandon you now, I'm afraid. Let the officers know if you're planning to leave the premises for any length of time … and if you're putting the kettle on I'm sure they'd be grateful for a cup of something." He turned, paused, then turned again to grip Jake affectionately by the shoulder and squeeze. "Look," he said, "I don't know what your plans are, but I hope it all works out this time. Nice to have met you, Rupert," he added civilly, before striding off through the orchard. He didn't look back.

Rupert's brows furrowed. "What did he mean?" He was struggling to decide whether or not a scarcely detectable undertone to Idwal's words was the product of his own hyperactive imagination. "*This* time? As opposed to some other time, or what?"

"As opposed to the last time I could potentially have got serious about a man, I suppose," Jake told him, heavily. "Unfortunately that never really got off the ground; his career was always getting in the way."

"Ah, so … ?"

"So … don't ask, don't tell, okay, Rupert? It was a long time ago, before I moved to London; we're both well and truly over it by now."

"Okay." But the implications were clarity itself; Jake had lost a lover to a demanding career in the past, and it had started to look as if that might possibly be happening again. No wonder he'd accepted that they were in no position to make long-term plans just yet; no wonder he'd been willing to take only what Rupert offered and not to ask for more; it wasn't that Jake was afraid of commitment, exactly - but it was beginning to look very much as if commitment might be afraid of Jake.

During the next half-hour or so they pulled themselves together enough for Jake to get a message to Bridget over the HT, asking her to let Helena know in guarded terms that Idwal and Sharon had completed their mission at Ship Meadow but for the clearing up. While he was doing that Rupert took up Idwal's suggestion of relaying coffee to the officers who remained on the farm, and returned with their gratitude ringing in his ears. Afterwards, although it was difficult to concentrate, they prepared the afternoon veg boxes, and then Jake and Toffee went to clean up after the geese.

The focus of the police operation had now switched to the inside of the railway tunnel and the main Diadem property beyond, and it was afternoon before anything further happened to disrupt their equilibrium. Then one of the officers from the satellite vehicle came strolling towards them, a strange quirky grin on his face. Clearly the assignments had changed at some point during the morning, because this was the lumbering beast who had so nearly overwhelmed them on the footpath; he was well over six feet tall and looked about fifteen years old.

"Ummm, Mr Goodall?" he began.

It was a moment before Rupert realised that the name belonged to him, and with difficulty returned his thoughts to the present day. "Yes?"

"My colleague at the main gate says there's a man asking to see you," the beast said, his tone clearly expressing doubt. "He says - and this is him saying it, mind, not me, and I'm not sure he's not winding me up – but he says Renfrew Sheppard's at the gate. You know, that bloke who does the cooking on the telly? He swears it's him, and he's asking to see you. I'm only passing on what I've been told," concluded the officer, without confidence. "It could be a total load of bollocks."

"No," Rupert assured him. "It may not be; I actually do know Ren Sheppard – I work for him, as a matter of fact – but I thought he was on his way to Florida. Or maybe I've got the weeks mixed up, I've completely lost track of time."

"So it's okay for him to come down, then, is it?"

"I suppose so – if it really is him. Assuming that's all right with you, Jake?"

"Yeah, no problem," replied Jake, gruffly. "Can never have too many chefs, in my opinion. Maybe we'll get him to cook our tea for us tonight, eh, Rupert?"

Ren, who was driving what appeared to be a hired BMW, climbed out of its luxurious interior looking carefully casual in expensive designer jeans and a very tight blue tee-shirt. His hair was artfully awry and he was wearing sunglasses which had certainly not come off a rack at the local chemist's. Incongruously, he was also carrying a briefcase.

"Bloody hell, it really is you," said Rupert. "I thought they were having us on. Of all the gin-joints in all the towns in all the world ... "

"I know, mate." Ren hugged Rupert enthusiastically. "I know. 'Allo, Jake - long time no see." He offered his hand, and Jake took it.

"Ren," he said. "How're you doing? And more to the point, why are you here?"

"I've been in Devon looking at the Orangery at Morchard Court," replied Ren. "We're doing a pop-up there for *Sheppard's Delight*, fantastic venue, really looking forward to it. I stayed overnight at a lovely place in Tiverton and I thought I'd call in here on the way back, because Andrew seemed to think it might be a good location for the second series – and anyway, I wanted to catch up with you both and see how you were getting on. Turned up at the gate and the place is full of coppers, so my first thought was maybe you'd killed each other or something." He waved away the tastelessness of this remark with an idle gesture. "I gather it's something to do with gangers and migrant workers on the farm next door?"

"Yes. They've been living in the old railway tunnel." Rupert gave him an outline of the situation; Ren nodded sympathetically throughout.

"It's the curse of agriculture in this country," he said, unexpectedly, as Rupert ground to a halt. "Supermarkets driving prices down, farmers cutting corners and looking for cheap labour – and guys like you who make a point of doing things to a certain standard get priced out of the market. Might make a good subject for a programme, actually; I'll have a word with Gary about that when I get back to London. Anyway, looks like a decent little growing operation you've got here," he went on. "Care to walk me round it for a couple of minutes, so that I can get a handle on the situation?"

Jake and Rupert exchanged glances briefly.

"All right," said Jake. "Why not?"

They started at the poly-tunnel, where the air was full of the scent of ripening tomatoes, and walked between the cultivated beds examining the onions, the brassicas, the Jerusalem artichokes, the Swiss chard, the marrows, Ren's gaze flickering delightedly from one burgeoning plot to another.

"It's like a patchwork quilt," he said, enchanted. "Everything neat and tidy, everything under control."

"We do our best," said Jake, "but the geese got all the radishes, most of the lettuce and some of the mint."

"Oh, well, they'll probably taste all the better when you come to cook them," replied Ren, philosophically. "Either that or they'll lay green eggs."

"Which would be quite a novelty item, of course; we shouldn't have too much trouble selling those."

"That's the spirit, turning adversity to account, making something out of nothing. Got good local customers, have you, apart from the stuff you send to London?"

"A few. Some cafés and restaurants, a few dozen domestic customers. We're only just getting the business off the ground at the moment."

"Understandable. But room for expansion, if you had the business to justify it?"

"Yes." Jake told him about the plan for the second poly-tunnel, and for a few moments after that they discussed asparagus, strawberries, sweet peppers and even lychees. "And of course there's the cider orchard; it's the only reliable income we've got, apart from what Helena makes at Caraways. A good harvest this year would put us in a much stronger financial position."

"Right. And how's it looking at the moment?"

"Pretty fair so far," conceded Jake. "Assuming we can get enough people in to do the picking, of course; that's always a bit of a gamble."

Ren was nodding thoughtfully. "Okay," he said. "Sounds as if you've got everything working nicely, although I suspect a certain amount of capital investment wouldn't go amiss. I suppose you've had problems trying to borrow money?"

"Not really." Jake's tone was flat and defeated. "We know it would be a waste of time asking, so we haven't bothered. We've had all the subsidies we're likely to get until we can take on more permanent staff, and I can't see that happening for a few years. We're between a rock and a hard place with it; there's no alternative to carrying on as we are and hoping for the best."

Ren took off the sunglasses and squinted at the pair of them acutely. "You both look knackered," he said, without even a pretence at subtlety. "Is there somewhere we can sit down and have a talk? Only I've heard some disturbing rumours about you, Rupert, and I wanted to find out if they were true."

"Inside," said Jake, indicating the bungalow. One by one they stepped over Toffee, who was on the threshold grappling with a rawhide chew, and positioned themselves around the table in the living-room.

"Does the ganging operation have any bearing on what might have happened to your brother?" asked Ren, as soon as they were settled. "Do the police reckon they're connected at all?"

Jake's eyebrows lifted in surprise at the directness of the question. "I don't see how they *can't* be," he admitted, "but they haven't said anything about it officially. Early days yet, I suppose; it'll all come out in the end."

"Of course, but it seems a bit of a coincidence, if they're not part of the same thing. The police'll tell you as soon as they know anything definite, I suppose?"

"Probably, yeah. But what was it you said about disturbing rumours? Is that anything we need to know about?"

"Ah." As though he'd been stopped in his tracks, Ren spread both hands on the table and scrutinised the backs of them contemplatively for a moment. "Yes, we should really discuss this while it's quiet. I gather there are children?" he added, vaguely.

"Two," said Rupert. "A boy and a girl."

But Ren wasn't listening; instead he was burrowing through the contents of his briefcase. "Oh, look, here's the Orangery at Morchard." He flourished a picture of elegant wrought-iron tracery. "They've just finished restoring it, cost them nearly a hundred grand. No, this was what I wanted – your contract for the Glasgow job, Rupert. It's not that

180

I don't appreciate the gesture," he went on, "and I get that you feel you owe me something – we'll have to talk about that later - but I know bloody well you wouldn't be happy in that job – and, more to the point, so do you. Things have changed, haven't they? You've got other priorities now."

"No, I … " Having made the decision, on however flimsy a basis, Rupert felt obliged to stick by it – even though he could feel the weight of Jake's eyes on him as he spoke. "I meant what I said to Andrew, I'm quite happy to do it."

"Andrew went too far when he talked you into signing this," continued Ren, scarcely pausing for breath. "He's bloody good at looking out for my interests, totally focussed on Nectarine and whatever's going to put money in my pocket, but he doesn't always see the whole picture. In particular he hasn't got the history with you that I have, Rupert. I need your expertise on the Glasgow job, and I'm not ashamed to admit it – but it doesn't absolutely have to be full-time, and you wouldn't need to live there if you don't want to. Supposing I offered you a consultancy contract instead of wages, for example, with an hourly fee and travel allowance? You could live anywhere in the country that had broadband internet and decent public transport, and you'd only have to be in Glasgow half the time. When you're not actually in the kitchen you're going to be doing a lot of networking, anyway … going to meetings, setting up marketing, video conferencing … there's a large part of the job that isn't site-specific, in other words, and it wouldn't matter where you were in the world for that."

"Fuck." This abrupt reversal was almost more than Rupert could reasonably process. He'd gradually begun reconciling himself to the idea that life henceforth would be carried on north of the border, among people he didn't know, while he paid his long-overdue debt of obligation to Ren; it had seemed fair to him, which was why he'd agreed to it in the first place. "But I know it's important to you to get Glasgow right," he added, in confusion. "There's a lot riding on it, isn't there?"

"There is," acknowledged Ren. "But hopefully I can get somebody in who'd be able to take on the day-to-day management of the place without supervision, and then you can run the Glasgow operation same the way I run London – at arm's length, leaning on a good strong *sous-chef* who's capable of taking the strain. I'm considering asking Graham to take it on, as a matter of fact; he's done his time in the trenches, after all, and I don't think I realised how much he'd grown professionally. He's almost as good as you are, mate," he continued, with a smile, "which makes me think I should probably be doing something to hang on to him before some bronzed Aussie adventurer – male or female - steals him away from me."

There was an awkward pause here, while Rupert struggled to make sense of an altered landscape in which Graham was to be offered the Glasgow post and he himself would be bumped up to a role almost on a par with Ren's. It sounded challenging and terrifying all at once, just the combination of attributes to make any proposal immediately attractive – but then, surely, if he accepted, it would only increase his indebtedness to his friend? "I owe you such a lot already," he said, weakly. "That was how I was finally going to pay you back."

"No." Ren spoke firmly, and his jaw had set into a stubborn line. "I don't see it like that at all. Look, the truth is I should never have let you go off with Cameron in the first place. Admittedly he didn't seem too bad at the time, but I was never comfortable about him and I should have said something about it. You ask Annabel – we talked it over and decided it'd be best not to interfere, but we had major reservations. The short answer is, I could have saved you a lot of grief and I didn't do it - and I've been feeling guilty ever since. So give me a chance to make up for it now, Rupert - will you, please?"

"You don't have … " Rupert stopped, feeling the words clogging his throat, then tried again. "Look, Ren, it's me who owes you … not the other way around."

But Ren was shaking his head in denial. "I haven't been keeping score," he said, "that's not the way it works. Don't ever try to repay me for anything, okay? Like I've said before, just pass it on instead - for example, if you can help Jake here with his business, well, we'll all benefit, won't we? You'll get a new direction in life and I'll get – hopefully – a new organic supplier for Nectarine. In fact, Jake, if you'd be willing to commit to an exclusive contract, I reckon I could see my way clear to making a sizeable capital investment in Ship Meadow Farm. What would you say to twenty-five per cent, for example? Would that help you out of the doldrums a bit, do you think?"

"I'd say," replied Jake, "that I can't consider anything until I've discussed it with Helena - but I'd definitely like to know more."

"All right, then – give me a day or two to get the lawyers involved and come up with a concrete proposal, and then we'll know exactly what we're talking about. And as for this, Rupert," concluded Ren, brandishing the contract under his nose, "I think I'm going to tear the bugger up. Assuming I have your permission, of course."

"Oh, but ... " But the objection had been involuntary, from force of habit, and there was no real power behind it. Letting go of one plan and accepting another had never been this difficult in the past, Rupert reminded himself, until he'd allowed himself to be fossilised by the feelings of helplessness which had arisen when his life with Cameron spiralled out of control; now he was going to have to get used to adapting to changing circumstances again; it was time to climb up out of his rut and get on with the rest of his life.

"We can do better than this, mate," said Ren persuasively. "Trust me."

Rupert took a breath, leaned back into the couch, and turned at last to look at Jake. "And what do you think?" he asked him. "What would you like me to do about it?"

"No-brainer, mate," was the confident response. "It's a fucking no-brainer, this is."

"It's a fucking no-brainer," repeated Rupert, feeling as if a weight had lifted from his shoulders, from his mind, from the entirety of his life. "All right, then, Ren, go ahead and do it - tear the bloody thing limb from limb for all I care, shred it into a million bloody pieces and throw them about like confetti if you want - and then let's go back and start all over again, shall we?"

21.

In the early afternoon Sharon returned; if she was at all surprised to discover a well-known TV personality sitting on the doorstep of the lodge making friends with an Irish Wolfhound she had the *savoir faire* not to show it, but settled for merely shaking hands and excusing herself so that she could talk to Rupert and Jake indoors. Ren, taking the hint, got to his feet and whistled Toffee after him, and together they went off to take a gentle stroll among the apple trees.

"Come on, Toffee my lad - let's go and scout locations for this pop-up, shall we?"

"You wouldn't have a picture of your quad bike, I suppose?" Sharon asked Jake, as the three of them settled on the couch. "Chassis number, VIN, that sort of thing?"

"Yes. It's all on the insurance paperwork – I think that's in the caravan at the moment. Want me to get it for you?"

"Not right away. Does this look like your bike?" The picture she had stored on her phone was small and indistinct, but apparently it was clear enough.

"Yes. I thought those bastards had probably got it somewhere."

"That and a certain amount of other small portable property which you may or not be able to identify," confirmed Sharon. "Resnik's copping to most of it quite freely; there was a concerted campaign of harassment against Ship Meadow, and the instructions for that came from Diadem management – effectively from the Roberts brothers themselves. They wanted you off this land so they could expand into it - which is what you thought all along, of course. He's putting his hands up to all the dirty tricks, only of course he's trying to shift the blame onto the Robertses. He swears he and Tesar never laid a hand on Martin Fisher, by the way – they reckon he just collapsed spontaneously – although he admits they didn't help him, just legged it out of there as fast as they could."

Jake was nodding sagely. "That seems to be the way they do things," he agreed. "Was that what happened to Tim as well, then? They manoeuvred him into a dangerous position, then buggered off and left him to get out of it by himself?"

Sharon cleared her throat before replying. "Look," she said, "some of it's not clear at the moment, but he admits they stole your brother's petrol on the night he died. Seems they were carrying a grudge that had nothing whatever to do with the Diadem campaign against Ship Meadow, and when they saw his car in the village they reckoned they'd got a chance to take some sort of personal revenge on him – as they saw it, anyway. Resnik swears blind all they wanted to do was frighten him; he says they were going to herd him out into the middle of the bridge and leave him there all night, but he panicked and jumped into the water of his own accord. Well, I suppose - if you thought those two were coming after you - you might possibly get desperate and jump, but I'm not really buying it; not the way they're selling it, anyway. Whether or not we'll ever have enough evidence to bring a charge of murder, though … " She sighed. "We'll keep working on it, of course, but it's looking as if we might have to end up charging them with manslaughter instead. That still carries a discretionary life sentence, although in my experience it's more likely to be five to ten years. On the other hand kidnapping and false imprisonment also carry life sentences, and there's no doubt at all about the evidence there, so one way or another these guys are going to be out of circulation for a while. There's every chance of the Robertses going to prison, too; I should warn you they'll almost certainly get bail in the first instance, but it'll be conditional on them not returning to the village. They'll have to go to a bail hostel – what we're now calling Approved Premises – and hire a manager to keep their business running, I suppose; I imagine that'd have quite an effect on their profit margins," she added, thoughtfully.

"Serves them right," said Rupert. "The way they carry on - exploiting vulnerable people, intimidating rivals; it's not exactly what you'd call an ethical business model, is it? I don't know how anybody does that and expects to sleep at night."

"It probably helps if you're ruthless," observed Sharon. "Or a psychopath. Or both. At any rate, if you can dig out the paperwork on the quad bike, Jake, we can add it to the list of charges. Might as well hit them with everything we can prove, all at the same time; more chance of getting a result that way."

"No problem." Jake had half got to his feet to comply, however, when a thought seemed to strike him and he returned to his former position. "No, hang on a minute. You said something about them not going after Tim because of the vendetta? You said they wanted revenge? What was that all about, then? Why would anybody be so pissed off at my brother that they'd persecute him like that? He'd never done anything to hurt them, had he?"

"Ah. Well, that depends on your point of view, I think," replied Sharon. "They did have something against him, actually, and they seem to think it was more than enough justification for hounding a man to death."

"Oh? And what might that be?"

"Your brother was a referee," she told him, sadly. "In his last match, on the day before he died, he sent off Resnik for violent conduct and awarded a penalty to the other side; they scored from it and won the game 1-0. Resnik was the goalie, you see," she added, as if that explained it. "He took it very personally. I don't imagine he actually set out to kill your brother, but I can assure you he isn't remotely sorry that he's dead. In fact I get the impression he thinks he's done the world a favour," she concluded, with a helpless gesture. "I'm really very sorry, Jake."

"Yes," said Jake. "So am I. It was even more of a fuckin' waste than I thought it was – killed over a bloody football match, of all bloody things. Just bloody fuck that sideways, Sharon – fuck it with a rusty chainsaw, and fuck the bus it rode in on, too!"

For a while after Sharon's departure Jake was almost inconsolable. Sitting on the step of the lodge - with Ren and Toffee maintaining a tactful absence - Rupert put an arm around Jake's shaking shoulders and did his best to offer comfort, although Jake had vanished into a curled ball of misery and was only communicating in expletives.

"Tim was a good bloke," he said, when he could bring himself to speak at last. "He didn't deserve that. *Nobody* deserves that, ever. If he jumped the way they're saying, it was because he was bloody terrified – and believe me, it would have taken a lot to do that."

"I imagine it would, if he was anything like you."

"He was better than me. A hundred times bloody better."

Rupert hadn't known Tim at all, and doubted he could literally have been a hundred times better than his brother, but he was wiser than to argue the point. "Actually ... " he began instead; it was difficult to articulate, but he was determined to say it anyway. " ... there's almost a case for suggesting that if Tim hadn't died, those people would still be living in the railway tunnel. They'd still be being exploited. I know it's no sort of consolation, but something good did come out of his death eventually – didn't it?" Spoken aloud, it didn't sound half as convincing as it had in his mind. "You saw how grateful Zdeňka was to be out of there."

Jake's response was a very long time coming, but when it did it was a considerable relief. "Yeah, you're right, and at least Diadem won't be doing it to anybody else again. That doesn't mean it won't still be going on in other places, though."

"True. Although if Ren meant what he said about making a programme ... it might give other people some idea of what to look out for, help to raise awareness ... "

"Maybe. He's not a bad bloke, is he, on the whole? Heart's more or less in the right place, anyway."

"He'll do," said Rupert, grateful to accept a change of subject. "He'll do."

"Think he'd stay on long enough for H to meet him?" asked Jake. "She's a big fan, she'd be sorry to have missed him."

"I can ask him, if you like."

But Jake's attention had wandered away again already. "How the fuck am I ever going to tell her about this?" he asked, his voice wavering. "How do I tell her Tim's life was thrown away over something as totally bloody stupid as a football match – and not even a real one but a tupenny-ha'penny village beer match? It's not like it was the bloody FA Cup or anything really important, for fuck's sake!"

"I'm not sure I *would* tell her that," replied Rupert. "Not just yet, at any rate. Tell her about the good stuff instead – about Zdeňka and Toffee and Ren. We can keep the rest to ourselves for a little while longer, can't we?"

"Probably, if you think it's a good idea." There was a pause after this, and then Jake said; "Does that mean you're going to be staying around, then? Are you going to be moving down here and living with me permanently, whenever you're not in Glasgow?"

"I could," conceded Rupert. "Although loving you and loving your awful bloody caravan are not necessarily the same thing, so I'm not sure I'd literally want to move in with you. Maybe I could find a house to rent in the village or something – at least they've got broadband over there - and we could spend the night together whenever we wanted? That would be ... " he thought about it " ... a lot less pressure all round."

"All right. But in that case what are you planning to do about your dog?"

"Rusty? I was thinking maybe she could come and live here, if that offer's still open; I suppose you'll need to give Toffee back at some stage, but it would still be useful to have a guard dog - and if I'm going to be on the road a lot I'll need to have someone reliable looking after her during the times when I'm away. I'll pay her vets' bills and everything, of course – and she needs a special diet because of her allergies, but we can go into all that nearer the time."

"Okay," replied Jake, "that works – and even if you get pissed off with me eventually, you'll still have to come and visit sometimes just to see her!"

"Well, that's true," conceded Rupert, "although I don't think I'm going to get pissed off with you – at least, not in the short term. Not as long as we don't try to rush things, anyway. No permanent promises, no lifetime commitments, not yet; let's just try to take each day as it comes, shall we?"

"Yeah, okay, one at a time – and be grateful we've got them, I suppose. Some people won't be getting any more days, after all – either good or bad."

"I know. But Tim would want you to live your life looking forward, not back. You've done everything you could for him, after all – you've taken responsibility for his family and business, and you've helped to find out why he died. If it'd been the other way round – with him alive and you dead - you wouldn't have wanted more from him than that, would you?"

"No," said Jake, "I wouldn't. You're trying to tell me it's time I drew a line under this and moved on, aren't you?"

"Well," replied Rupert, gently, "I wouldn't have put it quite as bluntly as that, but to the extent that it would actually be possible - yes, I think I probably am."

That afternoon, while Jake and Rupert went out delivering veg boxes, Ren took command of the kitchen of the lodge. By the time Helena and the children returned at tea-time he had made himself at home and, having cheerfully improvised a piping bag from an ordinary plastic bag, was creating decorative swirls of mashed potato on a baking tray. Helena walked in and took one look at him, as breezy and colourful as he appeared on any of his TV programmes, and shook her head in disbelief when Rupert performed the introductions.

"This is the second time lately I've come home from work and found a professional chef taking over my kitchen," she murmured, in bewilderment. "What's next - Heston in the bedroom, Nigella in the fridge and Jamie Oliver sitting on the loo?"

"Sorry, luv," replied Ren, chirpily, "just me, but I'm better than all three of those tossers put together. I've done sausages in red wine for tea, with Duchesse potatoes; you had the ingredients already – tomatoes, a leek, mushrooms … "

"We didn't have red wine," responded Helena. "If we had, I think it would have disappeared by now."

"No, fair enough," confessed Ren. "I had that in my car; they gave it to me at Morchard Court. I'm touring around scouting locations for my new show," he went on. "I reckon we could do a brilliant pop-up restaurant in a marquee down on the river bank here, using produce from your farm and others in the area. Be a fantastic advert for you, should increase your business by at least a hundred per cent. No, it's okay," he went on, responding to her panicked expression, "you don't have to give me an answer right this minute; have a think about it, talk it over with Jake, and we'll get into details if you're interested. Meanwhile, this must be the famous Finn and Tara; hello, sweetheart, would you like to help me with the cooking? You can make some of these potato squiggles if you like. And as for you, young man, I hear you like *Bob the Builder?* Well, so do I and so do my kids at home; I reckon you and I've got quite a lot to talk about."

"Effortlessly charming," said Rupert, his tongue firmly in his cheek, as Ren Pied-Pipered the children away and left Helena standing in the living-room shaking her head in disbelief.

"It was going to be ordinary bangers and mash for tea tonight," she said.

"Well, it still is," Rupert told her. "Only it's *upmarket* bangers and mash instead - with red wine."

"Okay, I reckon I can live with that. Since the day you first showed up here, Rupert, I've learned that the only really sensible response to all this is just to go with the flow. Nothing really makes a lot of sense to me any more, but I think I'm starting to get used to that."

"Good. Because Jake and I need to fill you in on what's been happening next door – and to apologise for not telling you it was going to be today."

Recounting the story of the release of the migrant workers didn't take long; voices were muted to avoid alarming the children with stories of prisoners being held so close to home, and only the most salient details of the police operation were exchanged. Even so, Helena was quick to make the obvious connection.

"And is there anything new about what happened to Tim?" she asked anxiously.

"Not yet. They're still questioning the two enforcers," said Jake, "but they might have more for us tomorrow. Oh, and it looks as if I might get my quad bike back after all," he added. "Bloody good job the insurance hadn't got round to paying out on it yet or they'd probably have made me scrap it - and I'd rather have the bike. Hopefully I'll be able to cancel the claim completely, and then assuming it's not needed for evidence they reckon I can just go over there and fetch it back. They say it isn't damaged at all," he concluded, optimistically.

Helena absorbed this without response. If she'd noticed the deliberate attempt to deflect her attention from the subject of Tim, she graciously declined to pursue the matter any further for the time being.

"Good," she said. "The money wouldn't have been nearly enough to buy a new one anyway, and we'd probably still have been waiting for them to pay out at Christmas."

"And your mum can have her demented bloody dog back, too, if she wants him," added Jake, in an apparent determination to twist the mood as far from the serious and tragic as he could. "Rupert's going to bring Rusty to live with us; she'll be a paying guest, and I reckon she'll be as good a burglar alarm as Toffee ever was."

"Really?"

"Really," confirmed Rupert. "I'll ask Ren to get Andrew to start the paperwork the minute he gets back to London, and she could be over here in a week or two – depending on the flights."

"Well, that'll work out very nicely all round," replied Helena. "The hospital are sending my dad home the day after tomorrow, and apparently he's supposed to get plenty of gentle exercise. They even suggested walking the dog would be a good idea," she added, grinning, "although in my experience you don't walk an Irish Wolfhound – it walks you. Anyway, it would be better if they had both dogs and then they could all go out together - so maybe we can take Toffee back home at the weekend?"

"All right," said Jake, "that's just what we'll do."

The notion of Helena's father being well enough to be capable of wrestling with anything as energetic as either Toffee or Fudge was a distinctly comforting one. Despite never having actually met the man, Rupert felt a considerable investment in Martin's Fisher's welfare; after all, he had come within an ace of being Resnik and Tesar's second 'accidental' victim in their dirty tricks campaign against Ship Meadow, and this time there could be no footling attempt at justification based on a past grievance – Martin had simply happened to get between them and their objective, and been brushed aside with impunity. Well, with a bit of luck and some diligent work from the prosecution, that wouldn't be happening again any time soon – and also, thank goodness, Martin seemed not to have been permanently affected by the experience.

Meanwhile, matters in the kitchen were progressing nicely. Ren and Tara were giggling together like a pair of naughty children, and Finn had produced his wax crayons and appeared to be drawing a picture of a man in a blue tee-shirt with his head on fire - which was instantly recognisable as being Renfrew Sheppard.

"We'll be eating in about twenty minutes," said Ren. "I hope everybody's hungry."

"What should you actually have been doing this evening, as a matter of interest?" asked Rupert, automatically moving to assist him.

Ren shrugged. "Evening off," he said. "Probably would've been watching something on the telly, that's all. I rang Annabel this morning and told her I might be late," he added. "These things happen. Listen, I've got a question for you – and for you, too, Jake; you're more likely to know the answer to this one."

"Oh? What's that, then?" asked Jake.

"You said those people next door – Diadem – had originally bought the old railway tunnel to use for workshops, didn't you?"

"Yes, they did – quite a while ago, actually, five or six years at least."

"Right. So, do you remember who they bought it from?"

"I do," replied Helena, rejoining the conversation. "The British Railways Residuary Board. They own all the old track-bed and any buildings that haven't already been sold off; my dad looked into it all at the time, I remember."

"Ah. That's more or less what I was hoping you'd say. So the old railway bridge, that'd be owned by the British Railways ... thingy ... too? And they're not bothering to look after it at all, they're not doing any maintenance, just waiting for it to fall down all by itself?"

"Presumably," said Jake. "They've put up 'Keep Out' notices and they expect that to be enough. Why, what are you thinking, Ren?"

Idly, Ren shrugged. "Only that if somebody actually bought the bridge, and invested some money into repairing the bloody thing, then the two halves of the village would be a lot closer together again – and it wouldn't take a fraction of the time it takes now to get from over *here* to over *there*." An expansive gesture with a spatula illustrated this remark.

"Well, no, it wouldn't. But why the hell would anybody want to put money into buying a broken-down old railway bridge in the first place?" asked Jake, in some confusion.

"Oh, I don't know," replied Ren. "Maybe because somebody really needs to take the damn' thing on so that it won't be a death-trap any longer – or maybe just so that the good people of Lower Hembury will be able to get to this side of the river to come to my pop-up restaurant. Tell your mum and dad I'm saving a table for them, Helena, by the way," he added wickedly.

But Helena was shaking her head in utter disbelief. "You've got it all figured out, haven't you?" she asked, unable to suppress a note of admiration at the sheer brass bollocks of the man. "Even though it's months away, if not years, and we haven't actually agreed to host it yet, you're already working on all the tiny little details!"

"Of course – although I wouldn't exactly have called the bridge a 'tiny little detail'. 'To fail to plan is to plan to fail', after all," he reminded her, his mouth twisting audaciously. "I like to think as far ahead as I can *whenever* I can; it's the secret of my success – along with being handsome, charming and incredibly talented, of course."

"Oh, of course," replied Rupert. "And I bet you've even decided what you're going to feeding everybody in the pop-up as well, haven't you?"

"As a matter of fact I have," said Ren, with the nonchalant air of one who smoothly delivers a rabbit from a hat. "How would you feel about serving roast goose?"

About Adam Fitzroy

Imaginist and purveyor of tall tales Adam Fitzroy is a UK resident who has been successfully spinning male-male romances either part-time or full-time since the 1980s, and has a particular interest in examining the conflicting demands of love and duty.

60616505R00111

Made in the USA
Charleston, SC
02 September 2016